Dollar To Doughnut

Edward R Hackemer

Dollar To Doughnut

Edward R. Hackemer

Dollar To Doughnut

(Book 4 - Throckmorton Family Novels)

~ a novel ~

Edward R Hackemer

ISBN-13: 978-1505245110

ISBN-10: 1505245117

OTHER TITLES BY THIS AUTHOR.

(The six Throckmorton Family Novels)

Sangria Sunsets
(Book 6 in the series © 2017)
ISBN-13: 978-1542615945

The Flying Phaeton
(Book 5 in the series © 2015)
ISBN-13: 978-1518707858

Dollar To Doughnut
(Book 4 in the series © 2014)
ISBN-13: 978-1505245110

A Bridge To Cross
(Book 3 in the series © 2014)
ISBN-13: 978-1494972820

The Katydid Effect
(Book 2 in the series © 2013)
ISBN-13: 978-1482669831

In A Cream Packard
(Book 1 in the series © 2011, 13)
ISBN-13: 978-1482662801

Plus:

PHRYNÉ ISN'T FRENCH
(The Truffaut Novels #1)
ISBN-13: 978-1975926397

Fables Foibles & Follies
(A collection of quirky tales)
ISBN-13: 978-1790613717

Titles are available in print and electronic format from online booksellers.

Visit the author's web page:
edhackemer.info

Acknowledgements and Credits

My proofer: Edny
My editor & pen pal: Letitia
My pen & inker: Amy
My reader: You
My inspiration: The songwriters, musicians, singers, sailors,
dancers & the Salvation Army doughnut girls

Cover photo & design: © *2014Edward R Hackemer*

Photo properties:
Latitude: 30.226278
Longitude: -88.001893
From sea level: 3 feet
Date: May 17, 2007
Location: Bon Secour Reserve, Gulf Shores, AL, USA

The Fine Print

Sincere effort has been taken to ensure that this novel contains the straight stuff for 1927-1934. Please realize that this novel is fiction except the little parts that are not. The needle and names have been changed to protect the record and only the record.

A novel is a work of fiction, therefore all characters in this book are fictional. Any resemblance in the description or name to any real person, living or dead, is purely coincidental and unintentional. No endorsement is given or implied for any illegal activity presented in this novel. Any name specific identification, dialogue, expressed or implied, comments or opinions used by any character or organization in this book are used solely for descriptive and entertainment purposes.

Any lyrics, songs or music annotated in this book are the intellectual property of individual copyright holders and are referenced only for descriptive purposes. The reader is encouraged to purchase the music, listen and feel free to enthusiastically tap his, hers, or its foot or feet. Finger-snapping is optional, but self-restraint is expected.

Retail, government, service, or religious institutions mentioned in this book, actual or fictitious, are not included as an endorsement or editorial rejection of their products or services. The descriptions of religious organizations, labor unions, political activists, governmental or law enforcement agencies within these pages, either actual or apocryphal, are included with literary license and no negative inference to or indictment of any current or past institution is intended. They are recounted solely for descriptive purposes. The reader is encouraged to research the history; some of it is nasty and not at all nice.

Verbiage and phraseology used in this novel is contemporary to the story except what ain't or never was. Some of it is not nice or acceptable nowadays. A short glossary of common early 20th Century slang is indexed at the back of the book. A superscript (*) indicates each word.

The Jazz

The Players

Leopold Throckmorton: 23

Phryne Truffaut: 22

Eloisa Ashworth: 20

Abner Mandelbaum: 35

The Stage

Buffalo, Los Angeles, San Francisco

The Set & Story

The Roaring Twenties, pre-code Hollywood,
The Great Depression, The New Deal

The Quotes

"Toodles ..."
~ Phryne ~ January, 1928

"It feels good to feel good ..."
~ Leopold ~ July, 1934

"Everything is difficult before it's easy ..."
~ Eloisa ~ May, 1928

"Your legs go all the way to Hanukah ..."
~ Abner ~ March, 1930

CONTENTS

FORWARD: THE NEWS PRINT

The following articles are displayed with spelling and editorial errors as printed Monday, August 29, 1927.

The Buffalo Evening News

Revenue Officer Dead
Violence at Peace Bridge

Buffalo, NY. 29 Aug 1927. Shortly after 1 am. August 28, Sunday morning an incident without precedent at the newly opened Peace Bridge resulted in the death by automobile collision of Customs and Revenue Officer Lionel P. Wiggins of Eggertsville, Erie Co. N.Y.

It has been revealed that the violent confrontation occurred Saturday night into Sunday early morning hours. Not all details have been released to this newspaper but what is known that a newer model, dark, four door sedan, possibly Cadillac model was involved. The total number of passengers beside the driver of the automobile is not known or released by the Immigration Dept. The public is informed the sedan will have impact damage to the front as well as gunfire damage. It was reported shots came from within the automobile, and officers returned fire after shots were reported coming from the passenger side. The total number of shots are uncertain, officials will not reveal any number or if Thompson type automatic machine-rifles were used pending complete investigation.

At press time it is also not clear what provocation led to the violence. The suspect automobile was to be inspected by the Customs and Revenue Secondary Inspection Unit when it violently drove into the barricade and struck and killed Off.Wiggins. The automobile subsequently exited the confines of the Customs Inspection Compound driving at high speed and escaped the pursuit of two squad automobiles of Revenue and Prohibition Police and Customs and Revenue Officers. The suspect automobile was last seen erratically driving south on Niagara Street, Buffalo. It is therefore suggested that the driver of the automobile suffered gunshot wounds. The incident is under joint investigation by the Buffalo office of the United States Customs and Revenue Dept., Ontario Prov. Police, RCMP, Canada Excise and Tax Dept., and Buffalo Police Dept. Contact: US Dept Customs Revenue; Canada O.P.P.; Cmdr. James P.Hines, Pct. 4, BPD.

Seven Souls Lost In Broadway Blaze

Buffalo, NY. 29 Aug 1927. A great conflagration set skies ablaze during the early morning hours this Monday. It is the most devastating fire for this decade. The dwelling and boarding house that stood at number 31 Adams Street was destroyed to the ground and neighboring structures at 29 and 27 severely damaged by flame and smoke plus explosion exposure, rendering them completely uninhabitable pending further city inspection.

At approximately 2:30 am. neighbor Mrs. Mildred Hutchinson noticed flames at the front stoop of number 31 and sprang to the Broadway alarm box to summon the fire brigade. At 2:40 Station No. 3 of the Buffalo Fire

Department responded but could not immediately sustain sufficient water pressure to effectively battle the flames. It was reported that the building was fully ablaze at that time. A tenant from the building, Mr. W. McTell leapt from a second story window to ground below and is now in hospital suffering a broken limb and burns about the body. When the pumping truck of the brigade arrived at 2:45 gas supply lines inside the structure apparently burst to create an explosive fireball that alit the skies orange and blue in color. Alas, total ruination ensued and the building was not to be salvaged. Two adjacent structures withstood severe fire and smoke and water damage plus debris spoilage. Broken window glass was reported on homes cross street. Three firehouses battled the flames, Stations No. 3, 7, and 1. The blaze was under full control at 6:45 am. The remains of seven souls were discovered in the abolition. Four females believed to be mother Wilhelmina Throckmorton, and three daughters Johanna, Ottilie and Hilde. An elder son, Leopold, was not located nor believed to reside in the home. A second son, Nicholas, was reported to be at his work at Russell Miller Inc. His whereabouts at this writing remain unknown. According to city records at time of press, three male boarders are believed deceased: Mr. Richard Arbuckle of no known address, Mr. Archibald Phillips of Schenectady, and Mr. G. Dominik Lopenzky of Rochester.

Recently, as reported by this paper, Mayor F. Schwaub has been active with Fire Department officers concerning apparent equipment failure and shortfalls, which could prove to be an official concern in this latest fatal blaze. The Office of the City Commissioner office has renewed the call to legislate the removal and permanent service disconnect of gas light systems in all private dwellings with electric service by year end and co-ordinate this with Ward Presidents. The investigation and determination of cause is ongoing. Contact: Brig. Comm. Abenstern BFC, Capt. D. Patterson II, BPD

Suspicious Death Investigated

Buffalo, NY. 29 Aug 1927. At 4:30 am. Monday a badly beaten body was discovered under the Michigan Street bridge at the river ship canal. It is suspected the death occurred sometime over this past week-end. Identification was tentative made of the deceased as that of Mr. Dillon I. Cafferty aged abt. 25 of Buffalo who is known to Pct. No. 2 police as a possible assoc. conspirator with the Black Hand mafia of the Canal District and New York City. Footprints of three men discovered on the soft riverbank are being examined. The Black Hand has been in the past implicated with prostitution rings in New York as well as Rochester and bootleg liquor smuggling from the Canada shore and to Lockport and Erie, Penna. No arrests have been made. The incident is under scrutiny by BPD Precinct No. 2. Contact: Lt. G. F. Krungel, BPD

1: BUFFALO, NEW YORK ~ 1927

~ PROLOGUE: THE BACK STORY ~

Who's Sorry Now

Monday, August 29

Between midnight and one o'clock in the morning on Sunday, August 28, a violent confrontation had occurred between agents of the United States Revenue Service, Customs officers and unknown individuals driving a newer four-door vehicle. Prompted by an order for a secondary inspection at United States Customs, the driver ignored commands to park the vehicle and began a wild escape. Federal officers rained gunfire upon the suspect vehicle, resulting in property damage and uncertain personal injury. Customs officer Lionel Wiggins was struck and killed by the driver of the suspect automobile during the murderous brouhaha and the subsequent wild escape through the streets of Buffalo.

Within hours on Sunday morning, the United States Customs office, in cooperation with the Buffalo office of the Bureau of Investigation, began an in-depth investigation of the International Peace Bridge incident at the busy border crossing linking Buffalo to Canada. A task force of Federal officers and City of Buffalo Police, led by BOI Regional Director Horace Shackleford, was formed. In Fort Erie, Ontario, the Canadian Department of Revenue, the Royal Canadian Mounted Police and the Ontario Provincial Police started a parallel investigation on their side of the border. The Mounties and OPP began their inquiries in Fort Erie and Niagara Falls, at nightclubs, dance halls and known blind pigs, or speakeasies. Without any significant leads, and no persons of involved interest, the Canadian investigators had no immediate results.

In Buffalo, by noon Monday, police informants and known members of organized crime had been rounded up and detained for questioning. The City of Buffalo Police was particularly interested in one individual: Dexter Perkins, a shameless grifter*, slipshod card shark, slapdash larrikin and bookies' runner. In the past, Dexter had proven his worth when prompted with a donation of a dollar or two. The police knew that, according to his thought process, quantity meant quality. More money bought more information, but the circumstances of this investigation were quite different from Dexter's usual dime-a-dance arrangement. The police rousted him from his bed at a flophouse* on West Chippewa Street, literally threw him into the back of a horse-drawn patrol wagon and dumped him into a holding cell in the basement of the Federal Building.

While no readily identifiable perpetrators were known, Federal agents literally swarmed onto Buffalo's streets, searching for answers. When the body of Dillon Cafferty was found under the Michigan Street Bridge, an indisputable connection to the Torricelli brothers and the implication of the Black Hand Mafia became obvious. In the past, Cafferty had been suspected of collusion in the distribution of Canadian bootleg liquor in the Canal District of Precinct 2, but police never had been able to link him directly to any illegal activity. The investigation into the Peace Bridge incident changed all that.

On the third floor of the Ellicott Street Federal Building, inside room 313, Dexter Perkins was sweating profusely. The interrogation by Special Agent Benson had begun over an hour earlier and had provided pertinent bits of information to the case, notwithstanding Dexter's openly evasive and self-preserving answers. Agents Rolf Benson and Daniel

Littlejohn were satisfied with their initial success gleaning clues and bits of evidence from the scruffy informant, who was unkempt, unshaven and stunk like the manure hopper of an Iowa hog farm in July.

Prompted by a convincing mix of physical persuasion, threats of prosecution and extended jail time, Perkins revealed the probable whereabouts of the vehicle involved in the Peace Bridge incident. A team of Buffalo police and BOI officers under the command of Benson and Littlejohn were hurriedly dispatched to a lower East Side address at the corner of Prospect Avenue and Hudson Street.

It was half-past two o'clock on a warm, hazy Monday afternoon when a dozen law enforcement personnel, armed with short-barreled shotguns and 32 caliber Colt revolvers rushed inside the dilapidated Prospect Avenue machine shop. Buffalo police and BOI agents broke through the wooden garage doors with the crash of axes and crunch of sledge-hammers. They surprised two men who were sprawled underneath a bullet-riddled, crippled 1925 Pierce Arrow, draining grain alcohol from the vehicle into galvanized buckets.

"Federal agents! Police! It's over, you mugs! Out from under the car! Hands up, behind your heads … up against the car! It's over!"

The men under the car replied, nearly simultaneously, "All right, don't shoot!" Both men gingerly slid out from under the rear of the car, shuffling their bodies across the dirt floor. They were handcuffed, held at their shoulders, pushed, shoved, and gruffly encouraged out of the garage and frog-marched into a paneled Buffalo police prisoner wagon. Agent Benson clicked the padlock onto the hasp over the back doors and barked to the driver, "Take them to Ellicott Street, and stall the paperwork. Remember men, we got a dead Customs officer in the morgue. These bums don't have a conscience, so treat them accordingly."

Back inside the garage, the BOI agents and Buffalo police detective Lieutenant George Krungel, along with his fellow officers began to examine the maroon and black Pierce Arrow. Without doubt, the car was involved in the fracas at the Peace Bridge during the early morning hours on Sunday. Scores of bullet holes, broken and cracked glass told the obvious, violent history. Inside the trunk, the officers discovered a bloodstained canvas tarpaulin.

Benson smirked and turned to Littlejohn. "Looks like somebody could have scored one for us. It could be somebody went and made a trial unnecessary for some dead rumrunner. Question is: who? This wasn't done at the border … somebody was wrapped up and stuffed in here before they came back across."

"Looks that way, doesn't it, Rolf? Could be a turkey shoot got started between the Canadians and the Torricellis and Black Hand over here, huh? A territory war maybe. Somebody wants a bigger piece of the pie … or maybe the whole thing. This car coming back from across the border and running the border and all that … and the booze inside. Never seen this set-up before. Looks like bladders inside the back seat … the cushions or frame … like hot water bottles or something filled up with the rotgut booze. These hoods* can think of anything, can't they? Smart ass, rat-bastard goons*."

Agent Benson turned and spoke to Lieutenant Krungel. "Go round up and put the pinch on all the guappo Mafiosi you know ... Torricelli's gang … nab them all, Lieutenant. And get office crew out here to go over this car … see if they can lift any fingerprints. And it looks like there's blood on the front seat besides all the blood on the hood and fender, so see if we can type that. Have your men go over the car, this whole place, everything. And carefully. Get it all."

Benson paused and moved his eyes around the garage. His gaze was that of a wolf stalking its prey: carefully, slowly, checking for movement, anything he may have missed.

"Look close, Lieutenant. Close. Tell your boys to look close. Me and Littlejohn are headed back to Ellicott Street … to grill them two flunkies and work them … and get the warrants made out … and make the judge work late today. Me and Dan ain't making this trip just for biscuits*, you know. We're going to get Torricelli … and throw the book at him. We're jumping in feet first, right up his Wop ass. Black Hand and all. Later, Lieutenant. Later."

Jailhouse Blues

On the third floor of the Ellicott Street Post Office and Federal Building, inside room 311, the two men arrested at the Prospect Avenue garage sat in straight-backed wooden chairs, having been handcuffed to a six-foot long oak table. Fifteen-foot ceilings of burnished tin tiles reflected the bright lights of two large, hooded ceiling lamps. Three eight-foot windows with vertical wrought iron bars allowed the bright sun to lay a deceivingly peaceful pattern of glowing light across the polished wooden floors.

The two men were Owen Healy and Michael Dunne, ethnic Irish from Buffalo's First Ward: extremely thin and wiry individuals with cold, steel-blue eyes. They were wearing their sailcloth work coveralls, and sitting in nervous apprehension -- sweat beading on their foreheads, soaking through shirt collars and underarms. The room was uncomfortably warm and heavy with stagnant summer humidity. Four table fans sat idle, unmoving on two desks against the far wall.

BOI agents Rolf Benson and Dan Littlejohn sat staring harshly at the prisoners, their eyes trying to pierce into the brains of Healy and Dunne. Benson lit one Chesterfield after another and exhaled the smoke across the table, looking over the top of his wire-rimmed glasses at the two subjects in front of him. He was a big man, and it appeared that the only comb that went through his thick black hair was his fingers. He had broad shoulders that he was barely able to squeeze into his Sears and Roebuck suit coat. Daniel Littlejohn was larger than his partner, taller at six-foot-four, and wider with a forty-four inch waist. A thick neck and wide hands made him appear much more powerful than Benson, if not outright brutish.

Only a few minutes into the questioning, the two men in custody proved to be willing witnesses. When they were told that they had been implicated in the beating death of Dillon Cafferty and his body had been found in the Buffalo Canal, it seemed to be all the incentive they needed to answer the questions being thrown at them.

Healy was the first to offer information, speaking in a pitchy voice with great apprehension, "Sunday morning, eight o'clock … when we got to the garage, on the job … me and Mike work the product, you see, drain the booze from the car… that's all we do, nothing else … it was then I saw the Pierce Arrow all shot up and crippled and I found Vinnie … Vinnie Torricelli in the trunk wrapped up in canvas with a hole in his head. It was then I got Lorenzo on the blower* and told him about the car and his dead brother. When Lorenzo got there, he was damn mad … and spittin' tacks at Dillon Cafferty, he is … was … the wheel man that drives … that drove … the Pierce Arrow and works the jazz in Canada. Then Lorenzo said it was time to dangle*, and he drove us and his cousin Johnny Minello to Cafferty's apartment on West Delevan and we rousted him out of bed, and brought him back to the garage. But we didn't kill him. They did … it was Lorenzo and Johnny that zotzed* him. Lorenzo wasn't happy with the way Cafferty handled the screw-up in Canada, I guess. I never seen him so mad. Him and Johnny kicked and stomped Cafferty to death right there in the garage."

Michael Dunne chimed in, "It wasn't us; we're not murderers! We're trying to make a living, that's all! Minello and Torricelli beat Cafferty to death, and then told me and Owen to stick him in the coal bin of the garage and then half an hour later made us load him back into Lorenzo's Chrysler again and then they left. I don't know what they did with ..."

Agent Littlejohn interrupted. "Cafferty ended up in the ship canal this morning. We told you that. It's pretty convenient that you don't know the whole story, isn't it? What else don't you know?" Cigarette ash fell onto the table.

Owen Healey anxiously chimed in and rapidly let his words roll, "Don't tell them any lies, Mike. Stop bumping* your gums and tell the truth! They're going to find out sooner or later. These guys are G-men*!"

Benson growled a question and his cigarette bounced between his lips as he spoke, "Are you bums lying? What are we going to find out?"

"They made us help them dump Cafferty over the Michigan Street Bridge into the canal. Then they drove us to Throckmorton's place on Adams … they were looking for him and wanted to find out maybe what he knew about how Vincente got that hole in his head. But nobody was there at Throckmorton's place, just a boarder … the whole family was at church the mug said. I think Lorenzo is mad enough to do something. I don't know what. But I know he's mad as a wet cat in a burlap sack. He said he's going back and he's going to even the score. That's what he does … he evens the score."

"Slow down. You two are giving us a lot of stuff at once. Let's slow down a minute. Let me get this straight." Agent

Benson crushed his cigarette into a large, green glass ashtray and put a pencil to the pad of paper on the table in front of him. He wrote as he spoke, "Torricelli and this Minello guappo beat Cafferty to death, then all four of you dumped his body in the canal, and then drove to … to … this Throckmorton fellow's house. Who is Throckmorton? Where does he live?"

"On Adams Street, off Broadway. That's where Lorenzo drove Mike and Johnny and me." Owen Healy was twisting in his chair as he spoke.

Benson held up a hand to silence Healy, and glanced to Littlejohn, leaned toward him and spoke into his ear. "There was a fire last night on Adams, killed everybody inside. Find out exactly where that was, Dan, and who lived there." Agent Littlejohn nodded and left the room.

Owen Healey moved his eyes across the room and watched the BOI detective open and close the heavy wooden door with a thump. He glanced over to his cohort Michael Dunne and continued talking, "Cafferty always took along Throckmorton and they went to Canada twice a month, sometimes more, and got the Pierce Arrow loaded up with hooch*. Up at the Lafayette in Niagara Falls, he told us. And they each always had a chippy* on their arms, dressed to the nines. Cafferty would brag to us that he was having his way with both of them … if you could believe what Cafferty said. We never saw them sweet patooties, only heard Cafferty talking about them. Good-lookers he said. Some babe with a French name and a blonde baby vamp that works in a bakery down on Hamburg Street somewhere. He called her his Ellie, like he owns her. Cafferty used the broads as snake-charmers*, they didn't know nothing from nothing, I guess. I don't know about that lug-nut, Throckmorton. Don't know if he was in on Cafferty's flimflam*. We never met him did we, Mike?"

Agent Littlejohn came back into the room, stood silent for a moment and then gave everyone the solemn news, "Bad news for you two. It was the Throckmorton house that burned to the ground, killing seven people … the mother, three daughters and three boarders. One boarder is alive, suffering broken bones, in Deaconess Hospital … he jumped from the second floor. One Throckmorton, a son, was spotted when he got home from work this morning and saw his home in ashes, burnt to the ground. According to the fire chief, there is another son, but he doesn't live at home. The fire Brigade Commander is an uncle to Throckmorton. We can check with him, I suppose. Maybe he knows which one was mixed up with Cafferty. Neighboring homes on each side were burnt too, but no other fatalities. The fire-eaters said the gas lines in the Throckmorton place lit up the street like a fireball. To me, it sounds like a professional torch job."

Benson spoke up. "So, it ain't looking good for you, boys. Or your boss, Lorenzo Torricelli. Could be at least nine counts of murder you're looking at now … and a Federal officer to boot … and arson. It looks like death row at Sing-Sing for you two micks* … then a seat on the hotsquat*. Yeah. It will be the electric chair for you, boys. The zap suit. Maybe they got green ones for leprechauns like you two."

Owen Healey and Michael Dunne looked sheepishly at one another, then at the agents and back down to the table. The agents leaned back in their chairs and lit cigarettes. Rolf Benson discarded a spent match to the floor, and filled his lungs with smoke before he growled at the handcuffed prisoners, "We are placing you two under arrest for violations of United States Code 27, and portions of the Volstead National Prohibition Act, under possession, transport and sale of intoxicating beverages. We are also going to ask the Federal Prosecutor to pursue charges of conspiracy to commit murder, arson, and the concealment of death connected with the Organized Crime Act of 1923. And that's just us. If that isn't enough to get you two fried, I am certain the locals and even the Canucks will have a few more charges they can hurl at you. So sit tight for now, boys. We'll get you started on your way to the hoosegow* directly. You got anything to add, Agent Littlejohn?"

With just a hint of a grin, he replied, "No. I think we're done here, Agent Benson."

The Prisoner's Song

Saturday, September 3, 1927

Three full days into the case, the BOI were finally able to detain and arrest Lorenzo Torricelli. He had successfully eluded capture by moving from one place to another under the cover of darkness and the long coat tails of the Black Hand, Castellammarese Mafiosi. Agents Benson, Littlejohn and BOI Regional Director Shackleford diligently pursued Torricelli under unrelenting pressure from the Treasury Department and the Customs Service. In bits and pieces, one arrest at a time, and with what they could glean from reluctant informants, they were able to capture Torricelli at a warehouse on the corner of Hertel Avenue and Niagara Street in Buffalo's "Little Italy" section of Black Rock.

Try as they might, neither BOI agents Littlejohn and Benson nor the Buffalo Police were able to extract any meaningful information from Lorenzo. Immediately after Lorenzo's arrest, criminal defense attorney Jerome Fischbein of New York City arrived to represent him. Fischbein was flashy, overbearing and considered to be among the best defense counsels money could buy, and carried an unsavory reputation among Federal Prosecutors in New York and the Northeast of jury-rigging and witness-tampering. The majority of the "leg work" in the investigation was completed in a matter of days, and the burden of due process for the deaths of Customs agent Lionel Wiggins and the rank Dillon Cafferty was now left up to the United States Justice Department.

Agent Rolf Benson had decided to direct his attention to Healey and Dunne's revelations concerning the probable occupants of the Pierce Arrow during the violence and fatal clash at the Peace Bridge on Sunday morning. Fire Brigade commander Abenstern, brother of deceased Wilhelmina Throckmorton, was able to confirm that 17 year-old Nicholas Throckmorton was at the scene of the Adams Street conflagration on the morning of August 29, in a state of shock, having just arrived home from his job at Russell-Miller. The BOI determined that the Throckmorton who was in the Pierce Arrow was most likely Nicholas' older brother, Leopold, aged about 23, who was employed at Urban Flour on Kehr Street. No photographs of the brothers were available, but Abenstern was able to provide a police sketch-artist with enough details to enable the creation of likenesses of Leopold and Nicholas. The fire commander stated that the brothers closely resembled their father, Hermann, and he had a wedding picture of Hermann Throckmorton and his bride Wilhelmina that he gave the police to work from. Further investigation indicated that neither Leopold nor Nicholas had gone to work since August 29, leading the BOI to conclude that the brothers had quit their jobs and left town.

Benson and Littlejohn were able to track down one of the young women Dillon Cafferty had used as snake charmers on his bootleg runs from Niagara Falls. They found Eloisa Ashworth working at Mama Farrachi's Bakery and Confections on Hamburg Street. Her arrest and interrogation late Saturday afternoon enabled the agents to tie up more loose ends. Under protest and strong exclamations of innocence from herself and her mother Esther, who was also employed at the bakery, Eloisa was placed under arrest and taken to Ellicott Street, where she was subjected to hours of questioning. Quite unlike his normal persona, Rolf Benson felt empathy for the good-looking blonde, blue-eyed young woman. It was, in fact, agent Daniel Littlejohn who administered the harsh queries, table-slamming fists, gruff tone and unsympathetic demeanor. Through her tears and sobs, normally withdrawn and demure Eloisa revealed that the occupants of the Pierce Arrow were indeed Dillon Cafferty, herself, Leopold Throckmorton and Phryne Truffaut. She also proclaimed complete innocence and unwitting compliance in any bootleg-running scheme, violence, or murder. It was a surprise worth noting to the agents, that she also stated that nobody in the automobile had any weapons or fired any shots at any Customs or Revenue agent or any policeman on that Sunday morning at the Peace Bridge. Eloisa told the agents that she suspected Phryne and Leopold had left town, and in her opinion, eloped. She insisted and guaranteed that she, Phryne and indeed, Leopold, were all unsuspecting, unintended participants in the affair. She gave the agents the local Buffalo addresses of her friends Phryne Truffaut and Leopold Throckmorton. Emotionally shaken, nervous and distraught, Eloisa sat in handcuffs, struggling with tears running down her cheeks. Her sobs shook her frame and consumed her physical strength. She was placed under arrest as an accessory to the murder of a Federal Officer and willful collusion in the illegal transportation of liquor under the Prohibition Act, and was remanded to the Erie County Holding Center for Women and Adolescents on Court Street. Standing in the atrium and reception area of the BOI offices, her father George and mother Esther watched helplessly as Eloisa was taken out of the building to a waiting Buffalo Police prisoner wagon. They had attested to their daughter's innocence to no avail.

Shortly after six o'clock, Agents Littlejohn and Benson, Buffalo Police Lieutenant George Krungel, detectives and patrolmen of the Buffalo police went off in an attempt to locate Leopold Throckmorton and Phryne Truffaut.

Throckmorton's Howlett Street apartment was unoccupied. The officers found only a man's suit, shirt, a lady's dress, stockings and undergarments inexplicably soaking in the bathtub. Two pocket flasks, partially filled with whiskey, sat on the bathroom shelf. An ashtray with cigarette butts, some with lipstick stains, was on the kitchen table. Mildred Flannery, the landlady who lived downstairs, said she had not seen Throckmorton for the past week and that his Model T breezer* was not parked in its usual spot in the adjacent alley. The rent for the month of September, however, had already been paid.

Seated at the dining room table of the Truffaut family home on Lombard Street, the BOI agents had a fruitful, early evening. Phryne's father, Bertram, had spoken to his daughter that very morning. She had made a transcontinental telephone call and had informed him that she and Leopold Throckmorton had purchased train tickets and left Buffalo on Sunday morning, were married in Chicago on Monday, and they were both currently in Los Angeles, California, seeking employment and an apartment. When Bertram Truffaut learned what charges his daughter could be facing, he was beside himself, and swearing to her innocence and that of Leopold. He explained that his daughter and Leopold became engaged to be married just a week ago, and he was willing to personally vouch for the young man's character.

Agent Benson nodded only slightly, looked at his partner Littlejohn and then back to Bertram. "You're not the first person to say Throckmorton, your daughter and Eloisa Ashworth are faultless in this mess, Mister Truffaut. But they are persons we believe have more than just coincidental involvement. The death of a Customs officer by a car driven by bootleg smugglers is a serious matter, and the Bureau of Investigation will continue to pursue this matter and the death by murder of Dillon Cafferty to their full resolution. And if your daughter and the Throckmorton brothers are in California, we and the United States Marshalls will find them and bring them back. Be assured of that, sir."

Agent Rolf Benson, of course, knew better and was aware he was only spewing hollow, meaningless drivel and that much of his work was simply an exercise in futility. In 1927, the BOI had no interstate jurisdiction for extradition.

Monday, September 5

On Saturday, the intense BOI investigation had paused for the long Labor Day holiday weekend. Benson and Littlejohn however, continued to press on. A Model T Ford with license plates linked to Leopold Throckmorton was discovered at the Lackawanna Railroad Terminal. After he saw the police sketches of the Throckmorton brothers, a ticket agent for The Nickel Plate Road said he recognized one of the men. He stated that the suspect was with a woman and they had purchased two tickets on the Monday morning *Nickel Plate One* express to Chicago only thirty minutes before the train was scheduled to leave the station. Benson asked, "What time did that train leave here, and are you sure it was only one man ... and not two?"

"The New York to Chicago train leaves here at six o'clock in the morning. Sharp. And I'm sure it was only one man with the dame*. Only one, I'm sure of that. I noticed. She was one hot mama, I'm telling you, and I remember thinking he was one lucky stiff. She hung on him like a tight fitting suit, if you know what I mean."

It was almost certain that Leopold Throckmorton and his girlfriend Phryne had left for Chicago after they ran the border with Cafferty. Buffalo fireman Wilbur Abenstern had placed Nicholas Throckmorton at the scene of the fire on Adams street Monday morning, making it impossible for him to be on the Chicago train. His whereabouts were still unknown.

Across the border in Canada, the holiday brought a bevy of party-goers to Niagara Falls and provided a unique opportunity for the Royal Canadian Mounted Police and the Ontario Provincial Police to closely examine what was going on at the pay-for-parking lot adjacent to The Lafayette Hotel in Niagara Falls. The Mounties had rented two rooms of the hotel that overlooked the valet lot on Ferry Street and Whirlpool Avenue. From their vantage point, they were able to determine which vehicles were being used to transport illegal alcohol into the United States. The Canadian authorities were able to take many evidentiary surveillance photographs. On Saturday evening, a handful of suspected American smugglers, and nearly two dozen Canadians working as either drivers, parking valets, car washers and even dock hands at a Garrison Street warehouse were arrested and charged with several violations of the Ontario Temperance Act and Revenue Canada Alcoholic Beverages Tax. The Americans were charged with smuggling and evasion of Revenue Canada export taxes. Barrels of bootleg liquor were dumped onto the streets of Niagara Falls.

On Monday, Agents Benson and Littlejohn crossed the Peace Bridge to Fort Erie, Ontario. It was Rolf Benson's idea to work on Labor Day. Littlejohn complained, "Rolf, we should be enjoying a day off, like everybody else in America and Canada, with a picnic of hot dogs and potato salad. We don't need to be chasing windmills and goosing butterflies over here in Canada."

Benson immediately climbed onto his soapbox and started to rant. Littlejohn knew he'd made a verbal misstep. He should not have said anything about working the holiday. He cursed under his breath, knowing he should have kept his mouth shut. Benson slammed his palm onto the steering wheel of the Chevrolet when he began his tirade, "This holiday means nothing to me, Littlejohn, and it should not be a Federal Holiday in the first place. This whole Labor Day thing is a joke. They created this Labor Day bullshit holiday out of thin air, nothing, absolutely nothing, only to satisfy and appease the anarchists, union bosses and the dumb masses of the Bolshevik movement. Plain and simple. And the Canucks don't even spell it right! L-A-B-O-U-R. What the hell is that?"

Agent Daniel Littlejohn did not argue nor offer an opinion. He knew better. He was silent for the rest of the way to their destination in Niagara Falls, Canada.

As part of the invitation and cooperation of the Canadian authorities, they were invited to sit in on several police interviews at the Portage Avenue OPP Barracks. For six hours, they heard portions of a handful of interrogations conducted by the Canadian police. Two of those were of particular interest: valet parking lot attendants Phelix Milton and Ian Withers. Specific details of the illegal operation behind the hotel had implicated Dillon Cafferty, the Torricelli brothers and the Lovejoy, New York, connection to Canadian organized crime. Their job at the Lafayette was to collect the correct amount of cash from the customer and ensure the product was delivered in the manner that the customer wanted. Several styles, sizes and shapes of containers had been used to smuggle the liquor across the border. Dillon Cafferty's Pierce Arrow used one of the most extraordinary: bladders inside the back seat cushions. With the Canadians' description of Cafferty and the car, it was apparent they knew the smuggling operation well. Milton and Withers stated that the Canadian mob wanted to control a bigger piece of the Torricelli bootleg imports and began to apply pressure on the Americans, hoping to assert Canadian control. The men had knowledge of Vincente Torricelli's murder and the subsequent placement of his body into the trunk of Cafferty's maroon automobile on that Saturday night in August. Although they were unwilling to be specific during the interview, they did not deny the police inference that the Rocco Petrozi organization of Toronto could have ordered Vincente killed.

With the help of RCMP Chief Inspector Jonathan Abbott, the American agents extracted testimony from parking lot valets Milton and Withers that stated Dillon Cafferty had been the only person whom they ever made contact with, and that no other person in his party was part of any interaction. Hearing that, Benson and Littlejohn asked specifically if they believed any of Cafferty's entourage knew what was inside the seats of the Pierce Arrow, and both men had replied they were ordered to communicate with Cafferty only. When asked about Vincente's body in the trunk, they repeated their claim that no one knew, least of all Cafferty, and that it was intended as a warning to the Americans.

Agents Rolf Benson and Daniel Littlejohn returned to Buffalo late Monday night. On Tuesday afternoon, following a conference with BOI Regional Director Horace Shackleford and Buffalo Police Lieutenant George Krungel, the murder and bootlegging charges against Eloisa Ashworth were dropped and she was released from custody. She was informed however, that a Federal Principle Witness subpoena could be issued and that her testimony could be required in the future.

Shackleford ordered jurisdictional appearance subpoenas for Phryne Truffaut, Leopold and Nicholas Throckmorton. The United States Marshall Service was tasked to locate them. The order was essentially meaningless paperwork.

Frustrated yet duty-bound, Benson and Littlejohn continued to chase windmills, hunt leprechauns, goose butterflies and run after rainbows.

Lorenzo Torricelli was released on bond and never brought to trial. In 1936, his bullet-riddled body was discovered in a rail yard off Hertel Avenue in the Black Rock section of Buffalo. The murder was considered mob-related violence and was never solved.

2: LOS ANGELES, CALIFORNIA ~ 1927

Makin' Whoopee

Saturday, September 10

Leopold and Phryne awoke with the sun poking through the only window in the small, ten-foot-square bedroom, rudely splashing buckets of morning light onto their faces and flushing the sleep from their eyes. The glass was streaked, dirty and dingy. No curtains hung from any of the windows in the twenty-five-dollar-a-month, partially furnished, three-room apartment off Figueroa Street. They had no bedding, and they had fallen asleep the night before naked, back-to-back, between two blankets they had brought with them when they hastily left Buffalo almost two weeks ago. A threadbare cushion from the worn sofa in the living room was their pillow. It smelled like an ashtray.

Everything was so very unfamiliar to them: a new apartment, together, married, far away from everything they knew for the first twenty-plus years of their lives. Phryne and Leopold Throckmorton, newlyweds in a new city, a new State, and a strange, run-down apartment with tattered furniture. They were the proverbial 'ducks out of water'. Leopold had finished his first full week of work at his new job with Famous Players Studios just the night before. Wide awake, and seemingly ready to begin another day, he sat on the edge of the bed, arched his shoulders, stretched and put his bare feet to the wooden floor. He had a troubling dream that night, and awoke with a solution to the puzzle it presented. He rubbed his eyes, and ignored a large insect of some sort, with legs askew and wiggling, that scurried across the room.

Phryne curled up under the blanket, holding her arms close to her chest, embracing her warmth. She longed to be held. She encouraged him to come back into bed. The last time they had shared intimacy was two weeks earlier, aboard the train from Chicago: *The California Limited*. Once they arrived in Los Angeles and learned the news of the deadly fire, it seemed the world had gone dark and the sun dimmed as if eclipsed by an ominous black moon. Leopold's passion had vanished. He was disinterested and detached. Phryne felt forsaken.

"Come and cuddle with me, Leopold. Please. I need your arms around me. I need to have you; all of you. Please make me yours and take me. It's been so long … too long ... it's been two weeks."

"You're keeping track now? I have things to do, Phryne. Right now I'm going to the hotel down the block, Sweetie, and try to make a telephone call to Buffalo. To the fire department … to that Wilbur Abenstern fellow … my uncle … and see what else I can find out about Saturday night. Saturday night … two weeks ago … Sunday morning. I want to find out what happened to Nicholas. I don't care if it costs me a double sawbuck* ... a third of my pay. I need to find out all I can. I need to do this. I had a dream last night … another bad dream … and I need to do this. If I don't, I may never be able to sleep. These dreams haunt me."

"I'll walk with you, and maybe we can get a bite to eat and a cup of coffee afterwards at that little diner … then maybe we can come back and make whoopie … like we used to."

Phryne was already pulling on her stockings. She felt a flicker of hope, but was nervous and wary of what could happen if her husband became upset again. When they had read in the newspaper about that fatal Sunday morning fire, it took two days for Leopold to get control of his emotions. The loss of his entire family was more than a shock. It virtually disemboweled him and mercilessly turned his world inside out. Phryne was impatiently waiting for things to get back to the way they used to be … back to before the Peace Bridge and the fire … back to when they couldn't keep their hands off one another, and he would love her.

They dressed quickly, and were on the sidewalk in a flash. Leopold walked with a purpose. He was driven, every step was quick, deliberate, and forced Phryne to struggle just to keep up. They were inside the lobby of the San Remo Hotel on Wilshire Boulevard in mere minutes. Leopold went directly to the desk clerk and asked to make a trans-continental telephone call. Required to first confirm he was able to pay and display cash, he was cordially directed behind the desk, and into the office.

Phryne sat in an upholstered Queen Anne parlor chair in the lobby, glancing through a tattered copy of last month's *Redbook*, flipping the pages nervously, hurriedly; wondering what the end result of her husband's telephone call would be. She was impatient and had no idea what she might expect. She repeatedly looked up to the hotel desk, trying to peer into the windows behind, looking for her husband, for something, for some kind of clue as to what was happening. She wasn't successful. Leopold was out of sight, inside the office, and she was holding the only magazine in the lobby.

Getting connected with Brigade Commander Abenstern required time, patience, three operators and two telephone calls simply to be able to obtain the number to Buffalo Fire Department Fire Station #3. After brief platitudes and hollow greetings, Leopold sat and listened as his mother's brother, Wilbur Abenstern, revealed everything he could about the fatal fire on Adams Street.

"The arson squad worked the fire and found some evidence of kerosene, fuel oil … something on the front porch and rear stoop. The Feds had Torricelli locked up right quick, but he got a shyster lawyer, a real mouthpiece* from New York and the torching evidence got lost from the Precinct. And two guys from his organization ended up getting themselves shivved to death in jail. The cops couldn't make any charges stick and the whole case is shot to hell. They're still working with the Canucks, though, I guess trying to get something to stick, somehow. Cafferty's murder case is going nowhere; the two mugs were knifed dead in the lockup* like I said. I hope you ain't involved. The Feds were looking for you and that beauty parlor girl you're with. They found your car at Lackawanna Station and figured it out from the train tickets that you're out there in California, but it doesn't matter a damn now. Not now. Torricelli is going to walk. There's a turf war going on now with the Lovejoy and Canadian mafiosi types, I heard. Maybe they'll bump him off and put him in a Chicago overcoat* at the bottom of Lake Erie."

Leopold was silent, dumbstruck. His uncle asked repeatedly, "Leopold … Leopold … are you there?"

Suddenly, Leopold spoke. "How about Nicholas? What about Nicholas? Does anyone know where he is?"

"I saw him on the morning of the fire. I asked him to come over to my place for dinner or something. He never showed up. Nobody knows where he is, not now … not that I know of … I haven't heard a whit."

Leopold's hand went limp and let the earpiece sink to his lap. He stared at the pedestal telephone, and slowly hung the trumpet back onto the receiver. The conversation was over. At that moment, he was not communicating with anyone, and least of all: himself. His shoulders sank under the weight of the world, his eyes focused somewhere beyond sight and his breath all but vanished. He paled.

The desk clerk hurried to the lobby. "Perhaps you should help him, Miss … the man you're with. He's in the office just sitting there, like he's in a trance or having one of them sleeping fits."

Phryne tossed the magazine onto a large leather ottoman and rushed behind the desk. Inside the office, she rushed to her husband and exclaimed, "Leopold! Leopold, wake up!" She did not get a response. She grabbed him by the shoulders and softly, smoothly shook his frame.

He jerked his head, pulled from her grip and shouted, "Leave me alone. Now." His voice sounded like that of a crazed man and his face had a look she had never witnessed: void of humanity, withdrawn, distant and lifeless within another world. He stood, his jaw locked in place, turned and started out of the office.

The hotel clerk protested, "Sir! Sir! The operator hasn't rang back with the telephone charges yet, Sir!"

Leopold turned like a cornered animal, glaring at the desk clerk. With a groan that was more of a growl, he reached into his trouser pocket and threw his money clip toward the man with a flick of his wrist. Phryne reached to pick it up, and watched as her husband shoved open the heavy hotel doors and exited the building. She could only nervously wait for the American Telephone operator to ring with the cost of the call. It seemed like hours before the call came, and she was able to pay the seventeen dollars and forty cents. She ran down the sidewalk to Figueroa Street, toward their tiny apartment, down to number 14 and rushed upstairs to the little bedroom and bath they had rented ten days earlier.

Her husband was in the tiny bedroom, stuffing his duffle sack with clothes.

"Leopold ... what happened? Tell me, let me help. Tell me about your telephone call. I can make a pot of coffee and I can toast some bread for us. We have enough for this morning, I think. Then we can sit and talk this out ... and work it out."

There wasn't a reply, only stillness, silence as deafening as death itself. It viciously sliced through her marrow like a double edge sword. She began to worry, not only for her husband, but for her safety as well. "Please, Leopold, please."

Phryne was begging, pleading for a response. She walked to the bed and sat. She was fearful; afraid of what might happen. Almost two weeks earlier her husband had a similar incident and withdrew deep within himself for days.

The first tears ran down her soft cheeks. She could only watch as he continued to jam whatever bits of clothing he had into the sack. "What are you doing, Leopold?"

She was controlling her anguish well, but could feel a clammy chill within her trembling form. It was growing, swelling, consuming her from the inside out. "What happened in Buffalo? What did your uncle, the fireman tell you? Did something happen? What are you doing? Talk to me, Leopold. Please. Please, talk to me, Darling."

He shoved his hands down into the bag, pushing the contents tight inside, and pulled the drawstrings shut. "What happened in Buffalo, you ask? Well, I'll tell you. My mother and three sisters were burned to death. My brother has disappeared into the wind like dandelion fuzz and now he's gone to who-knows-where. And it's because of me. And you ... yes, you, too, my dear, dear Phryne. It was you that introduced me to that sonuvabitch Cafferty and you that wanted to go out on party nights with him and his little kitten Ellie ... and it was you who wanted to do the jazz and dance and drink and party and whoopee* all night and now ... well ... my whole life is shot to Hell. Straight to Hell. Thanks to Dillon, thanks to you, and thanks to me. And I have no doubt you may even have known about Cafferty's shenanigans ... his dealings with Torricelli! Did you? Did you know? I bet you did. I saw him whisper in your ear more than once."

Phryne grabbed the bed blanket and held it in a wad to her chest. She experienced her husband's tirade with wide, burning eyes. She could feel her heart throb. She struggled with her breath. "No, I didn't know! How could I know? I only heard stories and rumors ... and what gossip I heard at the shop sometimes. But you heard the same gossip. You heard the same stories. But that was just talk, you see, and I didn't know anything... really! How could I? How could either of us know? How could we have known about the booze in the car?"

"Yeah, I heard rumors and gossip too ... plenty of it. And I should have paid attention. I'm leaving you, Phryne. I'm leaving. We were never in love. We are still just familiar strangers ... it was always just physical pleasure on and off the dance floor. Partying and doing the horizontal Charleston. That's all you ever wanted. Admit it, Phryne. You didn't want love, not me ... not real love ... just lust. I've been thinking about it and now I know so clearly ... I can see the truth. It wasn't love ... we were never meant to be married. You got me caught up in the excitement, and we never wanted it to end. Party, party. And ... the dishonesty, the secrets ... you and that lousy mick Cafferty, I saw him looking at you more than once. Did you have him? He called you his hot honey muffin* once! I heard him! I saw how he used to look at you. Did you let him take you? I wouldn't doubt it. You loved the attention. I know you did."

She broke into sobs, and her eyes welled up. "Did he tell you? But that was months before I met you." She took a breath. "And once right after. But that was before I loved you. I was foolish and not thinking. And the last time, Dillon was a brute, an unloving brute ... and that time he forced himself on me."

"Sonuvabitch! I knew it! You did! That proves it, Phryne, my dear. Or should I call you *Frenchie* ... like your sweetheart lover Cafferty did? Admit it! We never really had anything in common or a real marriage, anyway … did we? Did we? Hell, no! Our only connection was your boundless desire for whoopee and my greenbacks! You always seemed to have that … that … unfulfilled, unsatisfied, unrequited need to get your ashes hauled*. I'm surprised … surprised you can still walk … that you're not a bowlegged cripple begging for silver on some street corner ... or selling matches on the sidewalk outside a cigar store."

Still holding the worn blanket tightly to her breast, Phryne spoke through her weeping, "That was cruel. Vicious. Nasty. You dirty, filthy rat bastard. Do you really have that much hate in your heart? How can you say those things? I love you."

He was standing with the duffle bag at his feet, holding the cord clenched in his fist. His shirt was wet with perspiration, unbuttoned half way. Sweaty, unshaven and uncombed, he looked like a steel worker after a sixteen-hour shift. "You don't love me, but you're right, Sweetie: I am a rat bastard. You are absolutely correct with that description. I am a rat bastard. My behavior allowed my mother and three sisters to be burned to death. My behavior forced my brother to disappear into the wind. It's behavior I've got to live with now. I don't know about you. I don't know about you. I don't know how you will live with yourself. Good luck, I say."

Phryne gathered herself, and filled her lungs with air. She dropped the crumpled blanket onto her lap and wiped a tear off her cheek with the back of her hand. She spoke carefully and worked to say every word so her husband understood, "I admit my errors, Leopold. I admit my transgressions and I have regrets. But you must admit that you have made mistakes, and taken missteps. We both do … everybody does. You know that. We're only human. Don't hurt me, please. Please don't hurt me like this. You don't need to be so cruel. Don't put all the blame on me … nobody knew what Dillon was up to. Dillon deceived and snookered you, me and everyone around him … maybe he tricked me most of all, but we all make mistakes."

His anger swelled, and his eyes locked onto her. "Yes, I have regrets, and I admit that I made mistakes. And I'm looking at one of my biggest damned mistakes right now … right here in front of me … one of my biggest … you."

She forced her words, "Please, can't you pretend … can't you pretend that we are still in love? Talk to me. Comfort me. And I can comfort you. We can talk about this … we don't need to be alone … we can do this together … as one. Be my lover … love me, love me deep … if only just one more time … please. We can fix this. Let me try … please. Let me convince you. Love me." Her tears began to roll down her flushed cheeks. She was controlling her sobs and speaking between short, labored breaths.

He lifted the sack from the floor, and onto his shoulder. "You have just proven my point, Phryne. That's all you ever wanted … and that's all that attracted you to me … the physical stuff … the physical stuff, the whoopee and my money. Like a cheap floozie."

Leopold took four steps out of the bedroom, into the kitchen and turned. He picked up the pack of Chesterfield cigarettes from the table. His words began to crackle and pitch. "I'm walking away, Phryne. Remember that … walking … not running. I'm not going to trip and fall over you. And you sure as hell are not going to see me crawl … ever. You're a jezebel, Phryne. A possessive, spellbinding witch. A shallow, consuming woman. A damned jezebel."

She took a breath and forced out the words, "If you walk out that door Leopold, there's no coming back. Ever. I mean it. I will end our marriage."

He grabbed his hat off the kitchen table. The door closed behind him with a hollow thud.

Monday & Tuesday, September 12 & 13

Phryne had lived through a weekend of torment; alone, dejected, insulted, mentally torn and emotionally wounded as never before. She was, however, a proud woman, and not to be defeated. Her passion for survival had given her renewed personal dignity. She was determined to keep her sense and sanity. Her pride guaranteed that. She faulted Leopold for faulting her.

Saturday was an emotional firestorm: She cried more tears than she thought possible. No matter what she did, whether she stood, sat or laid down, her heart was on the other side of the small apartment, torn from her. Her mood was downcast.

Sunday was fog: past, present and future were barely visible or discernable. When she awoke Sunday morning, she reached her arm across the bed, just to be sure he wasn't really there. She had no concept of time; reality swirled and mixed with fantasy like a snow-globe blizzard. She could not be certain if Leopold had truly left on his own, was taken away, or would ever return. Her life was surreal. She fell asleep that night and dreamed she was dancing with Leopold in a gleaming, white ballroom.

Monday was clarity: realization, recognition and renewal. She got out of bed as a woman on a mission of self-preservation and freedom. She counted the bills in Leopold's money clip and added them to the money in the kitchen drawer. Ninety three dollars and change wasn't a bankroll, but it would be enough for what she needed to accomplish. Her spirit longed to be refreshed, refined, and redeemed.

She remembered what her husband had told her before he shut the door behind him, "… you sure as hell are not going to see me crawl." Those words meant more to her than

Leopold would ever know. Phryne sure as hell had no intention to crawl, either. She would continue to walk on, her head high. In the little cupboard next to the bed, she found a business card and the wrinkled *letter of introduction* that Irving Feinmann wrote for them when they met on the train from Chicago. She had decided that tomorrow she would take the letter addressed to Abner Mandelbaum to the Gower Street offices of Famous Players Studios. Exactly two weeks earlier, to the day, her husband made the same trip with success. If Leopold could get a job, so could she. There was no doubt about that. Phryne was certain of it.

First, she had to do just a few things; foremost was some laundry, then some shopping. She needed a pair of new stockings, fresh lipstick, rouge and eye shadow if she was to look her best while seeking employment in Hollywood, California. It was a busy city, full of beautiful women and men. Phryne was not going to be outdone, underexposed or outshined. She spotted her two pair of shoes against the wall. Another purchase was required: some boot polish and a brush.

She was sitting on the bed, the Monday morning sun managing to warm her back despite the dirty glass of the small window. She realized there was a lot of work to do before she could consider herself settled in her new surroundings. California itself was an experience far beyond what she had ever imagined. During the Pullman train trip, she heard stories and read articles, but nothing came close to the actuality of it all; the pride in the pomp and the dizziness of the dream. She had convinced herself to take one step at a time, one step forward at every opportunity and never, ever regret missteps… only correct and adjust course as needed. She would not fail.

After a cup of coffee and a stale, three-day old bagel, she left the apartment for the first time in two and a half days. The street, shops, people, trolleys, and traffic all looked the same.

It still smelled the same, too. A half block away was Oppenheim's Dry Goods, and it had everything on her little shopping list. She carried the handled paper shopping sack like a merit badge. She was on her way to a fate of her own making. Her success would be hers and hers alone.

She spent Monday afternoon riding the Pacific Electric trolley system that crisscrossed and zigzagged Los Angeles. She rode the Gower Street route twice, as a dry-run of sorts, on the Hollywood-Melrose line. She was trying to catch a glimpse of anything that could give her a clue as to what to expect the next day, when she would be taking the trip in search of employment.

Phryne was getting a feel of the city that she had impetuously accepted as her own. The sights, sounds, people and places of Los Angeles soaked into her essence. Phryne was getting her feet wet in California's unique river of life. She would conquer this new city, survive on her own, and someday she would view it all from the hills of Hollywood. She was certain of it. She felt reborn. That day, she knew she had crossed a significant threshold in the personal, emotive storm she had experienced when her husband shut the door behind him. After her afternoon of shopping and sightseeing, she had a spaghetti dinner at Georgiou's Mediterranean and walked back to her Figueroa Street apartment with a full belly and satisfied mind. She slept well that night.

First thing on Tuesday morning, she awoke, noticed the sunlight streaking into the room, and sprang from the bed with a task at hand. She grabbed the single undershirt Leopold had left behind, a pan of lukewarm tap water and a sliver of Fels Naptha soap. In short order, the little bedroom window was clean. The sunlight was no longer dank and dirty. It was bright and warm.

The small, shabby apartment had one justifying feature: a shower. Phryne had experienced a shower bath for the first time in Chicago, and decided that raining warm water was the only way to rid oneself of daily dust and wanton worry. She took an extended shower that morning, holding her face up to meet the cascade of water, rubbing her breasts with a bar of slippery Ivory soap, lingering in the sudsy foam, spreading the bubbling lather between her legs, down her thighs and basking her body in the refreshing stream of liquid warmth. She had carefully touched up her intimate grooming in the shower using Leopold's safety razor, and as she was rinsing off the blade, it occurred to her that he had not crossed her mind until just then … when she had finished. At that moment, Phryne realized that she would be fine, adjust and get a job on her own, however long that may or may not take.

By ten o'clock, she had smoothed the wrinkles out of her beaded, white chiffon dress and slipped it over her head without the usual camisole underneath. She decided to pair it with her red hook-and-eye boots, wide red ribbon belt, green lace-pattern stockings and green cloche hat. The kerchief hemline dashed teasingly just above her knees. She had curled her bobbed brown locks perfectly, allowing them to wistfully twist over the hat's right side. She applied her shining, deep red lipstick with care, forming the perfect Cupid's bow*. After a touch of purple eye shadow, black mascara carefully brushed over her lashes, a pinch and a blush of rouge to her cheeks, she was ready to meet Mandelbaum. She studied her reflection in the small mirror and wondered if she could control her nerves under pressure. She had never before actively looked for employment and had no idea what to truly expect, but had determined that her petite green, beaded pocketbook would be her hands-on accessory. Leopold had given her a cursory description of Mandelbaum, explaining that he was a smooth-talking man, full of himself and thought he was God's gift to women. For Phryne, that described just about half the men who walk the

Earth. The other half considered themselves to be God's gift to everyone.

As she stepped off the trolley at the corner of Melrose and Gower, her heart beat quickened and she could sense a tingle over her body. She was on a mission: employment, fulfillment, improvement. Anticipation and excitement alternated with every step of her feet down the sidewalk toward and through the red, climbing-rose covered Famous Players Paramount Studio archway entrance. The fleeting possibility of meeting Mary Pickford had crossed her mind, but she immediately passed it off as nonsense. Her excitement heightened as she entered the studio property and the place came alive with people busily crossing the streets, walking to and from barns, sheds, and tin-roof Quonset huts. A few automobiles and open-body trucks honked their way through the narrow streets. New construction was intermixed with what appeared to be random, ramshackle remnants of movie sets and backdrops. Common laborers, uniformed tradesmen, ladies in finery, women in neatly pressed suits, men and women obviously in costume filled the movie lot. Phryne noticed some men casting lengthy looks her way. She wore her clothes well and carried herself with pride. She smiled and continued along with gently swaying rhythm toward a grandiose white building, with a tall columned porch, terra cotta tile roof, decorative evergreens, huge flower urns of geraniums, and a red brick walk. Large brass letters over the center doors read: *Office*.

Behind an impressively large and long oak desk sat a lanky fellow in a deep blue, pin-stripe, three-piece suit. "May I help you, Miss?" His voice sounded like a field sparrow in April: lilting and sweet. His bow tie bobbed and quivered with his words. Phryne perceived a touch of mascara.

"I would like to see Mister Abner Mandelbaum. My name is Phryne Truffaut."

"He is currently in a production meeting with Mr. Balaban, and his meetings can be of undetermined length. You really should have an appointment, Miss."

"I have a Letter of Introduction, and I can wait. I'm the patient sort."

The thin man surveyed the twenty-two year old woman standing at his desk. He noticed that her makeup was impeccable, carefully applied and not blatantly overdone as was the unfortunate norm with most young female interviewees. "Who is the individual who wrote the recommendation for you, Miss?"

"Irving Feinmann: I am certain you know who he is." Phryne spoke in a tone of confidence, taking a chance that perhaps Irving's name was known, and that it would make her knock on Mandelbaum's door a little louder, and more audible than that of a winsome beautician from Buffalo. It worked.

"If you are willing to wait, you may take a seat in the *Welcome Foyer* and please make yourself comfortable. Hospitality staff should be around shortly with coffee or tea."

"Thank you, sir." She turned on a dime, and started toward the lobby.

Phryne's heels click-clicked across the polished marble terrazzo floor, stepping to a soft carmine red, arched-back love seat. It was positioned between two large, potted parlor palms and intermingled with several plushy upholstered chairs of Sherwood Forest green. Two men were seated in a large sofa to her left; one engrossed in the Los Angeles Times, the other was watching her. His eyes followed her from the desk to the sofa, not missing a movement. An elegant Oriental rug was under the men's feet. The receptionist left his desk with a small piece of note paper, opened a door behind him and returned immediately. Phryne assumed it was her arrival notice, and settled in for one of the most uncomfortable waiting periods of her life. She expected to be there awhile, and caught herself fidgeting with her pocketbook and decided not to light a cigarette despite the pedestal ashtrays scattered about. She fought back her nerves, and instead focused her thoughts on the room, its décor and the foot traffic in and out of the building. She was in a large atrium, with tall slender windows from floor to ceiling and a domed skylight. A formidable white wooden railing stretched across the second floor walkway.

A curvy young woman dressed in a sleek black dress and white apron startled her, and appeared at her left shoulder. "Would you enjoy a cup of coffee, tea or cocoa, Miss?"

"Coffee; black would be wonderful, thank you."

"Fine, and I'll bring a plate of biscuits."

"Thank you." Phryne was not expecting this level of personal accommodation. It came as a very pleasant surprise, and only added to her mysterious expectations of the place. She was puzzled. Leopold had not told her anything of his experience here. The curious gentleman on the sofa continued with his diligent attempt to disguise his glances. She smiled and curiously pursed her lips.

Single Girl, Married Girl

Within an hour, Phryne was escorted into Abner Mandelbaum's expansive first floor office. Two comely secretaries sat at desks on either side of the entrance to his inner office. He was standing behind his desk and sat as she entered, beaming a trifling, meaningless smile, "Come on in, Miss. Come on in, and take a seat, right there; right up front by the footlights, so I can get a good look at you, honey. I'm Abner Mandelbaum, Production Manager. What can I do for you, sweetheart?"

Phryne's eyes scanned the floor in front of his desk, discovered there were no lights, and realized he was only using movie talk. She sat in the wooden chair, slowly crossed her legs, placed a hand on her knee and smiled. She began to quickly study him, and search for hints as to what may lie ahead. He appeared to be near forty, perhaps twenty years her senior, greying at the temples, and nearly old enough to be her father. She caught a hint of Bay Rum aftershave lotion, but from his stubble, she guessed he had shaved at night rather than in the morning. A flashy dresser, his suit was impeccably tailored, shirt collar starched, tie sharply creased and silver cufflinks polished.

She gently, ever so softly, cleared her throat. It felt like her heart was up in her throat and blocking her vocal chords. "I am Phryne Truffaut, I have an introduction letter from Irving Feinmann." She handed the wrinkled paper across the desk.

"I've seen this piece of paper before, maybe two weeks ago or so, haven't I?"

"Yes, sir, you did. My husband brought it to you ten days ago."

"Didn't they hire him for set construction and maintenance or something?"

Phryne nodded slightly, "Yes, you did, sir. My husband has since left town and now I need a job. That's why I'm here today, Mister Mandelbaum, sir. I was married then. I'm single now."

He folded the letter and placed it on the desk in front of him. He had soft, pale blue eyes that looked like a clear sky in June, and defied his unvarnished complexion. Her first impression was that he was a man with conviction and not at all easily persuaded. "Really? I got your husband a job and he's already gone? You mean he's not around, then? He left you high and dry, just like that, did he? How long were you married?" His tone indicated his curiosity.

"Two weeks. I don't imagine he's here today. I don't know for sure, but I doubt it. He left without leaving tracks."

"Really? And why would he do that; walk out on you? I think that I have a right to be nosey if I'm going to give you a position … Fryné? Finey? Franny?"

Phryne continued to play the part of a coquette, and again crossed her legs. "It's P-H-R-Y-N-E. You pronounce it *fry-knee*. It's French." She noticed the glass doors behind him opened to a sunlit patio and lounge area, alive with palms and red begonias. "My husband left because he had trouble accepting the mistakes he had made back East. It's as simple as that. I couldn't stop him. It was his decision, indignant as it was."

"If I'm going to hire you as … as who knows … I want to know if you're going to be sticking around and not chasing after that man of yours tomorrow. It seems to me like it's an awfully big chance to take on a young, good looking tomato* so fresh off the vine, if you know what I mean. And exactly what is it that you do? What can you do? What's your talent? What have you got to sell?" He was teasing her now, and she caught it.

"I do beauty work, I do makeup and hair. I worked at a beauty salon in Buffalo for almost two years shampooing hair and doing ladies' nails and the last three years doing makeup, coloring and styling hair at the same salon. That shows that I'm stabile … reliable and dependable. And I'm good at what I do."

He leaned back in his wooden swivel chair and it creaked in protest. He was studying the young woman in front of him. His gaze slowly moved from her toes, up her calves, over her knees, a bit of stocking top, to her waist, breasts, shoulders and hazel eyes. "You're good at makeup, for sure. You did a great job on your own war-paint. And that dress fits just right. You say that you're a stable gal. I've got to give you that. We like our stables* out here." Unfamiliar with Hollywood slang, Phryne missed the camouflaged meaning.

He paused, and took a small round, red and white striped peppermint candy from the cut glass dish on his desk. "How about singing, dancing, or acting? Any good at that?" He had a hint of a smirk.

The way the conversation had been going, she wasn't surprised at his suggestive use of words, but wasn't sure if he had caused her to blush. At first, she felt apprehension, but it soon disappeared. His tone was ambiguous, but his demeanor was reassuring. His voice had charmed her. "I can dance the Black Bottom, Charleston and Baltimore Buzz. But I certainly don't act … and I don't sing, Mister Mandelbaum. Well, I do sing … I sing … in the bathtub … sometimes … usually in the shower." She did not want to seem as an unwashed, uncultured or unshaven Bohemian.

"Well, who knows? Maybe you will. You look as good as Colleen Moore, and certainly better than Norma Shearer. And I notice you have nice gams* to boot. Must be the dancing you do." He had a shallow smile. "I think we can find something for you to do: something that suits you. But what if your husband comes back tomorrow? Then what? What if he shows up just to gum up* your life?"

"He won't be back. Not with me. Not with me. I won't allow it. He's gone, and gone for good."

Silence settled in the room. Phryne awaited his response. Abner was sucking on his peppermint. His fingers were tapping the desk.

"How about you stand up? And turn around slowly … and walk toward the door … slowly, and turn around … and walk back … with your hands on your hips? How about that?"

She was certain she flushed at what she deemed a brazen request and asked, "Are you serious?" Phryne sounded indignant, but she only needed to be encouraged, not convinced.

His tone changed. "Yes …I am serious … please. I am serious. I want to see how you carry yourself, and exactly how you can move across the floor. I want to see your poise … your poise, that's all, so indulge me. Indulge me … please. Show me your poise, sweetheart."

She stood, set her pocketbook on the chair, gathered herself and took a breath. She did exactly as he asked. With each step, she could feel his eyes on her. She could hear him sucking on the candy as she turned and walked back toward the desk. She felt an inexplicable tingle.

She stood directly in front of him; hand on hip. He nodded, bit into the hard candy with a crunch, and motioned for her to be seated. On a piece of paper, he scrawled *makeup* and quickly scribbled his signature. He folded it twice, three times and hastily printed *Mabel Haverty* across the top. He stepped from behind his desk, walked around and handed it to her. He stood tall, with broad shoulders.

"Well, Miss Phryne, thank you. That was nice. You got poise under pressure. You are all set. Howard, my receptionist out there, will be more than happy to give you directions to the Hair and Makeup Department. And you tell Mabel if she has any questions … but I doubt she will … to call me. If for some reason she cannot use you, come back here right away and see me again."

Phryne was elated. The personal nightmare of three days ago had vanished and the useless, wanton worries were gone; washed from her thoughts. At least for now. "Thank you, Mister Mandelbaum. Thank you, so much." She reached out and welcomed his handshake. His warm, soft hand and gentle, surrounding grasp surprised her. It felt friendly. It felt good, comforting. She smiled wistfully.

"You are very welcome, Miss Phryne. And please, when it's just you and I, call me Abe." He placed his other hand under hers, gently holding it with his. "I am sure you will enjoy your work here. You will find that I … we … are very accommodating here at Players Paramount." She noticed his eyes had been momentarily fixed on the center of her scalloped bodice; staring directly at her cleavage. "And I can help you with a divorce, if that is where your marriage is headed. I know some lawyers and have had dealings with several, believe you, me. Just say the word, and I can help you start over and smooth over any difficult times." He moved into her and lowered his tone. "And … well … I could not help but notice that intricate silver and ivory breastpin on your dress. My eyes were drawn to it. It stands out. It's lovely."

She was taken aback by his offer, surprised and at a loss for a meaningful reply. She tenderly moved her hand from his. Her eyes and fingers went to the pin, and she gently brushed across it with her deep red nails. Her nipples pushed at her chiffon bodice. In a flash of modesty, she lowered her eyes and noticed his impeccably clean brown and white, two-tone oxfords. It was affirmed: without doubt, this man knew how to dress. "Thank you, sir … I'm sorry … Abe. My cameo was a birthday gift from a friend." She turned and started toward the large door. She felt his eyes, turned and smiled as her hand grasped the brass handle, "Thank you very much." Phryne was satisfied with her performance. She was smiling as she walked through the lobby.

Three weeks earlier, back in Niagara Falls, the brooch was her twenty-second birthday gift from Leopold. He had just proposed marriage.

Don't Put A Tax On The Beautiful Girls

The receptionist had given Phryne precise directions to the movie lot Cosmetics Studio on *Alvarado Alley*. It had a prestigious location on one of those little streets with quaint names. Her path took her over concrete sidewalks, stepping stones, cobbles, wooden pallets and walkways of wet, matted straw. On her first walk through Paramount Studios Phryne discovered that, if anything, a movie lot is a work in progress. Little alleyways and driveways had elaborate gas lights at every corner and hand-lettered street signs with names like *Persimmon Place, Cupid's Cove, Players Parkway* and *Lover's Lane*. It was an ever-expanding, ever-changing and messy hodgepodge of what was happening to Los Angeles. The film industry was taking over. She learned that when it gets down to brass tacks, nothing is as glamorous as it first seems. Phryne was in the land of dreams, the penultimate land of make-believe.

A large wooden portico covered the entryway to the Cosmetics Studio. A bold sign, lettered in flamingo pink script on a steel grey background read: *Through These Portals Pass The Most Beautiful Girls In The World.* When she had walked through the pergola she discovered that her destination was a forty-foot long Quonset hut. The Cosmetics Studio was nothing more than corrugated sheet metal bent into a half-circle and riveted to arched steel supports. Once again, Hollywood had proven itself to be the land of make-believe. Unlike the Production Office, there was no receptionist, no potted palms and no marble or wood parquet on the floor. It was sawdust. Entering from the sunlit lot and once inside, her eyes adjusted to the indoor light. Skylights and bow windows were along both sides of the building, augmented by a string of bare light bulbs hanging from the center of the steel structure. There were five-foot partition walls that certainly provided work stations, and a central concrete walkway that went straight down the middle to a lonesome exit door at the far end. It was warm and humid, almost like a gymnasium, with an inescapable, annoying tinny echo. Odors of perfume, lotions, waxes, peroxide, lacquer, grease paint and powder hung like fly-paper from the rafters. Music and ladies' chatter drifted through the building like dandelion seeds in a summer breeze. Two gigantic ceiling fans hung from the center support beam, churning the mixture of sounds, smells and sexuality.

A desk was to her right. The building had numerous occupants and buzzed like a beehive and swarmed with movement, conversation, bodies and voices. Phryne stood alone, studying her surroundings as a lost soul in paradise. Someone noticed.

Through the haze and clamor a woman's scratchy voice was heard. It was certainly seasoned with years of cigarettes and whiskey. "Can I help you, Sweetie?"

Phryne turned, and started toward the desk holding the neatly folded paper. "Mister Mandelbaum told me I should give this to Mabel." A handful of women instantly turned their attention toward her. They watched the precocious new girl with curiosity. Four of them moved away slightly, creating a spot up front for Phryne.

"Well, you found me, honey. I'm Mabel. What are you selling? Show me your wares, Sweetheart." Behind the desk was a buxom woman, standing just over five feet. Softy curled jet black hair rested on her shoulders. Her ample breasts were the only form visible under her otherwise shapeless, rose pink tunic. A narrow beaded belt hung at her hips. Like a gypsy, she was studying Phryne closely, her eyes moving over her form and then gazing straight into her soul. She reached out and took the paper.

"Myself. I'm selling myself. I'm a hair dresser and cosmetician. And I'm good at it."

Mabel curled an eyebrow, "Never heard it called that before. Hear that girls? We got a cosmetician here." A few quiet, scattered chuckles could be heard.

Phryne was not about to back down, certainly not now. "Well, some people do call it *cosmetologist*, but I prefer *cosmetician*. It sounds more professional, I think, don't you?" Somebody unknown snickered. Phryne glanced over the crowd of eight other women and smiled coyly. They all were wearing a pink smock, matching Mabel's.

"Where are you from, honey?"

"Niagara Falls: the honeymoon capital of the world. That's where I'm from. My name is Phryne. P-H-R-Y-N-E. It's French, and it's pronounced *fry-nee*." The white lie was an instant improvisation. Niagara Falls sounded a lot more exotic than Buffalo.

Mabel folded her arms across her chest, smiled and nodded. "Well, I'll tell you what, Phryne. You got nerve, moxie* … and I like that. I can use a … a cosmetician, like you say, with that kind of juice*. You got juice, kid. You be here tomorrow morning at eight, honey, and my lead girl, Thelma here will get you set up. We'll put you to work if that's what you want. You start at a flat hundred dollars a month, and seventy-five cents an hour you work over a fifty hour week. Raises when you prove you're worth more. Any questions?"

"No, Ma'am. I'll be here at eight. Thank you Ma'am."

Mabel stepped out from behind her desk, compelling the cluster of women to back out of her way. She reached out and took Phryne's hand, and held on after a brief handshake, covering it with her other hand, just as Mandelbaum had done. "Don't call me that … I'm not a Madam. Call me Mabel and I'll call you Phryne. I'll see you tomorrow, kid."

"Thank you, Mabel." Phryne was beaming as she walked from the studio.

No One Man Is Ever Going To Worry Me

The first few days at her new job were just that: new. She learned that the work was not a steady flow of faces in and out of a salon chair, but a rather unpredictable workload that was directly related to the movie studio's shooting schedule. She worked with a dozen other beauticians, all under thirty years old and wearing powder pink smocks. In the mornings, when the women donned their uniforms, they looked like a gaggle of pink geese, and sounded about as loud. She made friends immediately. Her laughter turned heads and her stories about Canada captured ears.

By the time Phryne had learned everyone's names, she had moved into a house on Preston Pointe, just a block from Sunset Boulevard with three new friends: Tracy, Pauline and Thelma. Drawn to her personality and mysterious nature, the women adopted Phryne as their newest close confidant. It only took a few days before the quartet became known as the *teepee* gang; created by the first letters of their first names. They shared giggles, gossip and an occasional gin. The giggles were good-natured fun, all about work, new fashions, music and men. The gossip was fierce, fiery and absolutely fabulous, filled with rumors about infidelity, parties, relationships and sex. The gin was consumed on their Saturday night jaunts to Hollywood's clubs. Every minute of the day was like reading the newest issue of *Screen Stars* magazine. The stories never changed much, only the characters. They were a busy quartet.

Abner Mandelbaum had visited her for the first time at the Cosmetics Studio on her third day. He had invited her to the first of a long string of casual dinners they were to share together. She enjoyed being seen in his company. Abe was a snappy dresser, acted the gentleman and drove a new Cadillac Custom. When he spoke, his voice bemused and soothed her, like he was casting a magical, romantic spell. His soft tone was not melodious, but hypnotic.

Phryne had tested the waters and landed her first new escort, a transplant from Texas that she had fished from the river of movie extras that flooded the Famous Players Paramount lot. His name was Fred and his fate was sealed before he could paddle his canoe around the pond a second time. He was sunk by the time he left the dock. "Phryne's friend Fred" just did not sound right.

After Fred, she had made the decision that certain first names would never again gain entrance to her intimate circle. And try as he might, overtly zealous sound technician Philippé Delacroix had no chance at a second night out, either. She was comfortable with Abe. He was reliable, predictable, established and as yet had not pressed her for physical favors. Phryne however, on occasion, did take the opportunity to invite herself to his plush residence on Pico Boulevard. To her, his first name was just perfect, and meant he was *able*.

The teepees regularly had casual male or even female houseguests, always out by morning. Overnight guests were always expected to completely vacate the premises at daybreak. It was a Commandment that never made it onto a stone tablet, or even crossed the lips of a living soul, but it was understood that no permanent relationships would be tolerated within their unconventional Hollywood sorority house.

Phryne became aware that she was one of the lucky few who were able to actually land a legitimate job in the Hollywood hills of Los Angeles. Celebrity was certainly everywhere, but there was also abundant debauchery, decadence and drugs. Prostitution was rampant up and down Hollywood Boulevard and life was not all beer and skittles*. Her new life was filled with distractions, something that she needed. Buffalo was a lifetime away. Unknowingly, she had a sort of self-imposed isolation, and had no desire to reconnect with her family or anyone from her past. At least not yet; her life had been so busy, and there had been no thoughts of Leopold for weeks. Like pages in a tattered history book, if left unopened, the wrinkles disappear over time. Her friendship with Eloisa was the only hole in her heart.

Phryne, Pauline, Tracy and Thelma soon became more popular as a coterie of cute party girls, based on their good looks, attitude and reputation. The four women were a handful of fun and an eyeful of sexuality. They continued to collect invitations to after-work parties both on and off the movie lot. Hollywood was a wide-open town. Clubs and dance halls the likes of The Tracodero, The Ball Room and Masquers' Club were frequent destinations. A lover was an essential part of their expanding, glimmering wardrobe. Of the four women, it was Phryne who seemed unwilling to start up new relationships that would last only overnight. After Fred and Philippé, she had recognized that she had grown familiar, comfortable, and content with Abe's companionship.

In mid October at the Club Casa Nueva, the arm she was on was again that of none other than Abner Mandelbaum's. Although he was not exclusive, he was the only man with whom she had consorted more than a few times. Phryne held onto a sense of trust and loyalty for Abe, not for any particular reason, but for appreciation. She felt she was building a friendship and had no need to meander.

On that particular night, the production executive made an introduction that she could capitalize on. Her new acquaintance was Ira Furst, a young attorney from Oxnard, and fresh out of Loyola Law School. It was surprising that despite his youth, he was obviously bald or balding, and was wearing a toupee that did not at all match his hair color. She was surprised that a man of means, a lawyer in Hollywood, would wear such a monstrosity of a hairpiece and be seen in public with a wrinkled suit. Her thought was: *nothing is more obnoxious than an obvious fake.* Nonetheless, despite his shortcomings in hairstyling and wardrobe, her August marriage was annulled within a week on grounds of unpredictable behavior. Her original petition to the court had listed the primary complaints as abandonment, emotional distress and financial derelictions. It seemed that attorney Furst knew his onions when it came to the law.

When Leopold left her, she had found herself mercilessly poured into a boiling cauldron of happenstance; alone in a strange new environment and without any form of financial or emotional support. Phryne persevered on her own, and was proud of what she had achieved. She had formed and shaped her life from a mold she alone had filled from torn pieces of her heart and broken promises.

She had written a few letters home, to her parents and brother, briefly covering the troublesome news about Leopold and their now defunct marriage. In her letters, she tried to paint her current situation only in the brightest and most cheerful colors, and used a wide brush. She was in fact very content with the way things were stacking up in her life. The replies she received from Buffalo were fluffed with platitudes, white-washed news and veiled pleas to return home. It wasn't long before she had begun to free herself from the written ropes of inked correspondence, and concentrate on rowing her canoe to the other side of the lake, and not come ashore until she knew the dock was secure.

Even the calmest of waters can become rough, and for Phryne, the ripples turned to waves on Monday, December 3.

Her doctor had given her a tentative due date at the end of June. She had experienced some occasional nausea at work, but when her menses did not occur in November, she suspected the reason.

When her husband left her in the lurch and walked out the door on September 10th, neither Phryne nor Leopold was aware of the life in her belly, a life they had created while traveling in a Pullman on the California Limited from Chicago. She was now caught in a life-altering quandary and tasked with a most important decision.

She had determined to keep her pregnancy private for as long as possible, allowing her to think through her situation. Phryne had options available to her in Hollywood that were kept deep on the QT* throughout the rest of the country. Additionally, she had been married, which meant she would be spared much of the social and morality stigmas attached to single motherhood.

By mid-December, she had begun to show. At work, Phryne's new best friend was her pink smock and she had decided to augment her evening wear with sweaters, tunic tops and drop-waist dresses.

She knew sooner rather than later, she would have to tell Abe the news. She was busy trying to find the right way to plead her case to him. Quite simply, she needed her job.

3: LONG BEACH, CALIFORNIA ~ 1927

Nice Work If You Can Get It

Monday, September 12, 1927

Long Beach is thirty miles due South of Los Angeles. When he had left Phryne three days earlier, Leopold Throckmorton walked down Figueroa Street and did not stop until he reached the shores of the Pacific Ocean. Emaciated physically, starved mentally and vanquished emotionally, he arrived to witness the sun dropping into the sea. He collapsed onto an expanse of oat grass beyond the sands and fell asleep; his duffle bag as his pillow and a suit jacket as his blanket.

He awoke before dawn and had thought it was the sound of surf crashing onto shore and the lamenting *caw-caw* of California gulls that disturbed his sleep. He had passed out from exhaustion the previous evening and did not notice the absurdly strange skyline that scores of oil derricks created up and down the beach. Massive wooden towers were everywhere: oil derricks, a hundred feet or more tall, pumping black gold from the Long Beach Oil Fields. What, in fact, did wake him, was the inexplicable mechanical humming, dull thump-thumping and metallic squeals creating a soup of noise so thick it was edible with a fork. His head hurt. His stomach ached. The noise was a contributing factor, but it was not the only thing that had pained his brain or socked him in the gut. He was in need of coffee and food.

Leopold stuck his hand into his pocket and found nothing but lint and flakes of cigarette tobacco where his money should have been. Struck senseless but for a few seconds, he realized the last time he saw his money roll was when he had thrown it across the room at the hotel clerk. After assessing his situation, he stuck his jacket back inside the sack, threw it over his shoulder, and walked in the direction of a cluster of worn, wooden, jerry-built structures a few hundred yards to his left, well above the tide water and storm line. Further away, up from the beach, were several long canvas-covered buildings that could be nothing other than bunk houses. Smoke was wafting up, into the morning air from crooked tin chimneys that were poked through the roofs. As he got closer, he recognized the smell of coffee and burnt toast rising from coal heaters and cook stoves inside the huts. The sun had not yet completely cleared the horizon and painted an orange sunrise that promised a glorious day.

Outside one of the larger wooden shacks, perhaps a dozen scruffy looking characters were milling about, smoking cigarettes, laughing and exchanging pushes, shoves and bumps. Their clothing could best be described as stiff, laundered filth; black and tattered. To a man, they needed a bath and shave. They had a rancid, heavy odor that reeked of tar. Leopold didn't feel so alone.

"Any work available here?" He was hopeful.

"Yeah, who's asking?" Loud, raucous laughter broke out.

"Me. I need work. I'm hungry, thirsty and need a place to lay my head tonight." He cautiously surveyed the group of men and anticipated that a surprise storm of hostility could blow in. He heard more guffaws, chuckles, and watched as the crowd pushed and shoved to get a closer look. Leopold took sudden notice when a giant of a man, with hands as big as melons, stood from an orange crate and took two steps toward him. Melon Hands gave Leopold a first impression he would not forget. Leopold had no doubt that Melon Hands was at the top of the pecking order here.

"You got any strength, bud?" His voice was like the bellow of a Brahma bull.

"I can lift you." Leopold immediately wondered if he made a mistake with that comment. The crowd was silent.

"Tell you what, wise guy. You pick up Otto over there, and then I'll think about getting you hired." Even more laughter brought more men to the growing circle of bodies around him. A dozen or so more curious laborers hurried from the bunk houses. Leopold was surrounded by an audience of ruffians certainly starving for any form of entertainment, any kind of distraction, any sort of ruckus. The noise got louder. The man who apparently answered to the name *Otto* stood and walked toward him. Leopold second-guessed his remark for a third time. Otto was indeed another large man, with a chest as big as a barrel, a neck as big around as a bushel basket, and legs like redwoods. He was easily twice Leopold's mass and even bulkier than Melon Hands.

He was forced to qualify his statement. "Oh, I can lift him all right. But there's no way I can fit my arms around that man." Chortles and boos rose into the morning air.

Melon Hands yelled over the noise, "We already got that figured out, wise guy. We've done this before! You're not the first freak in this sideshow!" Cheers, taunts and jeers emanated from each of the bystanders now. It was getting louder; anticipation grew.

The pack of men became a life force of one and began to act as a unit, gathering Leopold into its mass, and moving twenty feet away toward a large wooden scaffold at the end of an overhead ten-inch I-beam and conveyer line. A four-foot square wooden plate was flat on the ground, surrounded by half-inch, braided hemp cargo netting and one-inch rope attached to each corner, leading up to yet another platform twenty feet in the air. It was a freight lift, and they certainly had done this fascinating test of employment suitability before.

Otto went to the center of the wood plate, inside the netting and sat down smiling, his big arms folded across his body, sitting like a big-belly Buddha, awaiting the expected outcome. Nobody thought this obnoxious stranger could lift big Otto high into the air. Otto's massive legs were all a-kilter under his frame. His wide smile rivaled that of a cat in a sardine cannery. This was going to be fun.

The leader of this pack, the fellow he had named Melon Hands, stood next to Leopold, and said, "You climb up that ladder there, wise guy, and you get yourself up there, and grab hold of them four lines, and you raise Otto up to the loading level. You raise him straight up to Jesus. You do that, and you get hired. If you don't, the boys here can chase your sorry ass right into the ocean for all I care."

Leopold looked up to the loading crane, dropped his sack of belongings, and bounded up the ladder. The mob of men went silent, but not for long. Taunts and snickers began straightaway. From his twenty-foot high vantage point, Otto and Melon Hands didn't look so big.

"Come on, hot-shot. Lift!"

Leopold reached to the platform floor, and grabbed the four braided ropes. His head throbbed worse than a grain alcohol hangover. Confident in his plan and strength, he quickly twisted the ropes, and tossed them over the I-beam, grabbed the free end and drew it tight across the steel girder. His audience was quiet, but again, not for long. The mockery and jeers began again as he looked down.

He wrapped the rope twice around his forearm, grasped with his right hand, and in concert with his left, he began to draw the freight netting up to the loading platform. The hemp moaned, the mob continued to torment him with insults, and pull by pull, foot by foot, Otto was raised. His voice erupted from his thick throat, "Oh Lord, Praise Thee, Oh Lord! I've been lifted up!" It was a chant that was heard all the way to the Arkansas Primitive Baptist convention in Little Rock. First there was laughter, then the audience let out hurrahs and whistles. People like a winner. Mobs don't like to lose.

Leopold's back ached, his forceps burned, his head still hurt and Otto hung even with the platform. Two more pulls, and Leopold brought his human load sideways to the elevated safety of the scaffold. He graciously helped pull away the cargo net and offered a helping hand to the big fellow. "Pleased to meet you, Otto. My name is Leopold."

Once on his feet, Otto gave Leopold a hearty hand shake and yelled to the crowd below, "Hey, Larry! Now you got to hire this Monkey!"

Melon Hands introduced himself as Larry, the straw boss, and hired Leopold as a *roughneck*, which on an oil derrick can be any hired hand: a jack of all trades, a one-size-fits-all job title for hard, back-breaking labor. Two pieces of boiled bacon, a slice of bread and a glass of lukewarm coffee later, he went to work; following orders, getting scolded and derided, praised and pushed harder and faster. His pay was two hot meals a day, biscuits, board and twenty dollars a week for a string of five sunup-to-sundown shifts. He would be given one day off before it all was to begin again. Halfway through his first day, Otto gave him a nickname he would never forget: *Scaffold Monkey*, referring to his success at climbing and pulling him twenty feet into the air.

Thanksgiving, November 22, 1927

The hard work did not afford much opportunity for self recrimination. Leopold needed to be occupied and arduous physical labor kept his idle thoughts and worry at bay. For his first five-day stretch of twelve-hour days, his aching muscles and the unfamiliarity of the job did just that. When the sun went down, after the evening meal of beans, corned beef and bread filled his belly, there were a few hours of conversation, bawdy talk, and jokes before it was lights-out and time for sleep. A radio in the bunkhouse provided some limited distraction with news broadcasts from Los Angeles station KHJ, and not much else. Along with a handful of other self-made musicians, a transient roughneck from the oil fields of Oklahoma provided most of the entertainment with his ukulele. He answered to Erastus Lester and had a somewhat limited musical library to draw from, but if somebody could sing a tune or even hum a melody, his accompaniment skills came through. Although he had a voice that carried like a Swiss yodeler, it sounded like he was gargling with gravel. A few harmonica players were in the camp, one fellow with a Jew's harp and even an Irish fiddle player who was rumored to have escaped a German prison camp by overpowering and killing three guards during the Great War. Everyone gave Séan Duffy plenty of breathing room. The lights went out at eleven and the process started all over again at sun-up. After a breakfast of boiled bacon, biscuits and gravy, the day's production began.

The work was tough, the food barely edible and living conditions on a par with sleeping on the ground. The bunks were metal frames with wooden slats and two inch straw mattresses. There were two stations in camp equipped with potable well water that was suitable for cooking or drinking, drawn from the earth by hand pumps. It had a taste that hinted of turpentine, although the proximity to the oil fields probably mimicked the odd taste rather than pine pitch. No trees could be seen.

Most of the men did their laundry in the Pacific, which left a stiff, salt water starchiness to everything. A once-a-week laundry service picked up and delivered on Tuesdays, but at five cents a bagful, it was not worth a toss. Once the crude was pushed into the fabric, it stayed in the fabric. Leopold used only two of his shirts and trousers, and kept them separated from everything else in his duffle sack. Unwittingly, he was thinking of the future. Somewhere in his mind, he got the message he would not be staying in the oil field for any extended period of time.

Only two shower stations were available in the Seal Beach section of the field where Leopold worked. They were supplied with hand-pumped well water and heated by oil-fired vats secured above a wooden platform.

After two full months, he had a hundred and seventy four dollars to his name. He had sliced a two-inch gash into his mattress and kept his cash in the bank, so to speak. He kept to himself, and talked only when talked to. The sole person he allowed into his personal space was big Otto.

His melancholy subsided and his dreams weren't as vivid, but the guilt continued to blacken his spirit. He had nighttime visions of his mother and sisters calling to him from inside their home. As he would hurry to the door, and struggle with his steps, Dillon Cafferty held him back, flames would push up from under the door frame, lick outward around the window sills and raise from the clapboards. At that point he would wake, oftentimes in a cold sweat and out of breath.

The first day of Advent was Sunday, December 2. During the evening meal Otto had asked him, "You got plans to go anywhere for the Christmas shut down, Monkey?"

Leopold was staring into his tin plate of hash and cornmeal, his thoughts drifting into a lost vacuum of nothingness. Otto was sitting across from him at one of the flimsy metal tables in the chow hall. Leopold looked up at the big man. His eyes had the gleam of a six-year old and a smile that was equally as innocent. The kerosene lamp between them was set too high, flickering and belching twisted puffs of black smoke.

"I have no place to go, really. I think I'll just stay here and enjoy the quiet. You know: no noise, no machines, no people."

"Aw, hell, Monkey. That ain't no good. You ain't got nobody around here, then? No family, nobody?"

"No, I don't. It's just the way the cards were dealt to me, Otto. And the way I played my hand."

"You and me could take the bus up to Los Angeles. I ain't never been, and we can each find us a sweet mama* up there, I know we can. You know, we can do what the rest of the world does to pass the time, and get us some of that jazz in the hills up there. I hear it's jumping up there with dance halls and liquor and all the things a man really needs."

Leopold looked back down to his plate. "Tell you what, Otto ... you go ahead without me. I've been there. And I can tell you that the only difference between them dance hall dames up there and all the holes drilled in the ground down here is a pair of stockings, perfume and some lipstick."

The big man was puzzled. "Some dame kick you square in the family jewels when you was down, or what?"

"Let's say that I've learned my lesson the hard way. And I don't want to hear that school bell ring any more. It hurts my ears."

They finished their evening chow in silence. That was the last conversation he had with Otto. The next morning, long before first light, Leopold dressed in the dark and grabbed his duffle bag of clean clothing. He took the cash out of his mattress bank, stuck two fives in his pant pocket and stuffed the rest inside his shoes. He guessed it to be about two o'clock in the morning when he walked to the field office and knocked on the door.

Larry Melon Hands yelled from inside, "This better be good, damn it! What the hell do you want?"

"Larry, you can go back to sleep. This is Scaffold Monkey and I just want to tell you that I quit." Leopold could hear Melon Hands hurling curse words at him as he turned and walked out of Seal Beach the same way he walked in two months earlier: with his entire world in the bag on his shoulder. Two nights earlier, when he awoke from a dream, he could not get back to sleep. He stared at the canvas roof of the bunkhouse for hours. He was watching the indiscernible shadows and forms dance across the ceiling, and imagining what they could be. The pale moonlight and stars would flash tiny bits of light between the seams of the tattered sail cloth. The sparkling stars beamed a revelation to him, and a glaring epiphany that would change his life in ways unimaginable. From somewhere in the deepest bowers of his memory, he remembered something his father had said when he had spoke about the battle at Belleau Wood in The Great War: *Respond to fire with return fire.* He had decided to become a policeman and fight the fire, the mobsters that fuel it, and the arsonists that had set it. As a policeman, Leopold Throckmorton could fight the forces that murdered his family.

The Union Pacific rail yard was only a quarter-mile down Oceanside Boulevard. A gibbous, three-quarter moon cast its milky light around the railroad tank cars that crammed the sidetracks. Round, black, ominous-looking giants with large white lettering that read *Richfield Oil Corp.* completely conquered the landscape. Only one building large enough to resemble a railway office could be seen, but it did not have a passenger platform or travelers milling about. The murky yellow light of kerosene lamps was coming from within. To no avail, he looked for something that could be a ticket office. Three pumping stations at trackside sat ready to fill the empty black giants with crude pumped from the Earth. He followed the tracks to a boardwalk that ran between the structures, hoping to find a way to get a ride back to civilization. He had a pre-determined destination: San Francisco. Rumor had it that the city it had become one of the more prosperous and opportune places in California.

He heard muffled voices from the sidetrack behind him. He looked down at his crude-soaked, heavy work shoes and thought about the cash he had inside them.

Hallelujah! I'm A Bum

He stopped in his tracks. "Who's there?"

Seconds passed. A gruff voice spoke with sarcasm, "Ain't nobody here but us chickens, screw*."

"I'm not a cop. Hear me? I'm looking for the ticket office."

After rude chuckles of disbelief, "You ain't going to buy no ticket here, bud. But we thinks you could be a railroad bull." Two rough-looking characters rolled out from the undercarriage of the tank car nearest him, ready for a scuffle. One carried an axe handle and the other a filthy carpet bag. An eight-inch knife was shining in the moonlight. They stood studying him.

Leopold squared himself in front of the men. "I'm not a cop. I want to catch a train to Frisco."

They relaxed their stance, but continued to hold their weapons with malice. The tension was replaced by cautious distrust and curiosity. "Like I said, you ain't going to buy no train ticket here." The fellow with the bag and the knife chuckled again. The realization had hit home. Leopold now knew these men were tramps. "But if you want to catch a rattler*, you could ride with us. You got any money?"

Leopold was uncomfortable being on the defensive again. He feared this meeting wasn't going to end without trouble.

They continued to question him, "You running from something? You got money? You on the lam*?"

"I'm not a cop, I'm not a crook, and I think I have five dollars in my pocket."

"A fin? You couldn't buy a ticket to Frisco on a mule train for a half sawbuck, bud. And from your looks it seems like you came from that oil field over there and if you did come from that oil field, it means that you got more than five dollars. Come clean, what's your game? What you got in that bindle* sack? It's too damn big to be your bindle."

He was forced into a fast retort, thinking on his feet in anticipation of what could happen. "I left my wife last week down the coast in San Diego. I caught her with another man and I left. I made my way up here ... and I worked three and a half days on the oil derricks over there and I hated it. I quit this morning and I'm leaving for San Francisco. That's the whole story. All of it." He waited.

"Let's see that five bucks." They were ready.

"No. You tramps are not getting my money."

They came at him. He tossed his duffle at the fellow with the club. His right boot came up and hit the hand of the vagabond wielding the knife, sending the weapon up and into the yard behind them. He knew that was a bit of luck, and let loose a right cross that landed on the jaw with a crunch, dropping the thug to his knees. His left forearm partially blocked the man swinging the club, forcing it over his shoulder and it landing along his back. He gasped for breath. A crushing upper-cut caught that fellow at the bottom of his chin. A snapping sound let Leopold know that once again he had inflicted damage.

He had an instantaneous flashback and reflected on his teenage days at the Black Rock Boxing Club. He was thankful. Both men were on the ground holding their jaws.

The fellow that took the upper cut spit out a tooth in a bloody mix.

Leopold stood his ground. "Well, now what?"

The fellow that lost the club replied, "How about you give us that five dollars you got and we give you a ticket to ride with us? We can show you the way, and we know where the bulls and the cinder dicks* are." The other man slowly got to his feet and held his jaw. He stood with clenched fists, nodding at his cohort's words.

Leopold knew he could not trust these two and his options were limited; very limited. One man versus two carries a set of odds that usually doesn't hold up indefinitely. "How about I give you a buck apiece, and we ride together. That's the deal."

The hobos looked at one another, and without a spoken word, seemed to agree. "Fine. A buck apiece. But we lose you in Barstow anyway. That's as far as we're going. The train goes on up to Bakersfield, to the refinery there. You can jump off there, and catch a freight to Frisco." Both men snickered. "And don't call us *tramps* no more. We're not bums. We're hobos. We're looking for work … looking for work in Barstow."

Leopold tried to appear reluctant and only slightly apologetic, while still speaking in a stern tone, "Well … all right. But what's the game here? What needs to be done?"

Without negotiation, an uneasy truce was formed. "See that, mister oil man? You don't know it all. You pay up, then we'll talk."

For the moment, Leopold had the upper hand. He was the one with the money. "I'll pay you in Barstow … when we get there. Now tell me, what do I need to do here?"

"Two tracks over, that's the sign we read down the road. It's a slow mover to Bakersfield, by way of Barstow, on smooth

Santa Fe rails to north of Los Angeles with no bulls to worry about. There's no freight, just crude. You come with us, and we'll get you there … you and that sack of whatever-you-got. There's a bunch more riding, no doubt, but never mind them bums. We're the ones that get paid. You stick with us, and we'll get you there. "

"Understood. Let's go … I'll follow you two." One of them shuffled off and found the knife. He glanced at Leopold, and with a hint of a sneer, slipped it back into his boot.

On the far side of the rail yard, all three sat waiting in the tall scrub grass and bushes. Perhaps an hour later, a consist of tank cars filled with California crude began its slow, noisy and steady ride north to the refineries of Bakersfield.

Leopold followed behind the men, running, heads lowered through the bushes and grass to the stone, sand and ciders of the rail bed. One at a time, the men hopped onto the floor of the slowly moving tank car. His heart in his throat, he tossed his duffle up, and grabbed onto a support bar. The two hobos watched with big eyes and smiles. "You made it, oil man! You made your first good *run and hop!*" He cautiously maneuvered his body onto the railcar's narrow platform.

The train was moving at what could be the pace of a brisk walk. The consist was noisy, squeaky, unsteady and ever-so-slowly gaining speed. Each car was slightly less than thirty feet long, about sixteen feet high at the filling dome, and had a capacity of six thousand gallons of crude. The car was indeed a tank on wheeled rail trucks, and 'seating' was restricted to a three foot cat walk on each end of the car. The hobos sat at the right rear, side-by-side, knees to their chests and surveying Leopold. He was perhaps four feet away, leaning his back against the tank and left arm on his duffle. It was not possible to be comfortable. Man-ladders were fixed onto each end and middle of the car to access the fill dome on top of the tank, and two-inch iron reinforcing bars were welded from the car frame, up and around the tank that created a short railing. It was a warm morning, but the air rushing past pushed a chill through his body. It was a degree of discomfort that he had never before come close to experiencing. It was a barefaced fact that traveling as a hobo was dangerous and not at all glamorous. The tramps were staring at him, studying him with glaring curiosity. "So, what's your story oil man?"

"I'm Leopold. Leopold Throckmorton, from San Diego."

The hobos shared a look.

"I'm Hank. This is Gerald. We're from Nowhere. Got a cigarette, San Diego oil man?"

They were getting bolder. He did not want to provoke them, and offered his Chesterfields. They each reached and took one from the ragged pack.

"Need a match?"

They declined, and lit their own. In irony, Leopold thought the cigarettes were an Indian peace-pipe of sorts. The thick tension eased a little, but there was no talk; only looks. It was a long, slow agonizing ride. The wind, noise and fragile truce, combined with the precarious seating on the tank car, made for a most harrowing trip.

It was at least five hours and one-hundred-forty miles later that the train slowed and stopped for water in Barstow. "This is where we get off, San Diego."

Leopold handed the men a five dollar bill from his pocket. They looked to each other and grinned.

"How do I know when the train has reached Bakersfield?"

Hank yelled after they jumped off the train and hit the ground in a trot, "When it stops! … Smooth rails, San Diego! Watch the railroad bulls to Frisco!"

With the hobos off the car he was able to lie down, albeit uncomfortably and frighteningly. He was curled up behind the brakeman's wheel and freight rails, leaning up against his duffle and watching the arid landscape pass by. He remembered with mild relief that he did not need to worry about anyone with a knife or axe handle, at least for the remainder of this leg of his journey. His knuckles ached, a painful reminder of his first fistfight in years.

Waiting For A Train

Monday, December 3

The dark of night was approaching. The squeal of air brakes, the moan of steel and the lamenting echo of a train whistle from somewhere down the track was Leopold's cue: he had arrived in Bakersfield, California.

It was time to exit his free ride. Thankful that the agonizing trip was over, the concept of jumping off a moving mass of hundreds of tons of steel and crude oil was ominously daunting. The idea itself was awkward: jump with bravery, fall with grace and land safely. It was idiocy born of necessity.

The rail yard was about the same size as Barstow, but with some varied types of freight cars on the sidings and moving along on neighboring tracks. Hanging on with his left, he tossed his bag, jumped down and away in one lunging movement off the right side of the car. He landed with legs askew, moving quickly and trying to maintain his balance, while failing, and rolling on the grass and gravel. It was over as fast as it started. He stood, gathered himself, and brushed some of the dust off his crude-soaked jacket and pants.

Between the moving tank cars of his train, he could see lights, not kerosene lamps, but electric, about a half mile away, which lighted what appeared to be the main station. Looking back down the line, he saw the caboose fast approaching, and could sense the next part of his journey looming in front of him. Carefully, he made his way across five sets of tracks, jumping, hopping and running toward a road where automobile and sparse pedestrian traffic could be seen. Train whistles abounded and squealing metal echoed. He could hear sounds other than crude oil trains and moaning oil derricks. His escape was imminent. His sack felt lighter, and his mood brighter. As the sights and sounds of the station became nearer, he felt a sense of excitement akin to that of meeting an old friend after years of separation. He had a secret hope of new relationships mixed with a daunting fear of rejection, while sadly knowing that no one knew him from Adam.

He had indeed found Bakersfield's Santa Fe Station. Once inside, he sloughed off the looks he received and made a beeline to the Men's Travelers' Lounge. There he removed his stiff clothing, socks and union suit.

He washed his arms, face and hands in the sink. Compared to what he experienced in the oil field, a porcelain wash basin with hot and cold water in a train station seemed like the Ritz. He looked at his reflection in the mirror, and wondered why he appeared older than he remembered. His two-day stubble may have had something to do with it, but he placed the blame on California crude. He looked closely at his just-washed hands and back up to the mirror. The lines on his forehead, the little wrinkles at his eyes and corners of his mouth all were marked with the stubborn black stain left by the heavy crude. His hands, nails, cuticles, calluses and palm lines were all marked like a pen-and-ink drawing. He guessed that perhaps in six months or so the ground-in dirt could be washed away.

He dressed in fresh clothing from his duffle sack; clothing that he had originally packed when he left Buffalo on August 28. As he attempted to shake the wrinkles out of his trousers, and tried to smooth his shirt, a flash of thought crossed his mind. He wondered if Phryne was still in Los Angeles. It was his first such thought in months. He forcefully pushed it from his mind.

He decided to keep his oil-soaked work boots when he removed his wet, stinking bankroll from them and slipped it inside his brown oxfords, half in one, half in the other and a twenty dollar bill in his pant pocket, considering it was enough for train fare to San Francisco. He put on his wrinkled suit coat, took out his checkered golf cap, snapped it into place, put his grimy work boots in the duffle, and drew the strings shut. He thought how different his life could be in just a few short days. He wouldn't be Scaffold Monkey or Oil Man anymore, and there wouldn't be an Otto, Melon Hands, or Nowhere Men. His time as a roughneck was just that; it had taught him roughneck skills. It certainly helped him fight off two hobos back at Seal Beach.

His old clothes went into an open trash bin inside the station, and he wondered if any vagabond would grab them up. While he was riding on the tank car, he appreciated the oil-soaked properties of his jacket and pants. They were the perfect windbreakers, not letting the rushing air penetrate the filthy fabric.

The large clock hanging from the station's lofty ceiling read 7:45. A schedule was on the wall in front of the ticket counters. In large letters he saw that Santa Fe number 22 would depart at 10:45 and arrive in San Francisco at 11 AM tomorrow. It was just under three hours before the train was to board on track 4.

He walked to the Atchison, Topeka & Santa Fe ticket agent and purchased a one way coach ticket for $8.75. The Harvey

House restaurant enabled him to fill his belly with meatloaf, gravy, mashed potatoes and green peas for $1.35; quite a change from the cornmeal, hash and boiled bacon of the oilfield. He bought a fresh pack of Chesterfield at the newsstand for 20¢ and resisted the temptation to purchase a newspaper. No news is good news.

He took a seat on one of the long oak benches in the transit hall, lit a cigarette and began to watch the throngs of humanity inside the station. Every place he had been that day seemed like a place he had already been. Memories flashed through his head like lightning on a hot night in August. They crashed with a thunderous boom and disappeared in a deluge of gloom. He would work through this emotional downpour just as he had so many memories ago.

Buffalo and Phryne were in the past, somewhere down the line; along the endless ribbon of steel rails. He was going in the other direction. Leopold Throckmorton was waiting for a train and heading for a new life. He was on a mission: a mission of redemption. He was determined to become a cop.

4: HOLLYWOOD, CALIFORNIA ~ 1927-28

I Double Dare You

December 16

Friday night at the Tracodero night club was the place to be for personal encounters, drinks and intimate interludes. Phryne and Abe were there, along with friends Penny and Gus, and scores of other merrymakers. They were at one of Hollywood's hot spots; where pacts were presented, partners paired and partiers partied. The club was full of revelers; it was the holiday season; Hanukah, Christmas and New Year's. Everything flowed freely inside: business prospects, bawdy proposals, lewdness, liquor, dancing and deals. And like the rest of Hollywood and Los Angeles, prohibition was only a rumor at the Tracodero -- something the rest of the country had to deal with. If you could get in the front door of the Tracodero, you drank. Joey 'Iron Man' Ardizzone and Iggy Dragna ran the Southern California mob smoothly, in the open, under the noses of well-paid police sergeants and captains who were kept occupied with much more pressing matters; such as the yellow peril*, pachucos* and overt street prostitution on Hollywood Boulevard.

Penelope VanSylke was an aspiring young actress from Poughkeepsie, New York. The raven-haired beauty was fresh off the farm, barely nineteen years old with stars in her eyes. Penny's curvaceous five-foot-two frame was adorned from head to toe with everything sensuous; all of it paid for by someone else. Her someone else that night was Gustav Borgmann, an associate producer at United Studios on Marathon Street, just two blocks from Famous Players Paramount.

Phryne was eager to have the opportunity to talk to Abe alone and had hoped to get the chance tonight. She was nervous with anticipation, but while she was unsure how he would take her pregnancy news, she was confident that she had groomed the sort of relationship that was malleable enough to bend to her advantage. As a couple, they were well paired in what Phryne deemed important. He was caring, considerate, careful. He always asked for her input on their nights out, and his sexual zeal and stamina matched hers. It was clear as a bell that Abe was infatuated with her, and he had told her in so many words that he would do anything to keep her satisfied. Tonight Phryne would find out if he really meant what he had said, promised and whispered to her so many times over the past three months. She had a fondness for him, a comforting sort of puppy love that was unlikely to become dangerous or spin out of control. He was that sort of man - privately reliable and publicly reserved. So far, their relationship had been noncommittal. Tonight, Phryne was hoping for some kind of guarantee that she would not lose her job. It was a bold assumption for a pregnant woman to remain employed. She needed security and would try to convince her lover Abe to grant her some. Without it, she knew she would be wallowing in a serious predicament.

Phryne had pushed her chair up against Abe's and had been pressing her calf to his and teasing his inner thigh, running her hand slowly upward on his wool flannel trousers. As always, the band had been contributing to the atmosphere and played suggestive, ribald jazz.

Among the few dessert plates, coffee cups and ashtrays on the white tablecloth, two nearly empty bottles of Australian champagne sat off kilter, forlorn and floating in the melted ice inside the gleaming chrome buckets. Penny had nearly finished the first of three bottles by herself and became giddy, brazen, openly passionate and overtly suggestive, nearing but not quite turning into sloppy. Gus made a half-hearted attempt to rein Penny in, but that horse had already left the corral. She was whispering, tickling his ear with her lips and tongue. Her fingers were playing in his hair. Phryne had been watching the bawdy progression with curious amusement and chuckled to herself. She had decided much earlier that any alcoholic beverage with a kicking kangaroo on the label should be consumed in moderation. Gus' hand under Penny's dress did nothing to dampen or harness her ravenous mood. By eleven o'clock, Penny had Gus kicking in his stall like a mule, champing his bit and snorting passion like a stud in Spring. It was clear this wasn't her first rodeo, and she was going to bridle him like the galloping stallion she wished him to be.

He couldn't control it any longer and made his plea, "Penny and I need to make tracks*, Abe. Thanks for the evening. My girl Penny has a script reading tomorrow." That was about as fast as anyone could have fabricated a believable lie and made a quick exit without uttering a simple *goodbye*.

Phryne watched in delighted amusement and painfully held back a giggle as Gus nearly tripped over his chair and bounced, hopped two steps away, and struggled to keep his balance. Penny and her bucking bronco staggered across the parquet floor and through the large white doors to the anteroom and lobby, gone but not forgotten.

Abe pulled one of the last two bottles of bubbly out of its bucket "Would you like to wet your whistle one more time, Sweetheart?" His tone was suggestive and inquisitive.

"Sure. Just a little, I don't want to get tipsy. I like to know what's going on. I always do. You know what I mean?"

He smiled, and poured some of the last bubbly into their glasses. "So what's on your mind, Phryne? You obviously have something on your mind, I can tell. I can read you like a Charlie Chaplin script; no talk, just pantomime."

"I need help. I'm over a barrel … in a fix."

Abe did not respond, but nodded ever so slightly. She lit a cigarette knowing this chance could slip away and nervously felt the seconds ticking by. Her eyes moved from the ashtray, to the cigarette, to his. Still, he did not reply and did not flinch. He kept quiet and remained stoic. He was that kind of player. Phryne knew she had to take a leap. It was as if he had given her a dare; a double-dare, the serious kind. She decided to play his game, call his bluff and put all of her cards on the table, in plain sight; face-up and spread out.

"I'm pregnant … with Leopold's baby."

Abe bobbed one more gestured nod, and still, no words left his lips. Phryne felt tortured. It was yet another dare. He was playing her.

He picked up his glass, took a swallow of champagne and set it down without a sound. On stage, a pair of perky young vocalists from Toledo and *The Orleans Jazz Men* were working their way through '*Six Or Seven Times*'. An exasperated Phryne crushed out her cigarette, telegraphing her impatience and frustration with his silence. Abe noticed and decided to break his silence, "Marry me, Phryne."

"I've heard that line before."

"You don't need to be defensive, Sweetheart, not with me. I know you well enough to see that you had something on your mind tonight. I knew you were troubled." He took her hand and continued, "So, before you say anything more, let me explain something to you and lay it all out in the open. You mean more to me than any other woman that I've ever known … and I've known quite a few. From dolls to gold diggers*, pro skirts* and floozies to flappers. From the moment you walked into my office, you had me. I'm dizzy* with you, Sweetheart. That's the truth. When you're with me, I'm complete. I have never felt this way before. When you're with me, I'm confident. No other woman has ever made me feel invincible. I'll walk through walls for you, Phryne. I'll give you a bed, a home, clothes on your back and food in your belly. I'll provide for you. Without question, without doubt, with no second thoughts. You have nothing to fear from me. I'm a straight arrow, square shooter and most of all, I'm on the level. All I ask in return is that you do not shame me. That's all I ask."

He finished his champagne. "I am speculating that you have decided to have the baby?"

"Yes. The other option wasn't an option for me. It couldn't be."

"Marry me, Phryne. The child will have a father and you will have a caring husband." He came across as sincere, determined and straight up.

Phryne spoke without forethought, "I'm Presbyterian, Abe. I'm guessing that you're Jewish?"

She was afraid that she had spoken too soon, without thinking, and that her question was too forward. She immediately assumed that she had embarrassed him.

He smiled. Her fear and trepidation waned. Her worry vanished, and he did not hesitate with a reply.

"Let me explain that to you, Sweetheart. If a person is born a Jew, that person is a Jew until that person dies or follows another Faith. I'm as Jewish as President Coolidge. And just like me, he doesn't go to Temple either. Of course not! I'm joking, of course. Calvin Coolidge is not a Jew, but a Christian. I am just making a point. My mother and father emigrated from Saarbrücken, Germany in the last century. I was born and raised in Brooklyn, right in the shadows of the Williamsburg Bridge. My father, he was a tailor and haberdasher; died right after the Great War, and my mother passed three years later. I came out West the hard way, working job to job, hand to mouth, town to town. I ended up here in Los Angeles. You could say that I was in the right place at the right time. I loved it and lived it; got started with Meyer, then Lansky and here I am. And I believe that I could be in the right place at the right time again, what do you think, Sweetheart? And, it's true, I'm a thirty-five year old Jew who does not go to Temple in a town full of Jews. As far as I'm concerned, we can get married tomorrow, at the courthouse, in a chapel, in a synagogue, or wherever you want."

Phryne was sold. Her heart was his. She wasn't expecting this, but did not discount it. She felt victorious. She was elated. Opportunity had knocked. She answered.

"Well, will you marry me, Sweetheart?"

"Yes. Absolutely, positootly* I will. And I will never shame you. Never."

She kissed him. Abner wasn't in Temple. He was in dreamland.

Butter And Egg Man

Friday, December 30, 1927

Phryne had been rescued by her hero, Abe. In the nick of time, the damsel in distress was pulled from the railroad tracks and the good guy in the white hat ran the evil villains out of town. Her hero then swept her off her feet with a marriage proposal that she had accepted with glee. But it wasn't to be the end of Abner's Hollywood production; far from it.

Phryne's world was about to burst into bloom beyond her wildest dreams. On Monday, following his proposal, Abner went to work. Together, they had decided that the ceremony would be held between Christmas and the New Year, which delegated Friday, December 30th as the big day. The wedding was to be a production, a first-rate *Abner Mandelbaum Production* all the way from curtains up to the rolling credits.

The movie set used in the Clara Bow and Clive Brook Hawaiian-themed film *Hula* was the studio's romantic re-creation of a South Seas paradise on a Gower Street back lot. Crepe orchids, silk passion flowers, red and yellow hibiscus, potted banana palms and a bubbling stream were the backdrop for their wedding vows. Everything, from Phryne's costume department, flowing white wedding gown to the cleaning crew after the reception, Abe used Paramount's resources to the fullest. He had also invited some of the former talent that he had represented when he was an agent, current actors under contract and all of Phryne's co-workers at the cosmetic studio. Many of the studio's headliners were in attendance, despite the short notice and the holiday book ends of the wedding. He had arranged for the Wesleyan minister from the studio's chapel to perform a non-denominational ceremony.

Two tuxedo-clad musicians played Wagner's '*Bridal Chorus*' on classical Spanish concert guitars as Phryne walked down the aisle. Her escort was comedic actor Roscoe 'Fatty' McPhail, whose career had ended much too soon, three years earlier by an unwarranted sex and murder scandal. Phryne's three roommates, Tracy, Pauline and Thelma stood as her Maids of Honor, and Abe's Best Man was none other than traveling talent scout Irving Feinmann.

Standing in front of the orchid, passion flower and hibiscus blooms, with Abner by her side, and under a white trellis adorned with pink roses, Phryne knew that this was indeed, a dream wedding. She teared, and realized how fortunate she was to have been able to claim the man next to her as husband. The ring he slid on her finger was a rather modest gold band, if not for the five ostentatious ¼ carat rubies.

It was a wedding for the ages, something Phryne would never forget. Ironically bittersweet, it was the second wedding in less than six months that her family or close confidant, Eloisa could not attend. All together, a hundred-plus guests, a catered full-course dinner, a ten-man band with a sultry vocalist, contract studio photographer, and French champagne compliments of Vito Ardizzone made the wedding one to remember. The photographer took perhaps a half dozen posed portraits of the wedding party with his T-shaped flash lamp. The smell of the potassium chloride flash powder only added to the glitz and glamour of it all.

The big-name headliners like Fairbanks, Bow or Lloyd were not there, certainly having made earlier holiday commitments with other members of Hollywood's upper crust. The reception however, did have Phryne seeing stars regardless. She danced with actors George O'Brien, Millard Waters and Rudolf Klein, and shared champagne toasts with Simone Prevoné, Gladys Daultry and Mona Epstein. Abner was indeed an able producer.

The party had continued until two o'clock in the morning, after Phryne and Abner had left for his top-floor Pico Boulevard suite around midnight.

In her eyes, Phryne's new husband did in fact, hang the moon. That night, she had decided that she would dust the cobwebs off that moon. There weren't any.

Strut, Miss Lizzie

January 1, 1928

New Year's Day was the last day of their honeymoon weekend and work needed to be done. Phryne had moved her things out of the house on Preston Pointe that she had shared with the teepee gang. Pauline, Tracy and Thelma had helped Phryne bring them downstairs to the porch. The inevitable, regrettable, uncomfortable good-byes and well-intended platitudes of flaccid well-wishes cascaded as a never ending fountain of soft tears. Temporary friendships created out of necessity generally end in superfluous melancholy.

The realization of how much she had accumulated over the three short months she lived in the house surprised her. Phryne's wardrobe was significantly larger than it was back when she and Leopold had first arrived in Los Angeles. Abe had been busy carrying her belongings from the porch to the car. "That's the last of it, Sweetheart?"

"Yes, it is Darling, thanks. I'll be right there. Thanks so much." Her husband nodded and walked away to wait in the car. Phryne set her beauty case down, and started down the line of her housemates giving hugs, wishes and saying her goodbyes. She told them she would no longer be working at the Cosmetics Studio. One by one, they echoed back all of Phryne's goodbyes and well-wishes. After promises to keep in touch and final hugs and nuzzles, it was almost over. Pauline lingered, reluctant to back away and stayed close, whispering, "Phryne, I will always love you, always." With forethought, she placed her hand tenderly behind Phryne's neck, pushed her fingers into her bobbed hairdo, and placed a sensuous, soft kiss on the lips of her departing friend. Thelma and Tracy watched in amusement, knowing that while Pauline had always entertained partners of both sexes, she had in fact, covertly lusted after Phryne. A well disguised secret had just been revealed.

With brass, Phryne pressed herself to Pauline, returned the kiss, held her and whispered back, "I really wish you would have said something much earlier, Love." She savored the soft, musky almond fragrance of Pauline's *Heliotrope Parfum,* snuggled into her, gave her one more hug, lowered her arms along her body and waist, and ended the impromptu embrace with a little squeeze to her buttocks, pulling her closer. "I love you too. You're lovely. I'll stop by the studio, I promise." She could think of nothing else to say. Like any first kiss, this one was awkward yet titillating for her. Phryne could feel the twitching throb below. She knew her off-the-wall response was welcomed by Pauline.

Pauline put a handkerchief to her nose and spoke through her sniffles, "Please, do that. That would be nice." She too, was at a loss for words. Pauline's thoughts were in a state of dither and she tingled with the prospect of intimacy with effervescent Phryne.

Phryne put her hand tenderly on Pauline's shoulder, gave Tracy and Thelma a final wave and picked up her little bag. "Toodles*, girls!"

The women watched with mixed emotion and sentiment as Phryne swayed to the Cadillac that Abe had backed into the short, narrow, gravel driveway. He sounded the horn and waved, pulled out to the street and commented, "They look like a fun bunch. Are they?"

"Yes, they are. They certainly helped me get settled here; helped me a lot. They're a good bunch of girls, really ... fun-loving, hard-working girls." Phryne watched in the side mirror as the house disappeared behind them into the endless cluster of homes in the Preston Pointe and Melrose Avenue neighborhood. Her voice trailed away, "They really are good girls ... "

Her thoughts wandered as Abe drove the few miles back to Pico Boulevard. Hollywood's social etiquette was certainly no longer shocking to her and she had curiously observed lesbian couples in social situations. With the smallest bit of disappointment, she knew that she could not invite Pauline into her life or follow through on the promise she had breathed into her ear. For now, at least, it was out of the question. She was not genuinely comfortable with the thought, and had remembered her promise not to embarrass her husband.

From the day they were married, Phryne became a new woman, immersed and reformed into a new life. She was no longer striving to make a living by merely working in a giant beauty parlor, listening to tales of conquest, spreading gossip, or partying with co-workers she hardly knew. She became a member of an elite social hierarchy, part of a visual, celluloid phenomenon that the rest of America and the entire world could only dream of. She began to live, breathe, and fantasize everything Hollywood. She became infatuated with a real life fantasy: sharply contrasted by the dreamy lifestyle and stark actuality of the motion picture industry.

Her husband had made it all possible. She trusted him, adored him and gave herself to him. In two short months, she had become a glittering showpiece in the land of make believe.

Valentine's Day, February 14, 1928

Abner had eased quietly out of bed at five in the morning. He guessed that if Phryne would awake and notice the bed empty, it would appear only normal. His production schedule was so unpredictable that he often rose early and went to work. Today however, was different. It was their first Valentine's Day together and he had a surprise for his young wife: breakfast in bed followed by a short drive. His plan nearly came to fruition. It was spoiled by the smell of burnt bread and eggs, despite his gallant efforts to open every window on the first floor. His plans went awry while he was setting the table, percolating a pot of freshly ground coffee and noisily searching the kitchenette for the flapjack flipper.

Phryne appeared in the doorway wearing her flannel boudoir pajamas and lambs' wool slippers. Abner was at the counter attempting to hide his burnt offerings. She smiled, "Good morning."

"I'm sorry, Sweetheart. I guess I'm not a very good cook. I didn't mean for this to happen."

"Well, I wouldn't think that you intended to burn the building down, but tell me, what are you trying to make?"

"French toast. I failed." Phryne walked to the counter. They embraced and shared a kiss. He tried to vindicate his culinary failure, "Happy Valentine's Day, Sweetheart."

"We can fix this with more eggs, milk and bread, that's all. You didn't use them all up did you?"

"No."

Working together, in less than three-quarters of an hour, they had breakfast made, served and consumed. A colorful California sunrise shone through the glass patio doors of the suite, warmed its way across the parlor and into the small dining area. They sat with their morning coffee.

"I wanted to get a bit of an early start this morning, Sweetheart. There's something I want to show you. It's your Valentine surprise."

Phryne teased his calf with a bare foot, warmed by her slipper. "Get an early start? What's all this? What exactly do you have in mind? What are you going to show me?"

Abner continued to taunt her curiosity and remained secretive on the subject. He would only reveal that it involved a short drive to Hollywood Boulevard, and that they should leave the apartment at eight o'clock sharp. Her prying interest had been piqued. She knew there was the Los Angeles Auto Show downtown, and her heart jumped at the thought of an automobile of her own, but that was on Washington Avenue, not anywhere near Hollywood Boulevard.

Abe deviously suggested that they dress for a casual dinner, and perhaps facilitate an informal Valentine lunch. He had her flummoxed, and she didn't know what to expect. Predictably, when it became time to leave, Phryne was dressed for the Ritz. A drop waist, soft rose, chiffon sheath that ended at the knee and an extra long sheer black scarf around her shoulders disguised her five-month bulge. As was the norm, her makeup was perfect, aces up. Black lace-patterned stockings, two-inch heels and a creamy beige, floppy-brimmed hat rounded off her unscripted, ostentatious Valentine's Day outfit. The Pico Place Suites' doorman tipped his hat as they passed, and as his custom was, eyed every step Phryne took on her way outside to the curb. Abe, of course, noticed, nodded and touched his fedora at the fellow. He flaunted his young wife like a diamond pinky ring on the hand of a blackjack dealer.

Abe opened the passenger door on the Cadillac, and side-stepped to stand directly in front of her, blocking her path. He took her by the hand. "Phryne my dear, I love you. You do this all for me, don't you, Sweetheart? This primping and preening, I know you do, and you do it so well, you know. You make me so proud to be seen with you, my sweet, delectable orange blossom, you." He held her, and she pushed into him. Her hands were on his backside, pressing. He kissed her. "My little minx, I love you to bits."

She played to him, and pushed back. "Why Abner Mandelbaum, if I didn't know better, I'd say that you're trying to sweet talk me! And I'm guessing that you've been reading my résumé! I just bet you tell that to all the girls, don't you?!"

He leaned into her. They kissed passionately and Abner pulled her to him once again.

"You're a dream come true, Sweetheart. A dream come true." He meant it. When Phryne walked into his office five months ago, she also commanded every bit of his being; every molecule, every thought, every dream, every ounce of him. She consumed him with the zeal of a man-eater. He loved it, and felt as he was seventeen again.

She maneuvered herself into the car, and purposely flashed a bit of thigh and stocking top to the doorman. She reached and took Abe's forearm. He stood at the door. "Cig me, please, Darling." He didn't hesitate, reached into his breast pocket, brought out his silver cigarette case and offered it to her. She slid out an Old Gold. Abner struck a match on his pant leg and held it to the tip. Phryne inhaled, coyly turned her head, caught the doorman's eye, exposed a bit more thigh and blew smoke from her pursed lips to the outside. "Thank you, Darling. Let's motor."

It was a perfect, made-to-order morning for a drive: brilliant sunshine gleaming over the San Gabriel mountains to the East and warm, soft breezes wafting across the Pacific from the West Southwest. Her husband had remained quiet for the half hour ride thru Los Angeles to the Hollywood hills and Glendale. Phryne was beside herself with impatience; fidgeting with her hemline and scarf, crossing and uncrossing her legs. "Pretty please, Darling! Where are we going?!"

"Almost there." He turned his head ever so slightly and smiled at her. Indeed they were. He slowed, and pulled the car into a short gravel drive. The little stones moaned in protest under the tires.

"What's this place?" Phryne pulled her sunglasses down and off her nose, examining the property. It was a newer stucco, one story bungalow with a porch along the front, and a flagstone walkway leading to stone steps and a welcoming round-top, oak cottage door with a half-round, leaded glass window. A white picket fence that would make Tom Sawyer nervous ran around the yard. A large umbrella fig stood on the front lawn as a brave sentry. "Who lives in this house?"

"We do, Sweetheart. It's ours, and it's not a suite. And it's not just a house … it's a home. What do you think?"

She tossed her sunglasses onto the dash, slid across the front seat, and placed a quick kiss on her husband's lips. "Perfect. I love it, and can't wait to fill it up! Let's go and see inside!" A gentle push prompted Abe to open his door and get out. Phryne was right behind him, maneuvering her legs under the steering column, scooting along the leather seat and out the driver's door. Obviously, their new home was another masterstroke of Abner's personal production studio.

That evening, Phryne wrote a quick letter to Eloisa explaining her new marital status, her baby news and invited her for a visit.

Phryne and Abner spent the next two days shopping and decorating before moving in.

5. LACKAWANNA, NEW YORK ~ 1927

All Alone

Monday, December 3

Eloisa Ashworth was at a crossroads in her young life of twenty years, as were Phryne and Leopold. The old adage says: *bad things happen in threes.*

In late August she had been involved in a violent confrontation at the International Peace Bridge, suffered a gunshot wound to the shoulder, and her best friend, Phryne Truffaut had left town and eloped, spoiling her hopes to attend a wedding as Maid of Honor.

In September, she had been questioned, arrested and detained for three torturous nights by the BOI. Her life had become an agonizing ordeal that transferred to the rest of her family. In broad daylight, the BOI had arrested her at her mother's place of employment, Farrachi's Bakery, under the prying eyes of the entire city of Buffalo. She had been incarcerated in the Erie County Holding Center for Women on charges of accessory to murder and running illegal whiskey. Her father George held an honorable position at Bethlehem Steel as a foundry foreman, and he had endured the questions, rumors and whispers at the steel and iron works about his daughter's integrity and involvement with Cafferty and possibly, the Black Hand Mafia. George Ashworth never cared for the man, but begrudgingly gave into his daughter's desire to spend time with him. He had regretted that decision countless times since. His daughters had given him nothing but headaches over the last year.

In October, Eloisa was experiencing abdominal distress. She had missed her monthly cycles for two months, and after consultation with doctor Herbert Hurtzemn, she began a regimen of iron supplements and a disgusting potion of castor oil and powdered charcoal.

When November had arrived, and a bump appeared, the unimaginable came to fruition. Dillon Cafferty had fathered the child she was carrying. She had hoped for understanding and compassion, but reality tormented her. She knew what the consequences would be. Her family had suffered duress after her arrest and confinement, but an unwed pregnancy was unthinkable. Eloisa's pregnancy would force her father to eventually banish the young blue-eyed blonde from their home on Olga Street. Her parents' strict Welsh Anglican beliefs demanded it. Her parents initially disagreed, but her mother Esther reluctantly, inevitably relinquished the decision to her husband. Eloisa left her job at the bakery and was cloistered at home.

If there ever was a time that she needed a friend, this was it. Her mother's compassion was confined by her father's embarrassment. Eloisa longed for Phryne's friendship, understanding and advice, but her steadfast companion and confidant was across the country in Los Angeles. On New Year's Eve her elder sister Virginia had married Geoffrey Gibbons, a newspaper reporter at the Buffalo Courier. A week later Geoffrey had secured an assistant city editor job at the Sacramento Bee and relocated to California. Virginia and Phryne, her two closest confidants, were living on the other side of the country. It was a difficult time for Eloisa. Uncertainty, loneliness, fear and ostracism drove her into a state of despair that tested her will to live. She reached out for help the only way she could muster the nerve: ask for it not as a pitiful plea, but a subtle suggestion. She sought some kind of affirmation of love, or caring … something.

On the evening of December 3, her father had just set his fork down and finished his glass of water when Eloisa thought it might be a good time to tell her family the latest news. She spoke with trepidation, "Today, Mother and I went to the doctor's office and he gave me a due date sometime during the first part of April, Father. So there will be a new life to celebrate at Easter." Her words had hit a brick wall and fell to the floor unnoticed.

George Ashworth cleared his throat and wiped his napkin over his lips. "We do not need to discuss this further, Daughter. It does not matter. I do not wish to talk about it, and you know that. As the day gets closer, and your laces get tighter, you know what's going to happen. This has all been set to order by your mother, Reverend Kent, Father Burke, and I. All the details have been agreed upon and the proper donation has been made. You will have a place waiting for you there at the first of the year. There is nothing more to discuss."

Like so many times previous, Eloisa broke into tears, left the dinner table and slowly retreated to her upstairs bedroom. Her father saw the world as one-dimensional, black and white; Good versus Evil. Times had been difficult in the Ashworth home since all the trouble that had begun in August, and lately, Eloisa had been walking on egg shells. About to be put into exile by her mother and father, her nerves were shattered, her heart broken, and her future bleak.

She felt that her fate could have been written in stone by the Devil himself. Her situation and placement had been discussed with members of the clergy, the staff of Father Baker's Maternity Hospital and Our Lady of Victory Infant Home and Protectory. For her, admission to the home for unwed mothers and was not an absolution of her sin, but a solution to the problem and shame borne by her mother and father.

On January 1, she would be leaving the only home she had ever known, and moving into the Protectory for the duration of her pregnancy. Her baby would be adopted at birth by a family that was to be screened and selected by the Children's Home. It was settled.

I'm Going To Sit Down And Write Myself A Letter
January, 1928

Life in the unwed mothers' home was unlike anything that Eloisa could ever have imagined. The home had a comforting continuity and an expected sameness about it that was everywhere. In its own way, the place was consolatory, but there was nothing warm or comfortable about it. Everywhere, it smelled old and musty, with a heavy cloak of candle wax and match sticks. Every room had dark cherry wainscot with aging, brittle varnish that was cracked all over. The celery green, faded paint on the plastered walls was ubiquitous, peeling in the corners and under the windowsills. The lighting fixtures were wall-mounted, with shades of opalescent glass, and bare bulbs hanging from the ceiling under white metal shades. Various prints of the Sacred Heart of Jesus and the Sacred Heart of Mother Mary were in each room, as were small shelves with Holy statuettes and at least one carved Crucifix.

Eloisa's dormitory was a first floor room, longer than it was wide and could be best described as a library without books. Deep maroon draperies of heavy fabric covered tall windows on the exterior wall. A towering ceiling and polished wooden floors echoed every whisper, every footstep. The metal beds were arranged in three absolutely straight rows, lined up like books on a shelf. It was everything that one would expect in a home operated by an ecclesiastical institution: simple, orderly and clean.

Eloisa was segregated into a group of women in her predicament and not allowed to mingle with other members of the home who had already given birth. For advocacy and devotional gatherings, the women were separated by faith, either Catholic or Calvinist. Her Protestant group was encouraged to get support from certain qualified members of The Protectorate for their spiritual and temporal needs, so as not to appear ostentatious, confuse or scandalize the others and the little ones. To Eloisa, it was simply compassionate confinement; a convenient pregnancy prison without bars. She knew from what she had experienced in the Erie County Detention Center for Women.

She had accepted her situation months ago. In her view, the social stigma was an unjustifiable scourge, however unavoidable. She realized the rational resolution was adoption, and was comforted by the fact that the child would have a good home. The Protectorate thoroughly screened all adoption applications to ensure that the parents were Catholics of good standing with accompanying letters of recommendation from their local Parish. Eloisa looked at her stay at the home for unwed mothers as the singular legitimate resolution to an illegitimate problem.

Her day was divided between devotion, consultation and service to the home. She worked in the kitchen, and given her past experience, was assigned to the bread ovens. She made a few new friends, but the women were firmly advised that such friendships would likely end abruptly when they left the home. Connection to the outside world was limited to parents or adult family members; one visit per month, one hour and one adult. Her mother always had come on the second Monday.

In March, against the wishes of Eloisa's father, her mother brought Eloisa a letter from Phryne that had arrived in late February. Esther had considered everything that the letter could contain, and decided that her daughter had every right to read it, regardless of the contents. However, she told her daughter to keep the letter to herself; Esther did not care to know any of it. Like her husband, Esther believed that the isolation of their daughter somehow meant they were absolved of any further embarrassment or ridicule. In addition, her parents had kept Eloisa's plight from her sister Virginia, effectively putting the young mother in exile from her entire family.

That evening, after dinner and clean up, Eloisa sat at the edge of her bed and held Phryne's letter. The dim light of the dormitory cast a blanket of dull yellow off the walls onto everything in the large room. She studied the envelope, the stamp, postmark and return address. She was cautious, and slid her nail under the flap, along the top.

She pushed her finger inside, then her thumb, and pulled out the pages. Slowly, she unfolded the paper, and began to read her friend's words. She finished, and wiped a tear. Her heart ached. Her hopes soared.

Eloisa looked at the pages on her lap. The letter was a lifeline. It was her safety net. There was a way out of this dungeon of guilt after all.

Hollywood, California, February 14, 1928,

Happy Valentine's Day!

Dearest Ellie,

I know it has been too long since you heard from me. I'm so sorry that I have only sent those few postcards. I want to tell you I miss you. I deeply wish you are well.

Certainly, you and I have lived through troubling times these past six months. I'm sorry, Ellie, I haven't forgotten you, but my life has been a merry-go-round. Things have changed so much. First, Leopold and I are no longer married. We learned right away that things would not work out for us. The poor man could not get over his supposed guilt over the fire that claimed his mother and three sisters. He was extremely upset over how Dillon bamboozled us all. And nobody knows where his brother Nicholas is. The poor man would not open his heart and let me help him. Maybe I was selfish, and wanted only him and not his burden. I guess I'll never know. But I have some big news, Ellie, and I think you will agree that it's good news!

I am now married to the most wonderful man ~ Abner Mandelbaum ~ he's in the film business ~ Paramount Studios ~ they make the Douglas Fairbanks and Mary Pickford pictures! I would love to see you again, and cannot wait to tell you more. There is so much more!

We are living in our own little bungalow right in Hollywood, and it is too big for just us! And I have more exciting news, Ellie dear! I am going to have a baby in June. Leopold is the father of course, but I have no idea where he is. I have not seen or heard from him. It's so sad … but I cannot think about that. I have a delightful husband now. That's what matters the most.

If you can get away, I would love it if you could come to California and visit. You can stay as long as you like. I would love it, and so would Abner, and if you could stay, you are welcome to! I sure could use a friend. I know you would love it here.

Again, I hope you are well, and I hope to see you soon! Please write!

Love, your friend always ~~

Phryne 💜

Eloisa reread the letter and essentially had it memorized by the fourth read. She sat on the edge of her bed, oblivious to the other women around her, and reread it several more times. The letter was full of jolting news. She was flabbergasted to hear the news about Leopold. It had seemed that he and Phryne were so much in love.

The letter told the unbelievable news that her best friend had remarried and was going to have a child. Her thoughts went from elation to cautious curiosity. She longed for Phryne's company, her friendship and shoulder. Ostracized by her family, Eloisa had been starved of meaningful friendship and a sympathetic confidant for months. Driven by the daunting possibility of a new life on the other side of the country, and pushed by her moral banishment, she decided that she would accept Phryne's invitation and leave as soon as she was physically able and permitted. She replied to her friend's letter only two days after her mother gave it to her in March. She wrote that although she could not be sure of the date, she should be arriving in early or mid-April. She had decided not to mention her current predicament for two reasons. She did not wish to spoil the joy over Phryne's pregnancy and new marriage, moreover, by the time she arrived, her current situation would have become nothing more than water that disappeared under a bridge. She found it necessary to beg her mother to mail her reply back to Phryne. Esther Ashworth reluctantly agreed, and delicately took the envelope between two fingers as if it were addressed to Lucifer, and dropped it gingerly into her handbag.

Three weeks later, her mother brought a reply from an equally excited Phryne, which gave Eloisa her new address and some directions. Phryne's message was: *From the train station, take the Beverly Hills streetcar to Melrose Avenue, get off at Gower Street, and take the Glendale Pacific Electric Red Car to Gardner Place and walk to #16. If nobody's home, the key is under the pink rock by the steps! Can't wait! Toodles!*

Eloisa was beside herself with excitement. She read and reread those words, and set them to memory. To be safe, she carefully folded Phryne's short note and secured it inside her beaded pocketbook. She had another friend in California: her sister Virginia in Sacramento. It comforted Eloisa to know she would be heading toward warm weather, a good friend and a sister who would not shun or cast her out. After Phryne's last letter, there were two life events that she was eagerly awaiting -- one more so than the other. Leaving for California was the better of the two.

Love Me Or Leave Me

April, 1928

Eloisa was hospitalized on the evening of April 1. A cluster of nuns and nurses gathered on the Maternity Ward. Initially, she had been placed in a room with two other women, who already were mothers. Her water had broken a half hour earlier, and Eloisa was given some sort of sedation tablet, unknown and unexplained. She had no recollection of being moved to the delivery room, placed on the table and draped with clean sheets. She had no knowledge of the nurses, white gowns, needles or cold instruments. Between painful spasms in a dreamy, ether-induced, half-conscious state, she was oblivious to the world. At 1:30 AM, April 2, 1928, Eloisa Marie Ashworth gave birth to a six pound, four ounce baby girl. The infant was immediately removed from the birthing bed and placed in the infirmary under the care of a wet nurse. Eloisa did not hear the cry of her baby when she first met the cold of the world, nor did she feel the small incision the doctor had made or its subsequent repair. She awoke in a smaller room, alone, with no recollection of the birth.

The bright sunlight of a spring morning had pushed through the closed window curtains, turning the pale green walls of the room into a glowing chartreuse. Eloisa could hear footsteps, carts and chatter in the hall. The heavy oak door was open just a crack. Try as she might, she could not recall enough of the last twenty-four hours to make sense of the bits and pieces in her memory. She resolved that it was probably the best … if only everyone could forget their nightmares.

For breakfast, she was served a lukewarm, lumpy bowl of cream of wheat, a half glass of milk, and half glass of apple juice. Before noon, a nurse, nun, doctor and Reverend Kent of Prospect Methodist Church stood by her bedside. Eloisa was groggy from her ordeal, too weak and tired to be part of any meaningful conversation. She remembered being told the baby girl was healthy and strong before signing her name perhaps two times and being asked if she had any preferences for the baby's Christian name. Eloisa quickly studied the faces around her bed, and suggested that Sister Mary Katherine select a name. Her visitors commended her decision and reminded her of the consoling services available at the hospital's Lady of Victory Chapel. The visit was over as quickly as it had begun.

Alone with her thoughts, the emptiness within her seemed to expand. Her heart ached beyond belief, testing her faith with a feeling of loneliness that could only be described as suffocation; deprivation of the breath of life. She was agonized that her father and mother had both effectively turned their backs to her. It seemed that the assistance they had given was only to rid themselves of public humiliation and ridicule. The man with whom she had been so much in love and infatuated, was dead and had been exposed as a conniving, heartless fraud. Together they had created a life, only to have it given away. The two people she had considered to be her closest confidants and helpmates, older sister Virginia and friend Phryne, had moved away and married. Her most private, intimate conversations could only be shared with her conscience. Her thoughts were hers alone. She silently recited Psalm 23 and the Lord's Prayer, staring at the portrait of Christ on the opposite wall until she fell asleep.

That afternoon, baby Katherine Ann was Baptized by Father Patrick McNulty in the hospital chapel.

The next day, Eloisa celebrated her twenty-first birthday in her bed at Our Lady of Victory hospital. She had regained her strength and believed that with time, she could mend her soul.

She was to be confined to bed for five days, creating hours of lonely, if not empty hours. Of the scores of staff, one young nurse was especially helpful, friendly and overtly cheerful. Nurse Rebecca encouraged her to at least take advantage of the books that were available for loan. Over the next several days, she read Lucy Montgomery's *'Anne Of Green Gables'*, Francis Burnett's *'The Secret Garden'* and Louisa Alcott's *'Little Women'*.

On the third day after the birth, her mother visited for half an hour. On the fifth, she had dangled her legs off the bed, sat in a chair on the sixth and walked from her bed to the bathroom on the seventh. On the eighth day she was evaluated, counseled, and had two sutures removed. In the evening, she gathered her belongings and placed them in her woven railway bag along with a tightly wrapped oil cloth packet that contained her life savings; a sum of one hundred and twenty-six dollars. She was anxious and didn't get much sleep that night.

Her mother had made one last half-hour visit with her daughter the next morning, and brought along a small leather case packed with the dresses, stockings and blouses that Eloisa had worn before her trouble. She received a wide-brimmed, woven black horsehair hat with silk flowers and sheer red ribbons for the trip. "This is for the train, Ellie, my dear. And when you get to California, dress like a lady, and hold your head high. And always, always respect yourself." Esther hugged her daughter for the first time in months, and wished her a tearful goodbye. For Eloisa, it was an unnecessarily tragic farewell.

Just past noon, she took a taxi from the hospital to the Lackawanna Terminal, where she purchased a total of five railway tickets for her trip to Los Angeles, California: one each for coach fare to Cleveland, Michigan City and finally, Chicago. From there, she needed two tickets for the Union Pacific's *Los Angeles Express* Pullman to Central Station. She would arrive four and a half days later on the morning of Sunday, April 15. Eloisa assumed that Phryne would not be working on a Sunday, and would certainly be at home.

It was April 20, ten days later, that Horace and Bertha Dobbs arrived in Lackawanna from Syracuse, New York to bring infant Katherine Ann home with them. They were overjoyed to have been successful with the adoption. The baby girl was to enjoy two very loving parents.

6. SAN FRANCISCO, CALIFORNIA ~ 1928

Take A Whiff On Me

Upon his arrival in San Francisco, Leopold had secured bare-boned lodging at a ramshackle rooming house on Harriet Street for two dollars a week. The Ambassador Hotel had been struggling for twenty years, since the 1906 earthquake, and had nowhere to go but downhill and into the bay. From the exterior, it seemed like a run-down establishment, contending with a downward spiral of disrepair, neglect and perhaps mismanagement or ignorance. Looking at the interior, it was simply a dump.

Only three blocks from the Southern Pacific Passenger Depot, City Hall, and a short fifteen minute walk to the booming Embarcadero waterfront, The Ambassador sat on prime real estate. Through extortion and bribery, the hotel was a player in the illicit sex and drug trade operations controlled by the unscrupulous purveyance of brothers Peter and Thomas McDonough. The siblings were the uncrowned underworld royalty of San Francisco and virtually owned the city.

The accommodations at The Ambassador were in fact, better than what he had been accustomed to at the oil fields, but the toilet and washroom down the hall had neither hot water nor linen. He managed to shave his four-day growth and wash himself with a sliver of soap that he had discovered stuck, lost and forlorn, on the windowsill. His neatly trimmed, thin John Gilbert mustache disappeared into a wash basin months earlier. His room did not have a working lock on the door, so he propped the bedside table at an angle under the doorknob before he went to bed. He thought about installing a barrel lock on his own. That night, he slept fully dressed and with his shoes on.

Leopold's second day in San Francisco was spent getting to know his new environment, and feeling out the city. He walked the entire day, stopping on street corners and trolley stops; talking with newsboys, peddlers, or whomever would take the time to talk. His first impression of the city by the bay was that it was smaller, but at least as busy as Los Angeles and was home to much more of a mishmosh of humanity. Los Angeles had more Mexicans than Buffalo had Italians and Irish, but here the Chinese population was omnipresent.

On the third day he bought new socks, a union suit, a pair of blue dungarees, a shoe brush, two bars of Ivory soap, one bar of Fels Naptha and paid the scruffy Ambassador desk clerk for two hot baths at a nickel apiece. When he had finished scrubbing, and he climbed out of the galvanized fifty gallon wash tub, he was as tender and pink as a newborn. He managed to get the thick crude out from under his nails, in his hair and between his toes. His hands however, still had the black calluses of an oil field roughneck. Cleanliness has a special feel to it. After his baths, Leopold felt good.

On day four, the December weather dampened his mood. Cool temperatures and thick fog with a persistent, wind-driven mist created a grey gloom that pushed midday to twilight. He put on his best pair of suit pants, his only white shirt, suit jacket and tweed golf cap. Mixed up and mismatched, he walked six blocks to the San Francisco City Hall on Van Ness to inquire about becoming a city policeman. He was redirected to the Hall of Justice at 750 Kearny Street, and was given a snide "Good luck, buddy." At the time, he didn't give the remark any heed or credence. Outside, the gas streetlights flickered their feeble attempt to light his way. A short nickel streetcar ride up Van Ness and across Washington Street took him directly to the front steps of the ornate granite and slate-faced Romanesque structure that housed the city courts and police headquarters. Massive and impressive, the building cast a dark ominous forewarning through the fog and drizzle. He stood on the sidewalk, and briefly questioned his motivation for being there in the first place. He was surrounded by people, very busy people with coat and shirt collars turned up to the cold. He tried to imagine himself wearing a deep, blackish blue uniform, carrying a night stick and pistol with a badge pinned to his chest.

Inside, he sat in a second floor office with *General Inquiries* painted in gold letters on the door. He folded his cap, stuck it into his hip pocket and took a seat on a heavy wooden bench against the wall and faced a long, polished wood counter directly in front of him. From behind a partition wall, he could hear someone plunking on a typewriter, and the faint sounds of voices in conversation. A telephone rang, echoed to the tall tin ceilings and bounced off the granite floor. The rather plump man in police uniform behind the counter was penciling entries into a logbook of sorts. A six-inch brass nameplate sat off to his side on the desktop: *Desk Sgt. Gregory O'Rourke*. He had polished brass buttons, numbers and stars all over his blue shirt. He put down his pencil and cleared his throat as the words started, "What can I help you with?"

Leopold stood and took three steps toward the polished counter. "I was told to come up here from the desk sergeant down on the first floor. I would like to become a San Francisco policeman, Sergeant O'Rourke, sir."

"I'm not O'Rourke. He's off sick, and been sick for awhile." He studied Leopold. "Who sent you here?"

"Nobody sent me here. I'm here on my own accord."

He grunted and, "That's your first mistake. You can't get nowhere on your own; time you learn that. You need a recommendation, a reference, a sponsor. A councilman, an alderman, the mayor, the chief, somebody. You know the McDonoughs? They could get you in. The McDonoughs and some cash helps, the last I knew, if you want to go down that road."

Leopold felt his hopes crash like a porcelain tea set on a marble floor. "I don't know anybody in San Francisco. I came here because I want to join the police force."

"You came in here and you don't know nobody? Well, I'll tell you one thing for sure: you got balls, bud. Big ass brass balls, that's what you got. You might as well just turn around, go back to wherever the hell you came from and get back behind the plow. You ain't going to get to be a copper* here. No way in hell, bud. Not without a recommendation, anyhow."

He had a reason for coming here, and was not going to give up. "These McDonoughs you talked about ... where can I find them?"

"What's your name, bud? I need to know the idiot that I'm talking to."

Leopold kept his temper, and knew that this was not going to end well. "Throckmorton. Leopold Throckmorton. I'm from Buffalo."

The policeman shook his head. "A goddamn rube* from Nowhere-Ville. Where the devil is Buffalo? Kansas? Nebraska? Somewhere locked knee deep in Buffalo crap and prairie grass, I imagine ... well, I'll repeat myself, bud. You ain't going nowhere from here. Not without a recommendation. You ain't from here, so there's no chance in hell to get one; no chance in hell. And if you really want to find the McDonough boys, then try *The Corner*, two blocks down on Washington, toward the waterfront. Think of The Corner as the front door to San Francisco: your only way in. Just ask when you get over there. You'll find it easy enough, or somebody there will find you, wheat*. But you could do yourself good, do yourself a favor, and just to go back to Buffalo Town, Oklahoma. Crazy Okie*."

Leopold felt his body go cold, numb; like a January gale blowing across Lake Erie's ice. The insults did not phase him; the truth did. He stood dumbfounded. His dream became fogged over, distorted, then destroyed. He managed to speak, "The Corner?"

"Yeah, The Corner. You'll find them there, if you really want to take the bull by the horns. But, I would not advise it. They don't know you and you don't know them. Take my advice, and stay away. Go back to Oklahoma and be a copper there with your grass and cows and corn."

"Thanks for the help, Sergeant. And so you know, Buffalo isn't in Kansas or Oklahoma. I'm from Buffalo, Missouri, just north of Pittsburgh." It amused him to hand out a morsel of retribution. He enjoyed encouraging and nurturing ignorance by feeding it harmless, misleading drivel.

He left the Hall of Justice without uttering another word. Leopold stepped faintheartedly down the grey granite steps to the sidewalk, and turned left onto Washington Street toward a destination he was advised to bypass. The cold wind was at his back, driving through his suit jacket.

He discovered that The Corner lived up to its name, and sat wedged into the corner of Washington and Montgomery. Ruffians, drunks, longshoremen, ladies of ill repute and the occasional tradesman or shopper mingled on the streets like one big bowlful of churning humankind. A stone's throw from the Hall of Justice, he had discovered The Corner, and affirmed what he was led to believe. The disturbing truth indicated that The Corner was the linchpin, the driving force behind the police department and the government of San Francisco itself. The afternoon had not brightened, but had begun to embrace the dark of evening. He shivered, like someone had just stepped on his grave. The fog was getting thicker. There were automobiles parked tightly on both sides of the streets, barely leaving room for the streetcars to rattle down the center. Pedestrians boldly dodged everything on wheels, on rails and on foot.

This was not what he had left the oil fields of Long Beach for. He stopped in front of the place, about twenty feet from the front door, leaned his back against the clap boards and lit a Chesterfield. From inside, the music of a piano and brass jazz band filtered through the window panes along with the vulgar sound of rowdy and raucous voices. He had noticed eyes following him, and was taking extra caution not to return any glances, not at all desirous to initiate any interaction of any kind. He was living in a macabre Edgar Allan Poe horror. Regretfully, he already knew how this was going to end. He recognized the mistake he had made by walking down there.

Minutes earlier, he had been presented with a dilemma. He was now at a crossroad, standing alone, lost, and as an uninvited stranger in uncharted territory. Two tall, large men appeared from the entrance and walked along the sidewalk toward him. He dropped his cigarette and crushed it out. He wasn't surprised; the goons were obviously hired muscle to keep the riff raff at bay. They wore black bowlers, pin-striped slacks, white shirts, with vests and neat bow ties. He had seen fellows like these two erect apes many times; too many times, he thought, at the mob-controlled Hotel Lafayette in Niagara Falls that he, Phryne, Dillon and Eloisa had frequented so often in his not-so-distant past. He could feel his stomach churning. He swallowed bile. He had just stepped in it, a warm and steamy pile, and there was no place to wipe it off. He let out a sigh of desperation.

"Did you come here for a specific reason, Sir?" The redhead's voice was like rock salt; hard and coarse. The other gorilla was expressionless, standing with his jaw locked in place.

"Well, for reasons of my own, I came to San Francisco to become a police officer. And I just left their headquarters up the street there, and they told me if I wanted a job I would need a recommendation from the mayor or the McDonough boys. And long story short, I sure as hell don't know the mayor, and I was thinking maybe I could get a recommendation from the guys who run this establishment." He continued to doubt his forethought.

They pushed him against the building with a thud and manhandled him, no doubt looking for weapons. Leopold had wisely decided to allow himself to be putty in their hands. "Let's go ... inside." They shoved him ahead of them, pushing him into the building, through the room and to a table against the far wall. He went into the chair with a bump, squeak and a groan from its legs. "Wait here, don't move."

The place was a barroom; a bona fide wide-open speakeasy with overt gambling, drinking and whoring. Card games and numbers tables were scattered through the wide-open floor plan. It reeked of cigarettes, cigars, cheap perfume and gin. At least a hundred or more bits of humanity were scattered throughout the hall. Large wooden pillars were the only support for the upper floors; there were no interior walls. The place was massive. It was a boiling cauldron of illegal activity flourishing within a block and a half of the Hall of Justice. Leopold had one word for it: unbelievable. The organization that ran this place was indeed an organization of the highest, most fearless and lawless order.

He sat with controlled trepidation, forcing his anxiety back, and trying not to appear as nervous as he actually was. An unassuming fellow approached from his left, between tables of card players. Slightly behind him stood the two hoods who had pushed him inside. "Can I help you?"

"Well, like I told the two gentlemen with you, I was at the police department up the street and asking for work, and they told me if I wanted the job, I would first need a recommendation. So, here I am, asking for one. That's the whole story."

"What's your name?"

"Throckmorton, Leopold Throckmorton."

"Well, Leo, I'm Frank Daroux, and to make this as painless and short and sweet as possible, I have two things I need to ask you. Question one: do you understand the duties of a San Francisco policeman? And question two: do you have five hundred dollars?" Frank took a seat across from Leopold, folded his fingers together and set his hands on the table. He had a sheepish smile and continued, "If you cannot answer *'YES'* to both of those questions, you're in the wrong place, my friend."

Leopold shifted his weight and answered, "My answer to both questions is *'NO'*, so I am obviously in the wrong place."

"You're not from around here, are you, Leo?"

"No, no, I'm not. I'm from Buffalo. I came out here to find work, and I guess I'll need to look elsewhere."

The slick-talking Frank spewed a wisecrack, "There's lots of work on the docks, Leo, and you don't need a recommendation. Just a couple hundred yards down the street from here."

Leopold desperately wanted this conversation to end and simply walk out the door. "Thank, you, Sir. Mister Da-roo. Thank you, I'll think about that."

Frank starred at Leopold and bobbed his head in the direction of his goon companions, "Billy, Jake, … walk our friend Leo here to the door, and show him which way the docks are."

"Thank you, sir." He stood, and felt genuine relief as he started out. He felt the skin at the back of his neck crawl. The two alley apes* did not man-handle him on the way out, but he knew they were only inches behind him. Once he was outside, he did not look back.

He turned on Kearny Street and started toward the waterfront.

December 10, 1927

Leopold walked perhaps three hundred yards and turned into Molly's Canteen. He found a stool at the small counter and sat next to a fellow in brown coveralls. He was leaning over a cup of coffee that best resembled dish water; perhaps it was. A large woman in a tattered blue dress sauntered toward him. Every bit of flesh wiggled as she walked. A filthy white duck-cloth apron was stretched tight over her enormous belly. Her black grimy hair stuck to her sweaty forehead and down along one cheek. "What can I do you, mister?"

He wasn't hungry, not at that moment, not at all. His thoughts raced and he stammered, "Uh, coffee … coffee and a bowl of soup."

"Potato or cream of chicken?"

"Potato … potato soup and coffee, thank you."

She shuffled away. He wondered if she could be Molly. She looked like a Molly. His neighbor mumbled, barely looking up from his coffee, "You should have ordered a coconut and a can of sardines, buddy."

Leopold didn't know what to make of that comment. "Why is that?"

The stranger looked mysteriously around, as if he was checking to see if anyone was watching. He scratched and rubbed the top of his head, and made a low guttural sound like that of an irritated street cur. He looked around the diner again, leaned slightly toward Leopold and lowered his voice, "Because that's the only damn things they can't stick their dirty fingers into." Leopold needed a chuckle. It was like the fellow had read his mind. The brief levity didn't last long. If the guy next to him said anything more, he didn't hear it. He went numb again and his thoughts were somewhere far away in a bottomless pit of rejection. His time in the oil fields was for nothing. His effort to join the San Francisco police was without reward. His dream of self redemption disappeared like so much smoke along the track.

The big woman brought a piece of toast with a lonely fried egg laying on top and set it on the counter next to him with a hollow plunk. She set his soup and coffee in front of him, and smiled with a mouthful of brown teeth. "That will be ten cents for you, mister."

His soup looked and tasted like the coffee: dull brown and watery. The soup, however, did have a lonely morsel or two of potato and a layer of melted lard on top. The fellow in the brown coveralls had made quick work of his toast and egg with his fork, mashing the egg into the half-burnt bread and soaking up the yolk. The plate was chipped in more than one place along the edge.

Leopold came back to life. "I see what you meant about the coconut, my friend. Next time I'll take your advice and get the sardines."

The fellow looked around the diner once again, and whispered, "Shhhh! If you tell everybody, there won't be any left for us!"

Again, it felt good to laugh.

"Something bothering you, bud?"

"It's nothing in particular or even out of the ordinary; not for my lot. Lately, it seems the harder I try, the harder I fall. And all this falling down and getting kicked in the ass is starting to piss me off."

The stranger leaned away from the counter, turned to Leopold and stuck out his hand. They shared a handshake. "Well, see that, young man? You learned an important lesson today; if you don't aim too high then you don't have too far to fall. You need to remember that, and stop taking life so damn seriously, my friend. Elmore Leffingwell, that's me: chief labor force navigator and roustabout. I do it all and don't try doing what I know I can't. And one thing for sure, I don't look for work. Why look for something you don't enjoy? I let work find me, and when my belly's empty or I get thirsty, it usually does, and then I stop looking."

Leopold smiled, "I'm Leopold," and began to study this campy character. Elmore was grey, unshaven, tight at every seam and had a complexion that resembled a gravel driveway. He was well over fifty, with very short, wiry hair on his head, little tufts in his ears, and a curly mat of back hair climbing over his collar.

Elmore looked around the diner again. Leopold expected another winsome quip and got one. "Looks like you could use a drink of something other than that bilge water coffee that Molly pumps out of the bay, and I know just the place."

"You're not thinking about The Corner, are you?"

"Willikers*, no! My pockets ain't that deep. I know a joint* on Battery Row everybody calls *The No Name*. That's what it is, a place with no name. We can get a bucket of beer on the sly and maybe some stale pretzels." Again, he rubbed the top of his head with his open hand and made some sort of guttural sound, like a bear waking in spring: a low growl. "And you don't need to worry about falling on your ass. It's not a high class joint. How about it?"

"Yeah. Why not?" Leopold had a hunger to do something, anything. His day had been a total loss, and the dark of night was approaching. The beer might be a welcome novelty; he hadn't had any in months. Sometimes he had trouble falling asleep. This fellow looked amusing.

A block and a half away sat a row of derelict store fronts. The brick facades were partially gone or had completely fallen off. Elmore explained that it was damage from the 1906 earthquake and great fire. Leopold had seen other damaged buildings in the city, but had no knowledge of the event. He had been barely three years old, and living across the continent when it had occurred. He never knew.

Elmore stepped inside a doorway, and spoke in a near-whisper, "A word of advice, my friend. Inside, if anybody offers, even free, stay away from the white powder; it's too damn dangerous. It's cocaine from Vancouver, the Devil's sugar, and not worth the snuff. We're only here for the beer. In here, the tapster* is your only friend." He banged his fist on a door; three quick hits followed by two separate, short taps with his knuckles. It opened to reveal a round face sitting on a pair of shoulders no more than four and a half feet high. It appeared to be a man of sorts, with shoulder length, straggly brown hair. A cigar stub hung from the corner of his mouth. Despite his apprehension, Leopold felt he could trust Elmore. He emitted a reassuring bearing of a man with well-seasoned, varied experience.

"Elmo, my friend! Come on in, and bring your friend there with you. We got a seat or two left! Come on in!" The voice was disturbingly shrill, like that of a female cat bemoaning her Tom. The mascot at the door gave them a wide berth, welcomed them inside, and shut the door behind them with a creak and a clunk.

Inside, it smelled like an attic: cobwebs, mildew, moth-bitten clothing, dry rot and forgotten furniture. There was not a single electric light. Oil lamps and candles cast an eerie glow, and set all sizes and shapes of shadows dancing in every direction. For a passing moment, Leopold second-guessed his decision to accompany Elmore to this place. Then his vision adjusted to the dim light, and his trepidation eased. Without doubt, this place catered to a different class of customers compared to the clientele at The Corner. Regardless, he knew all too well that, once again, he was in unfamiliar surroundings.

A voice from somewhere inside encouraged, "Come on this way, Elmo. I got your usual spot for you." The voice leading them through the place was that of a buxom woman, who looked exactly like an aging Brunnhilde, with breasts of a Germanic goddess that completely filled the upper half of her grey dress and white eyelet blouse. Her hair was dirty blonde, messy and she had the hands and walk of a farmer. Elmore and Leopold followed her between tables, chairs, old settees and sofas. Inside, the place had a cross section of humanity; working people every one: laborers, tradesmen, teamsters, warehousemen and the omnipresent dock hands. Here and there, either sitting upon a lap or leaning close, were working girls in smeared eye shadow and misplaced women of fleeting opportunity. A hand-cranked Victor Talking Machine was spinning a scratched black shellac pressing of Margaret Young's *'Red Hot Henry Brown'*.

The two men sat in a corner, at a round table with a quarter-circle bench that looked like a pew, and belonged in a broken-down 18th century castle somewhere in the highlands of Scotland. Elmore ordered a bucket of beer, asked for two glasses, gave Brunnhilde two quarters, a kiss on her plump left cheek, and thanked her, "You are a lovely woman, my Rose, thank you, my dear." The men settled in, and relaxed. Leopold felt at ease for the first time in days and hadn't noticed any white powder. When the tin bucket of suds arrived, he reached to his inside pocket and took out his deck*. He offered Elmore one of his Chesterfields, lit it for him and took another for himself.

"See that, my friend? Rose proves the point, and she does it so well. *True beauty is in the eyes of the beer holder.* So, Leopold, tell me ... what the hell were you doing at The Corner? It's a clip joint* full of shylocks* and trouble boys*. You got to explain that to me, my friend. That's not a place where you would go for a shave and a haircut, so what the hell were you doing there?"

He thought for a moment or two and answered, "Learning life lessons, that's what I was doing. Earlier, I was at police headquarters and inquired about becoming a copper. The desk sergeant sent me to The Corner." Telling his story, Leopold had validated the wicked paradox of the whole affair. He recognized how foolish it seemed.

Elmore laughed briefly, coughed, stopped abruptly and injected, "I'm sorry, buddy. I'm not laughing at you. I'm laughing at the cold hard facts of life in San Francisco. I mean, what does it say about this city if you got to see the mob before you can become a cop? Oh, I mean crime is on the down low ... there's no more gang wars, and no union riots ... not now, but willikers ... hell, I mean ... the McDonough brothers allow this place right here, that we're in now, to pour beer ... for a price. Well, what I really mean is; you can't fight city hall, can you?" He nodded in self-affirmation and dumped more beer into his glass. "Not too long ago, I realized that there are two kinds of men in this town: those who drink and those who pour. Me, I'm both; a fully functional, walking, talking booze hound*." He rubbed his head with his open palm, moaned like a dog and swallowed half of his beer. A lion's purr; that would be the sound of Elmore's head-rubbing grunts. "Tell you what, Leo ... we'll finish this bucket and I'll take you on a tour. A sight-seeing tour of this fair city. So you can experience life without the McDonough brothers ... under the dim lights of Portsmouth Square. Your night has only just begun, my friend." Elmore coughed again.

"Where?"

"Chinatown, Leo. Chinatown." He swallowed his glass of beer, poured himself another, hacking, and clearing his throat.

"I prefer to be called Leopold, Elmore." .

Curious and inquisitive, Elmore exhaled an eruption of cigarette smoke from the corner of his mouth. Another glass was refilled, and the bucket emptied. He belched and, "Oh, all right … but why?"

"Well, I don't want you to think that I'm a crumb*, but that's the name my mother gave me: Leopold."

Elmore sat back against the bench, once again rubbed his head like it was a pet dog and let out another low growling sound. "I like you, Leopold. You're on the level, and I like that. Drink up. We're going to Chinatown, buddy."

Chinatown, My Chinatown

The sun always sets in the West, regardless if you are able to see it or not. The dank greyness carried by the fog and mist of day was transformed into the murky, damp darkness of night. The Mission Rock foghorn echoed down the streets and bounced off the cobblestones. Gaslights on the street corners were only guideposts and not a source of illumination. Their senses numbed, and with a bucket of beer in their bellies, Elmore and Leopold shuffled along the streets of Chinatown.

Elmore redirected the course of conversation into the abstract needs of men for pleasure, satisfaction and fulfillment. He expounded, "You're going to like it here, Leopold. You see, my friend, Chinatown is more than just a wide spot in the road on our journey through Life. The Chinese think inner peace comes from meditation and self-discovery. Well, here you can discover yourself. Back at Molly's you were complaining that lately you have been getting kicked in the ass and falling down. Well, like that Chinaman Confucius said, *Don't worry about falling down, worry about getting up* ... or something like that. Tonight we're not going to fall down. We're going to get up. You will discover that in Chinatown, it's too damn easy to feel good. And me, well, I sure like to feel good. And at my age, I try to feel good as much as I can."

Leopold laughed only briefly, and asked, "Where did you learn so much about Confucius and Chinese philosophy, Elmore?"

"Right down the street here in Chinatown, where else? Down here at Da Hung."

It was another world. It was China. Everything was in Chinese. Although the vast majority of store fronts was closed for the day, the streets were bustling. Most of the ethnic population was dressed in Western attire, leaving the odd Chinaman with his pigtail queue and mandarin jacket. It was easy to identify the establishments that catered to the English speaking population; English got top billing on their storefront signs, however, there were only a few of them. Most businesses were identified only in Chinese, while some others were easily discernable simply by pictures, such as loaves of bread, cuts of pork or washboards.

"Tonight I'm going to show you Heaven on Earth, my friend, and it will only cost you eight bits*; two more for a bed. You should pay for the bed. You're coming with me, right, Leopold?"

"Where?"

"Right here, *Da Hung Tea Parlor*; it means *Big Red*. And that Chinese chicken scratch right underneath says *pipes and lamps always available*."

Leopold was nervously anxious, but thought he could trust his new acquaintance, at least to the point that he didn't fear for his life. He had an inkling as to what was in store: opium. The beer had kept his desperation at bay and dampened any misgivings. He considered that he had nothing left to lose. He had heard about the Hong Kong opium trade and was aware that, right or wrong, it was associated with Chinese culture and the work of authors such as Elizabeth Barrett Browning, Edgar Allan Poe, Lewis Carroll and detective extraordinaire Sherlock Holmes. He was also aware that it had been outlawed, but just as alcohol was to Prohibition, opium was to countless drug laws. Opium use, although denigrated and publicly vilified, continued to bear a spiritual and physiological mystique.

Elmore walked in with Leopold following behind. The tinkle of little porcelain bells hanging from the beaded doorway curtains announced their arrival. Inside, there were a half dozen small, low tables to accommodate seated customers. Three of those tables had squatters sipping tea. A beautiful young woman in a carmine silk tunic with intricate embroidery on the collar and cuffs welcomed them. She had coal black hair and glorious, deep brown almond eyes. Under her red jacket she wore billowing dark blue silk pants and black slippers. She bowed and gave Elmore a personal greeting, "Oh, welcome, Noble Grey Ox. Come in with friend." She led them around a linen-covered half-wall partition, down a short, narrow hall, stopped at a curtained doorway, motioned them to enter, bowed and departed. Leopold was amused and very intrigued. They started down another dark narrow hall, with several curtained rooms along the way that ended at a wooden door. Some of the curtained rooms had shoes on the hall floor. A sweet, flowery odor was pervasive.

Elmore knocked three times, spoke low and quickly, "Do what I do, Leopold. He'll ask if you want a woman, you can accept or decline, and if you intend to stay the night. Like I said before, stay the night, regardless of any female company." The door opened and revealed a man smiling ear to ear. He bowed, invited them with a hand gesture into an anteroom of sorts with four other doors, and closed the door. He was also dressed predominantly in red, wearing a yi chang, secured around the waist with a wide black sash and a tight fitting jin cap.

"You will sleep? Do you wish for company?"

Elmore gave Leopold a passing glance and began, "I would honor a lovely woman in my bed and I will stay the night."

Leopold allowed himself to be forced by circumstance and answered, "I will do the same; honor and sleep." His thoughts immediately jumped around all the plausible probabilities and he began to imagine what a Chinese prostitute could look like. He had no prior experience in the trade, either Oriental or Western.

They each paid two dollars, which was accepted with repeated bows and superfluous gratitude, and were shown into one of the rooms. Elmore took off his shoes, gestured for Leopold to do the same and explained, "When you set your shoes outside the door, it signals that the room is occupied."

There were two low beds, covered with large rattan mats with pillows and cotton coverlets scattered across them. The walls looked like paper, black and brown, held in place by two-inch strips of lath. A small side table was next to each bed, with the opium lamps and pipes*. Two oil lamps burned on corner shelves. The air was thick and sultry, with a musky floral scent that was close to oppressive.

"This is what's going to happen, Leopold … a coolie* will come in with the black tar and get our lamps lit … we'll relax, settle in and then the sideways* muffins will appear. It'll be a new experience for you, I'll tell you. Believe me, they know their business. She'll stay all night with you if you like. Just show her respect. That's important, especially if you think you could be coming back."

"They know you here? The girl outside called you *Grey Ox*?"

"Yeah, 'grey' because I am and 'ox" because that's the Chinese sign from the year I was born. The Chinese Year of the Ox. I was born in December 1865 in Natchez, Mississippi, son of a Canadian fur trader and a Cherokee squaw. But I suppose some people could argue that I'm called *Grey Ox* because I ain't no *Spring Chicken*."

"Seems to me that you can hold your own, Elmore."

"Not so much, but that's the main reason I visit this place. Not to hold my own, but to have ring-a-ding*, I mean. The smoke lets me feel that youthful flame, that lust again, if only for the night. It does, you'll see. Keep the right mind, and don't take it for granted. Remember that … it's important. And heed the tar vapor. Always. And honor the girls. The girls here are respectable, if there is such a thing among sideways whores. These girls ain't the ones you see on the street. Wong Wai, the yellow* that took our money, he runs a closed shop. They're his girls."

That night was the first of many at Da Hung for Leopold. He had experienced a glorious euphoria, an out-of-body experience that seemed to last the entire night. The girl who shared his bed wore a scent that evoked Lilies of the Valley. At one point, in the middle of the night and after the lamps had burned out, he drifted from this world and entered a Paradise beyond description. Elmore was right.

I'll See You In My Dreams

Leopold awoke alone on his rattan mattress. Elmore and the women were gone. He returned to his room on Harriet, gathered his belongings and got lodging on John Street for a dollar a week, half of what he had been paying. The John Street address was within a quarter mile of The Corner, the waterfront wharf, docks and Chinatown's Da Hung.

He considered looking for employment at the docks within the week. It didn't happen quite so soon. The bankroll he had saved from the oil fields had provided him with a steady supply of opium vapors and the company of one particular girl named Hui Zhung. Her only English was *'I love you'*.

He had met Elmore by chance one more time at Molly's Canteen, and once again they ended up at The No Name to share a bucket of beer. His friend was out of sorts, and wasn't rubbing his head or growling like a dog that night. He had turned down Leopold's invitation to join him at Da Hung. Leopold was never again to lay eyes upon Elmore, but never gave it a thought until many years later.

Wong Wai, the owner of Da Hung, drove Leopold out for good on New Year's Eve after he had tried to gain entrance in a knee-crawling state of drunkenness. He had committed the ultimate disrespect, and even went so far as calling out for Hui Zhung, but, like Elmore, she also was never again to be seen.

January was a bad month for Leopold. His money was nearly gone, his appearance and hygiene suffered, he was unable to find work, and he had once again come to the stark realization that he was alone. He felt like the trap door to Hell had opened underneath him. He plunged feet first into a cesspool of self-pity and loathing. He had pestered, bartered and convinced Molly to allow him to sweep the floor and wash dishes in return for a bowl of soup or whatever sustenance she could provide. She too, eventually began to shun his presence, and ultimately set him out on his ear with the help of a few longshoremen.

One of the few opium dens in Chinatown that was not particular with their choice of clientele was the *Sing Lee Laundry*. It was a hovel, a den of depravity that Leopold began to frequent out of desperate necessity. When the trap door to Hell had opened, his pride went with him.

The smoking rooms at the laundry were no more than ten feet square, with mats strewn directly on the floor, chamber pots and defecation buckets placed perilously against the walls and prone to spillage or faulty aim. Patrons in varying stages of stupefaction would lie with bodies askew anywhere there was room. The air hung heavy with the sweet, putrid odor of the drug's vapor, and the walls were blackened by years of smoke from the burning poppy tar. The Sing Lee Laundry had a chilling silence that permeated Leopold's inner self and overwhelmed his conscience. It was as quiet and morbidly still as a mortician's workbench.

At Sing Lee, his dreams were transformed into nightmares, and one pipe was no longer enough for him to achieve that state of blissful reverie. Again and again he would relight the lamp, reheat the black lump he paid for, and repack the bowl. He would then draw in the vapor, allowing his eyelids to close and hands to go limp, mimicking the pose of a dead man. Then, without forewarning, what was once Heaven had turned to Hell. On several occasions, he woke himself with his wailing and cries over one or more of his recurring dreams. The once dreamy vapors could no longer keep the troubling demons of his past at bay, nor could they vanquish them. His tormented past kept coming after him, breathing down his neck, and never was more than a few puffs away. He found it increasingly difficult to escape his dungeon of dreams and began to dread sleep itself. He would fall hard from his stupor, crashing to the cobblestones. His sleep was consistently distraught, full of nightmares born from the smoldering shadows of his past.

He dreamed of hoards of Chinese swarming onto the street and blocking his path, and pointing to a steam locomotive, tender and a consist of Pullman cars sitting at a desolate, abandoned passenger station nearly buried by snow drifts. He envisioned Phryne, bleeding from wounds to her hands, beckoning to him from a window in one of the cars. He would try in vain to make his way through the blowing snow, and always awoke in trembling terror.

His nightmares were more than hallucinations; they were torture on the most vile level. He saw his tuberculosis-stricken father as a skeletal figure pushing a derelict rag-and-bone junk cart, gasping for breath, reaching and begging for pennies. No-account Dillon Cafferty stood laughing as if possessed and menacingly tossing lit matches onto his mother's porch. He would see his beautiful wife Phryne as a painted whore in makeup so thick it hung like concrete wallpaper, wearing a mascara and lipstick stained camisole, enticing and calling to him from the doorway of Shea's Hippodrome dance hall and motion picture house. Eloisa Ashworth was sitting on the curb outside her family's home, destitute, disheveled, begging for money and drinking from a pocket flask, her clothing torn to shreds. Leopold stood atop a grain silo and could see his brother Nicholas trapped inside and helplessly swirling within a whirlpool of wheat, about to be ground into flour. His mother Wilhelmina, and sisters Johanna, Ottilie and Hilde appeared as charred walking souls, drifting away with their backs turned, their scorched clothing falling from their burned, cadaverous bodies. He would awake in a night terror, in a cold sweat, wallowing in his personal stench of sweat, tobacco, and the drug. His underclothes were glued to his wet, shivering body. The sweet aftertaste of the opium pipe triggered an involuntary reflex to retch and gag. His violent convulsions became part and parcel of each nightmare.

At first, he blamed it on the poor quality of Sing Lee's opium, or that it could actually have been an inferior Indian counterfeit rather than a product from Hong Kong or Shanghai. His bad experiences got progressively worse, and he railed against the quality of the drug in the streets outside the laundry. In a matter of days, he was permanently banned from the Sing Lee parlor also.

Leopold persisted with his addiction, and was barely able to support his demons by schlepping anything, anywhere for nickels or dimes. More often than not, he was thrown out to the curb and soon found it nearly impossible to gain admission to even the seediest dens. His self esteem melted like a pat of butter on a hot cast iron skillet. He pawned his wing tip shoes, suit and the few pieces of wearable clothing that remained in his duffle sack. Out of pure desperation, he included his father's silver money clip in the deal. The exchange netted Leopold and his habit a total of forty-five cents.

He awoke on a bench in Pioneer Park one Saturday afternoon in early February, clutching a tattered copy of The San Francisco Examiner to his chest. By sheer accident, he had spotted a small advertisement for ongoing boxing competitions at an athletic club in the Tenderloin District. Leopold considered it a stroke of luck and a fortuitous chance to make a dollar or two. He did his best to clean up his appearance in the Men's Lounge at the Union Pacific terminal and walked to the club to answer the ad. He discovered that he could make a few hard-earned dollars by billing himself into second-tier matches at the O'Farrell Street Boxing Gym. The marquee fights were staged, and the winners were predetermined by none other than the McDonough brothers' organization. His San Francisco boxing career lasted six rounds: the duration of two very short bouts. He tragically admitted that he could no longer pull his weight in the ring and recognized that he was a beaten man, a worn-out pug* weakened by the poppy. He had no further to sink than his grave. Bruised and broke, he found himself in a perilous state of desperation. He had barely managed to tread water and keep from drowning in a sea of self pity for one more week. The void of money activated a primal instinct of survival that kept him from total surrender and ultimate disaster. Stopping the opium however, did not stop the dreams.

Wednesday, Noon, February 15, 1928

Leopold was standing outside the Salvation Army Waterfront Help Center on the corner of Battery Row and Union Streets, a stone's throw from The Embarcadero waterfront and Pioneer Park where he had recently spent a cold night or two. He had been aware of this place, and on occasion, pitied those waiting in line for a warm meal, shelter or guidance. He was battered, bruised and beaten. His nose had been broken for the third time and his ego had taken a knock-out blow. He recalled his father's words of admonition: *There, but for the grace of God, goest thou.* He had not eaten in two days and had been unable to find work, beg or borrow enough for a meal or a bed. He was light-headed and needed to steady himself against the clapboard building. He could not recall how he got there and had no firm concept of time or date. Moments of clarity would arrive and disappear.

He stood in queue waiting to warm his belly, and it crossed his mind that not too long ago, Leopold Throckmorton would have had no pity for the likes of the men in line with him. He quietly studied the people in front, and those in line behind him. There were three categories: sorrowful, worse, and hopeless. He regretfully placed himself in the last; his realization only added to his shame. He was hoping that here he could attempt to correct his course yet again, right the wrong, knowing full well that he'd had the same aspiration before and had failed. Once again, he understood that he had to do something. Elmore had said, 'In Chinatown, it's too damn easy to feel good.' He remembered that, but his mind was unable to summon up what the old fellow looked like.

The line moved steadily along and once inside, he was greeted by two young, uniformed Cadets. The line was being culled and he and two other men had been segregated out. Obviously the bottom of the barrel, his group was taken aside and encouraged to accept the opportunity of a shower-bath and a change of clean, dry clothing. Taken aback, groggy, stunned, and ashamed, he accepted the offer without comment or protest, and in the company of only one of the two others, they followed one of the young Christian soldiers to the men's shower. Standing under a stream of barely warm water, steadying himself with on open palm on the cement block wall and a hand on the faucet, he recalled that it had been at least a month since his body had experienced soap. When he took his place in line that morning, he had expected some degree of humiliation. So far, all things considered, it had been worth it. He was hungry to the point that his belly button was tickling his backbone. The shower had refreshed him and his filthy, putrid clothes had been replaced with used, but clean dungarees, oversized shirt and jacket. His dizziness was displaced by fatigue. His eyelids hung as heavy as horseshoes.

After his meal of mashed potatoes, mashed peas and barley soup, he was politely asked if he would consider taking advantage of some additional services that the Army could provide. He suspected that they would attempt to preach to him; after all, it's what they do. He accepted, and was praised for his honesty and willingness to embark on the path to redemption. He met with seasoned Salvation Army counselor Major Allen Burrus and a very devoted spiritual advisor,

Lieutenant Mary Singleton. Major Burrus was a twenty-year veteran of the Army, having finished his officer training shortly before the devastating 1906 earthquake and fire. The Lieutenant, a spirited lady in her forties, was attending theology classes at the Corps College on Valencia Street.

The Salvation Army Waterfront Help Center was a soup kitchen and community outreach post that provided urgent assistance and aid for San Francisco's wharf district and Chinatown. They had reached out their hand to Leopold and he accepted it. Before dark settled on the city that evening, he was aboard the Market Street trolley, accompanied by Cadet Fergus Abernathy, and on his way to the Salvation Army Dolores Street Shelter. Once inside, Cadet Fergus and two other soldiers helped him to bed. The first night and part of the next day was spent in a quarantine room, strapped in bed with leather restraints.

His first days there were tortured outbursts of paranoia, triggered by his persistent dreams. Emaciated and exhausted, his first full week as a resident was spent battling insomnia, hallucinations, malnutrition and confusion. Army Captain Ellis Cornwall was also a practicing physician, and had seen a good deal of opium addicts. He placed Leopold on a regimen of controlled doses of laudanum for his opium withdrawal and goat's milk with an emulsion of castor oil as a purging laxative. His initial diet was oatmeal, fat back bacon and watery pea soup.

Get Happy!

A large, narrow building, the Delores-Mission Shelter was hastily built immediately after the '06 earthquake as emergency disaster housing for victims of the quake and subsequent fire that had destroyed the city. Since then, it had been under constant renovation and repair. The daily routine was structured in an efficient, quasi-military manner by Major Burrus. He had seen countless men in Leopold's situation, and had created a successful schedule of spiritual inspiration, rehabilitation and reintroduction that had worked very well according to his standard. The Major was proud of his recidivism success rate of 50%. Residents were granted a time limit of thirty-days in the shelter, which was renewable on a case-by-case basis to a maximum of ninety days. Hot breakfasts and dinners were provided for the residents.

Leopold had worked through several temporary jobs from the onset of his stay; his first being at a piggery, where he sorted out edible municipal and city waste for a population of seventy-five porkers. He began his longest and most current employment as a warehouseman at Bay Grocery Distributors on March 1st. Major Burrus had been pleased with Leopold's progress and following several counseling sessions, Burrus agreed that Leopold should secure private living accommodations. After four and a half weeks in the shelter, Leopold returned to his first lodgings at the Ambassador Hotel on Harriet Street and once again paid two dollars a week. He had entered into an agreement with the Major that he would first attend services at the Booth Universal Christian Chapel on Sundays, and volunteer at the shelter afterwards.

The population at the shelter was in a constant state of flux. Resident turnovers were a daily occurrence. Most of the time, people came and went without notice. There were never more than a handful of women and a very few children among the fifty-odd population of homeless and they were segregated to separate quarters under the supervision of female Army officers and cadets. Leopold had many passing acquaintances while at the shelter and had made a handful of casual friendships during his stay, but his longest and strongest connection was with two-year Ensign Amanda

Hugg. An aspiring officer in the Army, she was his assigned duty nurse from day one. She had continually encouraged and comforted him since his arrival, and eased him through the early episodes of hyper anxiety and nausea. Nurse Hugg had even shaved Leopold's month-long stubble as he lay incapacitated during his first nights at the shelter. She had worked closely with Doctor Cornwall for the duration of the month-long opium withdrawal regimen the doctor had devised for Leopold. Little by little, she was getting to know him and attempting to piece his puzzling life together. She felt empathy for this man, convinced him to regrow his mustache and saw a promise in his muscled body that needed to be fulfilled.

From the start of his rebirth, she encouraged him. She gently ran her finger over the crooked profile of his thrice-broken nose, and whispered in his ear, "It's time to pick yourself up off the mat, Leopold Throckmorton. Wipe your bloody nose, bandage your self-esteem and stand up straight. The bell is about to ring, signaling the second round of your life."

He acknowledged that he had to change his ways. "I can speak from experience, Nurse Amanda. When I started to hold the pipe, I certainly did not intend for it to overtake my mind. I thought I could just walk into the room and sit in the back row without getting noticed. It didn't work out that way. The opium rooms are full of the fumes of Hell itself. And when it comes to Hell, I know from where I speak." He then gave her an amicable foreboding, "You need to be careful when you use the sword of the Lord to fight my demons, Nurse. If you don't have a good hold on it, a firm grip, it could cut you too."

They had begun a relationship that played on their personalities and teased their emotions. He saw Amanda as his guide, lighting his way through the dark alleys of The Embarcadero and down the brick and cobbled streets of Chinatown, around scoundrels, thieves and no-accounts. She ignited a spark within him. The twenty-two year old nurse was an enigma Leopold wanted to solve. Her puritanical uniform was just the outer wrapper of this mysterious young woman. She had intense brown eyes that mirrored his, and flowing, deep brown locks. She wore a high-collared white blouse and a navy blue skirt that ended four inches from the floor. Her nurse's cap was also blue, with red ribbon trim, and an embroidered "S" at the front. The only hints of color were her glowing cheeks and pink lips. She had an endearing smile that hinted of mischievous innocence. Her form was hidden underneath all too much cotton and wool, but in the reflected sunlight streaming from the windows on the east wall, he was able to catch a fleeting glimpse of her shapely silhouette. He wondered if her body had ever been exposed to light, and could only imagine her milky white legs, waist, shoulders and bosom. When she wore her blue-black cape, its only distinguishing feature was a brass pin, with three interconnected letters "S"; proclaiming the Army's motto: *Soup, Soap and Salvation.*

They had become close friends and had many cautious conversations, each realizing the delicate situation they were in. Leopold especially wanted to proceed with care. They each had a secret desire to pursue the advancement of their relationship, and between them, it was Amanda who was forced to use the most restraint. Going back to her maternal grandparents, her family had been Christian Soldiers. Her mother and father were active officers in the Army; Major Aloysius and Captain Maude Hugg. She was living in the family home on Haight Street with her younger brothers Duncan, 16 and Oliver, 15. The boys attended Lucas Adams Secondary School, volunteered at the shelter on weekends and they too, got to know Leopold. Her parents had been working in Mexico since late April, helping to establish a new Salvation Mission in Juárez, just across the border from El Paso, Texas.

Weeks ago, when Major Burrus had allowed Leopold to leave the shelter and seek accommodations off-site, an opportunity arose that the young couple had been waiting for. The moment Leopold was granted off-site housing, Amanda extended an invitation and gave him clandestine directions to her home. He used an alley off Scarborough Place and stole his way to the back door where Amanda spirited him inside. For Leopold, it was to be the first time he consciously had relations with a woman in nearly six months. Every one of his Chinatown trysts were experienced while in an opium fueled trance. For Amanda, full intimacy with the enigmatic Leopold could not have happened soon enough. The tall, lean, muscular fellow from Buffalo fascinated her. The suitcase full of secrets that he kept hidden from her was a temptation akin to Pandora's Box or the Forbidden Fruit itself.

On that warm June morning, she invited him to her upstairs bedroom. He removed her clothing slowly, like it was a ritual of passage. She moved her hands over every inch of his naked form, tasted the salt on his brow and the passion in his kisses. "Love me, Leopold. Love me like you have never been hurt."

He tempted her with his tongue and teased her with his touch.

She breathed, "Are you trying to lead me on?"

He taunted her, "I am trying to get you in bed."

"I think that's where I am, but you go right ahead and keep on trying."

Life lessons learned

Sharing a cigarette, she was resting comfortably on his arm. "How can I ever wear a gown of white, Leopold? I walk around every day with blazing scarlet red ribbons on my uniform. However you interpret that meaning, it's convoluted. And furthermore, the Army proclaims that *'We believe that our first parents were created in a state of innocence, but by their disobedience they lost their purity and happiness, and that in consequence of their fall all men have become sinners, totally depraved and as such are justly exposed to the wrath of God'*. Truly? I mean, if you take that literally, we're all evil and going straight to Hell!"

Leopold saw his chance to egg Amanda on, and see how far she would take this conversation. "I think they call it the *original sin* or something; Eve ate the apple, didn't she? And I agree, all the churches and all the governments cannot successfully regulate sin or legislate morality. Murder is illegal, yet it happens every day. We're not perfect, are we? Once Humpty Dumpty went over the edge, it was over. Just take a look at what happened in the Garden of Eden. Eve broke God's law."

Amanda had a wry little grin. "Sure, but I'm not talking about apples or snakes or Cain and Abel. The Church stands for one reason only: to facilitate your forgiveness, to save your soul. Well, if that's the case, in order for the Church to exist in the first place, people have to sin. Or the Church doesn't have a job to do." She sat up and let the sheet fall to the mattress. Her deep brown hair curled over her shoulders. He gently tugged at her locks, and she laid down once again, lifted a leg and pushed herself to him, wriggling her warmth to his hip. She looked across the pillow and directly into his eyes, "So, just think about this … all right? Do you think people only just started to hanky-panky and kadoodle and make whoopee and commit all this sin? It's nothing new to mankind. How do you think all the graveyards got filled up? People make people."

He teased, "All right, go ahead, and continue my theology lesson. But, to expand our discussion, I think it's only a sin if you know it to be wrong. It's impossible for the deed to be a sin if there is no standard for right or wrong. So, go ahead and explain. I'm all ears, Sweetheart."

"Well, think about this: The Church saves your soul. The only time they are able to save your soul is after you sin -- after the fact. So, it only stands to reason that you need to sin in order to give the Church something to save. *You got to sin to be saved.* To me, that's just crazy. If you ask me, the more sinners there are, the more the Church has to do. I think we need to keep the Church in business, that's all. That's all I'm saying." She made her point by giving him a gentle poke in the ribs.

He touched her, wiggled and teased her dewy den with his fingertips. Her rosy pink nipples were hard and as big around as a stack of ten dimes.

She breathed, *"Like they say, you got to hold the glass if you want to taste the champagne."*

After a moment of thought, she added, "So obviously, the only way to get my message across is action. You know what I mean. I'm talking about one more dance around the ballroom; the horizontal Charleston, sir." She let out another little laugh and rolled on top of him. "It's an hour until my brothers get home."

That evening, Leopold had dinner with Amanda and her brothers Duncan and Oliver. After a few spirited games of checkers, he gave Amanda a peck on the cheek and caught the Market Street trolley back to his room at the Ambassador on Harriett Street.

It was the beginning of an intensely physical relationship they took every opportunity to enjoy. Amanda's parents were expected to return from Mexico in early July.

Monday night, June 11, 1928

It must have been around midnight. The skies were dark as pitch, with a full ivory moon dangling, suspended directly above, as if hanging by an invisible string. The lone streetlight at the corner was a flutter of activity. Whippoorwills darted in and out of the light beams, catching and feasting on a hearty meal of moths, flies and June bugs buzzing around the lamp. The air was thick, heavy and curiously unmoving. Lawn crickets moved their legs in a frenzied mating call; squeaking and chattering. Oppressive midsummer humidity covered the city's neighborhoods like an unwelcome woolen blanket. A thirsty man could quench his thirst by waving a spoon through the wet, soupy air.

Vanilla moonbeams filtered through the leaves of towering elm trees down onto the green grass, grey sidewalks and red brick streets below, creating an illuminated pathway skyward, to the heavens above.

Eight shadowy figures in street-length overcoats exited a large four-door sedan that was parked at the curb. Had they not arrived in an automobile, they could have been mistaken for eight prophetic horsemen dressed in rawhide dusters. With damned determination and manifested malicious intent, each moved slowly from the large car, carrying Thompson automatic machine rifles alongside their frames. Their identities were mysterious; all facial features were hidden deep in the shadows of the tilted brims of their black fedoras. Only their eyes were visible as heinous glowing pools of blood-red. Their hats had distinctive wide white bands that emitted a foreboding glow in the moonlight. Lit cigarettes hung from their lips with the burning intensity of red hot coals. The eight men moved toward the two-story, wood frame Victorian home and stopped short of the wooden steps that led up to the covered porch.

Four brown bats exposed their fangs, chattered, clicked, chipped and performed aerobatic swan dives above the heads of the eight dark strangers, feasting on mosquitoes and gnats.

A knock sounded, and it echoed up and down the street, but no one appeared at the door. A lamp came on upstairs and another in the parlor.

When the front door opened, orange-red flashes of light and the piercing sound of gunfire brought the wrath of the Evil One down upon Adams Street. There was no one standing behind the open door. From the street, only the vacant hallway, the empty stairway, and the bare parlor could be seen. There was no life inside the home. The eight men laughed along with the Devil's hellion choir.

The home burst into a fireball that lit up the sky, illuminating the city, blanketing everything in flaming red. A demonic scream from the deepest depths of Hades called out: *"THROCKMORTON !!!"* The eight horsemen aimed their machine guns at him.

Further down the block, coming from within a cloud of the blackest smoke, the harrowing whistle of a monstrous steam locomotive was heard. "All aboard" was the shrill cry of the mummified conductor. Grey flesh fell from his bones as he stood waving his lantern. Phryne emerged from the coal-black cloud, taking the form of a ravenous, winged hag on the fly, swooping upon a painted oriental girl dressed in scarlet silk. Eloisa was as innocent and beautiful as a spring bride, unscathed by the blazing cataclysm, smiling and pointing to his derelict Model T, without a roof or wheels.

Leopold's mother and sisters were beckoning to him, riding atop a horse-drawn hearse, racing across the International Peace Bridge. The horses spooked, reared, whinnied and jumped from the bridge into the roaring waters of the Niagara River below. Dillon Cafferty stood on the shore, hands-on-hip and laughing in a tone shrill enough to evoke apocalyptic terror from the Archbishop of Canterbury. His younger brother Nicholas stood at ringside, and rang the bell that signaled the end of Round One. His father was peddling penny-a-bag peanuts.

Leopold awoke in a cold sweat, trembling, terrified and frantic. All night long, newsboys, boxers, bankers, poets, swordsmen, devils and preachers had screamed fire deep within his skull. His bedding was on the floor, and his bed was askew. He was bewildered, afraid and sick to his stomach. He had shared his nightmares with Amanda, but had never mentioned Phryne, Dillon or Eloisa. This was his worst night.

My Melancholy Baby

He didn't leave his room until late that Tuesday morning, and did not go to work. The nightmare had troubled him more than any of his other hallucinations. What went against the grain this time was the fact that he had not been under the spell of opium for nearly four months, and yet he had experienced his worst nighttime apparitions since he left Buffalo ten months earlier. His head ached as if split by an axe. As soon as he walked down the stairs, and reached the lobby of the old hotel, the innkeeper called him over to the desk, and informed him that he was to be evicted that day. The landlord seemed to be a bit timid, and unsure of Leopold's demeanor. He nervously said that the remainder of his rent for the month would be refunded, and further explained that there were numerous complaints from other residents in the rooming house that had forced his decision. One guest had suggested that the police should be notified, and judging from the sounds that were heard coming from inside the room, a murder could have been committed.

Leopold was in limbo; a lucid, yet catatonic state. He knew where he was, who he was, but had no concept of intention, purpose or direction. He apologized to the landlord and promised that he would be leaving by nightfall, "I'll be back to gather my things soon."

Kicked out on his ear, he had no idea where he could go. The sun could have been blazing, it could have been raining cats and dogs; regardless, he was in a fog and had decided to seek refuge at the one place he could rely on: the Salvation Army Mission. Amanda would help.

He started down Market Street, and his eyes drifted to a handbill nailed to a telegraph pole. Among all the others that were tacked to the pole, weathered, torn and ripped; his eyes focused on the freshest, newest one. It depicted an impressive red flag waving in the breeze, embellished with a large, white dollar sign upon it. He could have stood there for hours, reading and rereading the advertisement under the picture. Life went on around him, but he was standing alone in his own world. For reasons he could not explain, at that moment in time, he had decided on a new direction, a new focus with an abstract solution to his plight. First, he would tell Amanda; it was imperative. He didn't imagine that she would understand this new course of action. He couldn't expect her to understand. He didn't. He was grasping for a life-line that he wished she held in her heart.

Nurse Amanda Hugg was surprised by his visit, and invited him to the rear courtyard. He waited patiently for her behind the shelter, on a bench that was in dire need of paint and positioned close to a lopsided, weathered table.

Amanda brought out two mugs of hot cocoa and a small plate with three doughnuts and sat next to him. Leopold took one of the tempting fry cakes, and tried to think of a way to explain his new plans. After two sips of cocoa and half a doughnut, he was ready. He had considered that the logic behind his decision would seem flawed to her, and that he needed to appeal to her compassion and understanding.

"I've taken many missteps and I have stumbled more than a time or two on my walk through life. I should have been more appreciative of the people around me when the times were good ... the people that loved me, my family ... back when I was younger, back in Buffalo. Right now, I appreciate you beyond explanation, Amanda, but I'm afraid of hurting you. I do not want to hurt you. That's something that I would never intend to do."

She listened to each word and answered, "No matter what you are trying to say, I can tell you one thing for certain, Leopold. You hold the rope that leads me on. If you yank it too hard, I will go right over the edge, so you better be careful. When I first met you, all jazzed up on the smoke, shaking, struggling and sweating, I could not forsake you. I reached out to you. You didn't know your own name; you were that bad. In only a few weeks, you had your tent pitched right on the outskirts of my mind. And I let you move in. And finally you moved right downtown. You drove the tent stakes deep. And now, well, I'm afraid you have moved in permanently. And made your bed, too."

He swallowed the last bit of doughnut. "I'm trying to tell you what happened, and what I decided. Last night I had another dream, a bad one, a real bad one. They are kicking me out of the Ambassador ... it was that bad."

"Peace of mind and Salvation are not porcelain souvenirs you can pick up at some Market Street curiosity shop. You have to take control of your life. The Mission will help you find another home, Leopold. That's what we do ... we help people. I can help you once again. But you have to be willing to do some of the work yourself."

He finished his cocoa, and set the cup on the ground between them. Amanda turned to him, and he took her hands.

"I'm leaving, Amanda. Going to sea. I have to be somewhere that allows me no escape. This morning, I was tempted to return to the numbing damnation of the opium vapor. I almost took the Chinatown trolley. I cannot let that happen to me again. On my way over here, I saw a bill posted on a telegraph pole for deck hands ... above and below deck ... ships are sailing almost daily, loaded cargo steamers to destinations all over the Pacific ... China, the Philippines, Japan and Australia. I need to put myself in isolation, away from temptation, and perhaps I can find peace and come to terms with myself and my damning dreams. I cannot stay here. I'll drown. I do not wish to take you down with me."

She bit her lip. "The broth always boils down to what you can live with, or the soup ends up burnt to the pot, doesn't it? You're running away, Leopold. That's what you're doing. You cannot face your demons by running away. You've been a millwright , a roustabout, a warehouseman, a viper* and you have even tried boxing to feed your addiction."

"I'm not running. I'm bouncing off the ropes and pouncing back for the next round." He remembered that he had spoken nearly the same words to Phryne.

She sniffled, blinked and wiped a tear. She was far beyond disappointment. She was aggravated. "I really have tried to unravel the secrets you have twisted around in your memory, Leopold. I thought you were a fighter, a champion. You're not. You're retreating to your corner, aren't you? You're messed up, crazy and acting like a doughboy* with shell shock*. You're giving up, throwing in the towel and looking for the easy way out. How's that for a sucker punch, Mister Prizefighter? It's the cold, honest bucket of truth I just tossed on your head. So, you go right ahead and be a bell bottom*. You go right ahead and sail away with my heart."

"You're hurt, Amanda, and I'm sorry. I know you're trying not to show it. You're trying to slap me conscious with smelling salts and scripture. But show me some faith, understand me and bandage my bruises. I have to do this, for my peace of mind. I have to fight these hellish dreams my way. I have to accept my mistakes and win this round with my mind, or I will become my own prisoner in my own dungeon in some back alley, either on the waterfront or Chinatown. I'll win this fight, and I'll be back."

She stood and started away. The remaining doughnut fell to the ground.

Amanda was halfway to the back door of the shelter when he called, "I'll write to you."

She did not turn around. "Don't bother." She brushed away one last tear as she entered the building.

7. GLENDALE, CALIFORNIA ~ 1928

Everybody Loves My Baby

When Eloisa Ashworth arrived at Los Angeles' Central Station, she had finished an epic cross-country journey across grassy plains, over snow-capped mountains and through barren deserts. Every mile had been an adventure and it was a trip that she would never forget. Inside the station, she sought out the Travelers' Aid booth and got the help she needed to arrive at Phryne's home address. As it was, the route she had written for Eloisa to 16 Gardner Place was a little off. Phryne had assumed that Ellie would be arriving at La Grande Station aboard the Atchison, Topeka & Santa Fe, and not the Union Pacific's *Los Angeles Limited*, which made her written directions a bit off kilter. Eloisa got the help she needed and was quickly on the corrected course.

From the windows of the Melrose streetcar, she could see the hills over Los Angeles and the giant white letters that spelled out HOLLYWOODLAND. The bright morning sun made the sign gleam. Her pulse quickened.

She arrived at 16 Gardner place, and stood on the sidewalk in front of the home. A two-tone, grey and black Cadillac Custom Eight sat in the drive. The bungalow was white stucco, in Spanish Mission style, with wide arcade arches along the front patio, and terra cotta clay roof tiles. Everything was awash in morning warmth. There was no doubt she was in California.

It was just past eleven o'clock when she carried her bags along the flagstone walk, up the steps and set them onto the porch. She pinched her cheeks and bit her lips for color, adjusted the brim of her hat, squared her shoulders, and knocked. She had dressed on the train for this reuniting, wearing a light blue, fitted waist chemise dress she hadn't worn since her pregnancy. Her blonde locks, in tight finger waves, contrasted well under the black hat. Eloisa looked wonderful, and felt better than she had in just about a year.

The frantic bark of a tiny dog brought a winsome smile to her lips. She recognized Phryne's voice, "Easy there, Wiggins. Control yourself puppy, we've got company."

The door opened and Wiggins, a black and tan Yorkshire terrier, ran out and circled Eloisa, jumping enthusiastically up and down on little hind legs and emitting tiny, high pitched, teeny tiny doggy woof-woofs. Gradually, the hugs turned to smiles, curious little questions and dinner mint platitudes. The women were beside themselves with happiness. Over Phryne's shoulder, Eloisa saw Abner, standing with folded arms across his chest and amused at the display of loving friendship.

"Come on in Ellie! You must be hungry; are you?"

"I really didn't have much for breakfast on the train … I was too excited."

"Well, good! We can fix that! Come on in, and meet Abner … there he is! And I'll ask Connie to make us up a nice lunch."

Phryne was referring to Consuela Delgado Marquez, the housemaid Abner had hired a week after they moved in. He had insisted on securing house help over the mild protests of his wife, but it certainly wasn't long before Phryne had become accustomed to the situation. Connie lived on the property, in an two-room, one bath, efficiency garden house twenty feet behind the main dwelling. A bronze-skinned, green-eyed beauty of twenty-five, she was fluent in English, having worked nearly ten years as house help in Los Angeles.

Sardine and cucumber sandwiches, cream of celery coup and iced tea were followed by a bottle of *Monastery Reserve* that Abe had brought up from the basement larder. They went to the sun room after lunch and relaxed on a white wicker sofa with oversized floral print cushions. Wiggins hopped up and found his spot next to Phryne.

Eloisa was curious when Abe set the bottle and glasses on the tea table. "There isn't Prohibition in California?" It was an honest question.

Abner explained as he twisted the cork screw, "This is from Saint Paul Monastery, in the valley east of Frisco. So it's legal, it's for religious purposes, you see. It's actually a Sherry, but the Spaniards are so damn particular about that name, the monks can't call it that. So let's simply say that it's a very, very righteous wine. And I have some very righteous friends." He poured three glasses and relaxed into his Morris chair.

"Not really, Ellie. Abe's pulling your leg. Out here it's nothing like it is back in New York. Things are a little different in Hollywood, you'll see. It's easy to be spoiled out here." Phryne was right. With money and good connections, you could get just about anything in Los Angeles.

"And I've got to say, you really look beautiful. You must be taking care of yourself. You're beautiful."

"I'm not doing anything different, Phryne. I'm still the same old me, and afraid that I'm a little worse for wear."

Abner interrupted, "Ladies, I know you have a lot to chin wag* about, so I'll leave you two at it. I think I'll pop over to Hillcrest and perhaps shoot nine holes … or maybe the full eighteen. I'll be able to pick up a foursome right there in the club house. So, have at it ladies. I expect that I'll be back by seven, Sweetheart. Before dark. I'll grab my clubs and I'll be on my way."

He stepped toward the sofa and extended his hand, "Very nice to finally meet you, Ellie. Phryne has spoken about you so much, I feel like I already know you. We're so glad you were able to come out and visit." He gave his wife a peck on the cheek. Wiggins let out a woof in mild protest.

"Thanks, Honey; have a good game. I'll figure on dinner at about seven, then, thank you. Toodles ! Bye!" Phryne and Eloisa were eagerly awaiting the chance to really catch up. Abner's golf game was his way of graciously yielding the floor to his wife. He blew a kiss to her from the front door and gave a little wave in Ellie's direction. As soon as the door was closed, Phryne began, "So, first tell me about your trip. Everything went well?"

"It did, it went fine. The trains were on time and all in all, it was a pleasant enough trip. But I didn't sleep a wink from Buffalo all the way to Chicago I think, the train made so many stops, and in Chicago, that's where I got a Pullman berth, and I paid for both the upper and lower so I could have the privacy. And as soon as the train left the station, I think I was asleep. I slept all the way to Omaha. Really! I passed right out, I was so tired."

"You're looking so good, so fresh and healthy, Ellie. Your shoulder, where you caught the bullet, it healed all right then?"

"Yes, of course it did. It was only a scratch really. I told Father that it had happened during a fight that broke out at the Lafayette, and that satisfied him at the time. But enough about that … tell me what happened with Leopold. I was stunned to hear that your marriage was over, and now you're pregnant and you're married again. You said in your letter that your life was a merry-go-round … I think that's a bit of an understatement."

Phryne poured a little more sherry into Ellie's glass and just a splash into hers. "The long and short of the story is that

Leopold and I never should have married. Never. I now know that his marriage proposal wasn't at all thought out, and it never would have worked. And I admit it: I was too quick to say 'yes'. We both were caught up in the excitement of things, of everything, and weren't thinking straight. And what pushed everything over the edge was that night at the bridge, and all the violence and Dillon unfortunately hit and killed that officer. Bullets were flying, you got shot, and everyone was afraid for their lives. Dillon had used my Leopold as a patsy* and you and me as dumb Doras*. He used us all and had us wrapped around his finger."

Eloisa listened intently, trying to retain every single word, every detail. Phryne had begun to open up and express her feelings as she never had before.

"When we left Buffalo, we thought we were running for our lives. Perhaps we were. Looking back at it now, I think it was just an excuse to run away. So was our marriage, I think, just an excuse. And I ran with him. I know that now. It had bothered him to no end that he broke ties with his mother, and he carried all that guilt with him, I think … and the belief he had let his mother down after his father died. And when he heard the news about the deadly fire, it was too much for him. And Nicholas was missing. And then his night terrors and haunted dreams started … the heebie jeebies* got hold of him and he couldn't stand it any more. He lost control. When Leopold left me, he said that he wasn't running away. That's bullshit. He's been running since the Peace Bridge fiasco. He's been running away from himself. And that's something you just cannot do. Your shadow always stays with you. The shadows that you cast, they never disappear and they follow you everywhere. You can't lose your own shadow. I don't think Leopold is a bad person, but he said some really mean, nasty things to me before he left. I don't think it was him talking. At the time, I thought he was possessed by the Devil. He was terribly upset, but now I think he meant everything he said when he said them. I have no idea where he went or where he could be and I haven't heard one word. Not one. I cannot forgive Leopold for leaving me. Only God can truly forgive and it's His job, not mine. That night back in Buffalo, Leopold had told me that we had to leave to be safe. He was running away then and I didn't like that idea. Sure, I wanted to go with him, but I wanted to go somewhere. First he said Cleveland, and then he said Chicago. I finally suggested that we should stop thinking about going away and start thinking about going somewhere, like going to a destination, toward a goal. And I suggested California, and Bingo! Here I am. He's gone, and still running probably. But not me. I just didn't leave Buffalo, I went somewhere. I went to Hollywood."

"You've kept in touch with your family back in Buffalo, haven't you?"

"I've written a few letters, but to tell the truth, I've decided not to dwell in the past, and deal only with the future. I was getting lectured, scolded really, with every letter I got, and I don't need that. That constant ridicule and criticism is nothing but poison. After you hear so much of that, you can start to shrivel up inside and rot away."

"When did you find out you were pregnant?"

"That's another story, isn't it? Well, it was after Leopold had left, and he had no idea, either. It happened on the train on the way out here. It had to be ... on the train. We left Buffalo in such a hurry, he had forgot his lambskins*, of course. He dropped his seed into me a few times and I ended up pregnant, but I didn't know it until months later. But let me say that I had some fantastic finishes on that train ... all those vibrations and that rocking motion. Sometimes when Leopold was asleep I would set myself off by just laying flat on the bed, on my belly and pressing myself into the mattress. Of course, my fingers helped. And the image of that steaming, powerful, big black locomotive would swirl in my brain. I still daydream about that. That was a part of the trip I will never forget ... those fantastic finishes."

Her thoughts had drifted and she began again, "Anyway, we started to get settled out here, and got a little apartment, Leopold got a job and then he goes all haywire* and leaves me high and dry. So I got a job ... I had to ... I started working at Paramount Studios, doing make-up and hair. At the end of October I had my marriage to Leopold annulled ... I had no choice. Why would I stay married to a man who left me? It just didn't make any sense. And then in December I found out I'm pregnant. I knew I had to keep my job in order to survive, so I told Abner about the mess I was in. That man is a prince, Ellie. I know he doesn't look the part, but he is. I landed a good one this time ... he's one of those men that honor their woman. He asked me to marry him and I said yes, positootly."

Eloisa interrupted, "From what little I've seen, Abner seems to be a fine man, Phryne. I mean, look at this place ... you're doing all right, I'd say. And you're pregnant? You're not very big ... are you sure you're due in May?"

"Yes, May or June. I was at the doctor last week and he said everything is all right ... he could hear the baby's heartbeat ... it's just the way I am, I suppose. He wants me to eat more, but how can I eat more than I do? I mean, I can only eat so much, you know. But, it's your turn now, Ellie. I've been chin-wagging long enough. What have you been up to? Tell me everything."

"Hang onto your hat, Phryne. There's a lot." Eloisa took a sip of sherry, and began with her arrest in September. Phryne was at the edge of her seat as she listened to her friend's account of the arrest, interrogation and three-day stay in jail.

"Father and Mother were very upset and ashamed by my arrest and time in jail; charged as an accessory to murder and conspirator in bootlegging. It was quite public, you know, the Feds came right into the bakery and put me in hand irons. And it was in the papers too. And then the rumors started. But when the cops dropped the charges, that news never got in the papers, did it? They never printed that. But that's not all. It got worse, much worse. The real brodie* hit in October when I found out I was pregnant. Just like you: surprise, surprise! And I would not take it away ... that's something I could never do ... never. It happened over the 4th of July and Dominion Day weekend. Dillon forced himself on me, more than once. The second time I was weak, let my guard down and I just gave up."

Phryne's eyes opened wide, and she exclaimed in surprise, "July?! When we all took the *Canadiana* ferry to Canada, spent the night and watched the Crystal Beach fireworks? I don't believe it! Dillon forced you ... he raped you that weekend?"

"Yes, it started that way ... right after the sun went down ... behind the sand dunes. Don't misunderstand, it wasn't my first time at bat, but I wasn't comfortable outside on the sand and grass. He had to have it his way. He forced himself on me anyway, held me down and took advantage. I got dirty, and I cried, went inside and went to bed. And then again, later on he woke me up in the middle of the night and that time I didn't resist. I lost my fight, and I let him do it all over again. I was weak. He gave me the sweet talk, told me he loved me and a whole boatload of hokum*. Maybe you and Leopold were still dancing, I don't know."

Phryne looked away, her thoughts drifted again. "Yes, we must have been ... dancing or drinking. We drank a lot of Fergie's Foam that weekend ... we all did ... a lot."

The next bit of news disturbed and hurt Phryne: Eloisa's rejection and banishment to the unwed mothers' home.

Phryne let out a gasp in disbelief. "I'm surprised you didn't get any compassion from your parents, Ellie. You didn't get any? None at all? Not even from your mother?"

"No. It was all my fault, you see." The sobs started, they held each other, gave solace, held hands, and shed tears.

"Never mind that Dillon used me as a floor mop and I let him. Remember we convinced our parents that you and I were staying in one room and the men in another? Well, after he found out I was pregnant, Father rubbed my nose in it until I bled. And Dillon was murdered by the mob, so the marriage option was out the window. My father would have permitted that just to avoid scandal, you can bet, no matter who the father was. He would have insisted on it; demanded it. My sister had to get married because she was pregnant. You know how it is. Never mind the fact it's 1928, I'm free, white, twenty-one and have the right to vote. Women are evil, evil, evil. You and I have seen it before. If you sin, if you step over the line, you get ostracized for life and might as well be on a desert island somewhere. I'm not the only girl that went to this party, not by a long, long mile. I'm not the only girl some scum of a man led down the primrose path to condemnation. Father Baker's in Lackawanna is full of babies like mine. My daughter was lucky and was adopted at birth. Some of those children are there for years, and it's the only home they will ever know. Some grow up, graduate from school and get jobs right from there, for Pete's sake. My little girl was one of the lucky ones. As for my father, he thinks the road through life is straight as an arrow, and there's no *if* … no *and* … and … no *but* about it. And Mother, well, she thinks the road is smooth … as long as she has Father showing her the way. However, me and my sister Ginny … I hope … know better. I know I do. Virginia was always the quiet one, and she always seems to know more than she ever lets on. *Everything is difficult before it's easy* … everything. She used to say that."

"If I would have known at the time, Ellie, I would have brought you out here to California with us when Leopold and I left." She asked, "Your sister, Virginia, couldn't she help?"

"She and her husband Geoffrey have been out here in Sacramento since January. It's a nine hour train ride from here, I checked. He took a job offer at the paper there, the *Bee*, I think it's called. Mother and Father haven't told me anything, and there hasn't been any communication between them or Virginia ever since. They have never opened any of her letters ... none that I have noticed. But I don't hold hard feelings toward anyone over this. What happened is over and done with. I have considered that if I had broken it off with Dillon after he took advantage of me, none of our misfortunes would have happened. But I didn't, and kept seeing him. I was foolish and I made a big mistake. I have come to terms with that, and there's no sense to fret over it. It happened, it's done. The end."

That afternoon, Phryne and Eloisa rediscovered just how much their lives had changed since the previous August. The next few days were spent catching up and shopping. With Abner's help, Ellie began working at the studio's posh *Spotlight Café* as a kitchen assistant, which included everything from washing pots and pans to slicing celery. The work kept her busy and helped her sleep at night.

Thursday, May 10, 1928

Phryne went into labor in the early morning hours of May 3. Abner drove her to Hollywood Hospital where she was admitted to the Maternity Floor, and although she had been sedated, it was a long, strenuous ordeal that ended in late afternoon with the birth of a five pound, four ounce baby girl.

Doctor Howell had estimated that the infant was approximately four weeks premature.

Millicent Mae Mandelbaum died of respiratory failure on May 4, 1928. Phryne was released from the hospital six days later, to attend her daughter's funeral and burial the following day at Hollywood Memorial Cemetery.

Although Eloisa had witnessed Hollywood's flash, and had experienced some of its flair, baby Millicent's tragic funeral was her first total immersion into the resplendent, trendsetting lifestyle that her friend Phryne had become a part of. It had begun when Abner arranged for a dressmaker to measure and fit the women for their dresses of black and ended abruptly as everything returned to normal immediately after the burial. The crowd at the service and interment was a veritable mass of celebrity and influence. What struck Eloisa as bizarre, was how quickly it had come together, seemingly without effort: the sumptuous wake and ornate service. When Abner left for his office the next morning, it appeared that everything had been set back into its rightful spot, the past had been forgotten and that order had returned to the world.

Friday had turned out to be a glorious spring day. A pair of Bullock's oriole were showing off their singing talents in the garden. Connie had brought a breakfast of toast, cream cheese, anchovies, orange slices and boiled eggs to the patio. The women were quiet and conversation was subdued. Eloisa unwrapped the towel from around the pot and poured more coffee. She was dressed for the day, in a drop waist shift of layered soft green silk. Phryne was in full makeup as usual, but still in her plush, ivory dressing gown with the feathered black collar. A wisp of stray hair brushed along her cheek. Her plush pink day slippers had a small, one-inch heel.

"You could have went to work today, Ellie. I think I'm able to manage on my own now. And really, I think I would prefer it. I don't want anyone to hover over me … I'm fine, really. It's a tragedy that was written in the stars. It's over, and life goes on."

Ellie spoke softly, "All right. I think I'll go to work tomorrow then, if you think you can be alone."

"Of course, you go ahead. I'm fine, really. And of course, I can be alone." She took a red-tip Marlboro from her silver cigarette case, slipped it into the four-inch black Bakelite holder, lit it and poured another splash of cream sherry into her coffee. "I'm over the worst of this ordeal, Ellie. I've come to accept that Life is what it is: all bad unless you make adjustments. That's it in a neat little package: *Life is what you make it.* And I'm going to make those necessary adjustments. And I'm making those adjustments so my life is livable; endurable. The other option isn't an option for me. I refuse to be miserable. I flat-out refuse. I will not be a pathetic old hag."

Ellie tried to shift the downcast conversation to cheerful. "I was thinking of asking my sister if I could take the trip to Sacramento and stay with her for awhile, and allow you to get back into your own rhythm, and give you some peace and quiet."

"Sure, Ellie. That would be nice for you. And for your sister, too."

Eloisa had found herself at a loss for words more often than not over the last week. Things got uncomfortable at times. Phryne would drift off into her world of private thoughts, and become silent, creating a fragile eggshell of soundless awkwardness that surrounded her and everyone in her company.

Phryne finished her coffee, and filled the cup with the last of the milky liquor. Two hours earlier, it had been a fresh bottle. She placed another cigarette in the holder, and lit it. Her gaze was far out in the garden. "I left Buffalo with my life in pieces. I was afraid and without foundation, leaving for an unfamiliar destination." Her eyes went back to Eloisa, "And then Leopold and I discovered the terrible fate of his family, and the unnecessary, tragic, violent death of poor Dillon. And then my husband suddenly decided to walk out on me, crumpled up my soul like a wad of paper and threw it away with my heart … and now … my sweet baby Millie has died. A part of me has died. A part of my Leopold died. She was a part of both of us, regardless of where he is now. A part of me for eight months. A part of me died. I cannot get over that fact. A part of me is buried in Hollywood, California. Just think about that, Ellie. I can never leave here. Ever." A tear ran down Phryne's cheek.

Eloisa picked up on something that her friend had just said. "You were upset at the news of Dillon's death? That troubled you? His death?"

Phryne did not bat an eyelash. "Yes, of course. You never forget a lover. Especially one that's well-endowed." She took a hearty swallow from the coffee cup and smiled softly.

"What did you say? A lover?!" Eloisa wondered if it was the alcohol talking. She feared the truth. Dillon was a snake, but a deceitful friend that hides hurtful deeds and harmful, intimate secrets is a poisonous, vile viper.

Phryne suspected that she had just crossed the line, but it was far too late to jump back across. It was an impossible hopscotch leap even if sober. "I'm sorry Ellie. I shouldn't have said anything. I'm sorry. I shouldn't have said a word about it. I spoke without thinking."

"Sorry?! You shouldn't have said anything?! When did this happen?"

"It was only two times … twice, that's all. The first time was after we celebrated Leopold's birthday, on one of our first trips to Canada … and my Leopold got so drunk he passed out and slept all the way back to his apartment. And you and me and Dillon all helped to get him upstairs; remember?

Dillon dropped you off, and then … me and Dillon … we drove to Sperry Park and me and him struggled all across the front seat of his car and got intimate with each other. But it didn't mean anything, it was crazy lust, that's all. It don't mean anything if you don't take your stockings all the way off or smudge your mascara. You know that. But I'm sorry, Ellie. I didn't feel a thing … in my heart, I mean. I felt all the rest, I sure did ... Dillon made certain of that. But it was just sex."

Eloisa felt her heart was ripped out and trampled upon. She sat wide-eyed, finding it difficult to believe what she had just heard. "When was the second time? The next time?"

"I had almost forgotten about it until you mentioned that 4th of July weekend up in Thunder Bay; at Crystal Beach when you said Dillon had forced you into whoopee. You had gone to bed early, I remember now that you were terribly upset at Dillon … he did something that had you peeved … and then Leopold and I left Dillon at the bar singing some of those silly Irish drinking songs like he used to. We all were drinking a lot of Canadian beer that night. We got upstairs to the room and Leopold passed out before I even kicked off my shoes, and that got me upset, you can imagine. I mean, he was useless. He couldn't even move; he was so drunk. I wasn't ready for the night to end. So, I went back down to the lounge and had a few more beers with Dillon. He had his hand on my thigh and I figured why not; why not let the party go on and on. I was furious with Leopold anyway. I needed a man. The fireworks show was starting at midnight. They really did … bang, boom, bang. Me and Dillon went outside to the parking lot to watch and after a few sloppy kisses, he lifted up my dress, told me he wanted me, turned me around and pushed me head-first against the grill of his car. I remember how ready I was; I certainly was. He filled me from behind and I mean he really filled me. I was hanging onto the chrome grill of that big red and black Pierce Arrow with my outstretched arms and white knuckles. The whole time, my eyes were fixed on that hood ornament, you know, that chrome archer with the bow and arrow on the radiator cap. Dillon drove his arrow into me with the burning passion of white hot steel. I remember how much I trembled. I quivered. I thought my toes were going to fall off. It was some kind of rough and tumble, tough guy attraction, I guess. My world shook. Damn, I was rattled until my spine wiggled. And good God in Heaven, Dillon performed wonderfully ... I took every inch of him. It's a terrible thing to admit it now, but that was certainly one of the best releases I ever had. One of the best. Never mind the fireworks, I had my own explosions. More than one, for sure." She extinguished her cigarette and finished her cream sherry. Her eyes were glassy; her movements shaky.

"My God, Phryne! Do you take fornication as a hobby?! That was the weekend I got pregnant, that exact weekend, that exact night! That was the night Dillon forced himself on me!" She spoke between short, shallow sobs, and holding a dainty cotton handkerchief to her lips. Her anger was dampened by her disgust.

Phryne was staring out into the garden again. "Dillon used a rubber sheath that night, I think ... it was black, like a locomotive ... I think he called it a Trojan horse or something. I'm sorry that I upset you, Ellie. I didn't mean to ... it was foolish and unfeeling of me to bring this up ... I'm sorry. I really should not have said anything." Phryne rose from her seat a bit too quickly, and teetered before catching her balance. She said she was going back to bed, and wavered across the patio, into the house and into her bedroom.

Eloisa was jolted into a trance and realized that her friendship with Phryne had just been torpedoed like the Lusitania. She was too traumatized to shed another tear. She gathered her nerves, stood and walked to the house. Her heels clicked across the floors to her room. Inside, she hurriedly stuffed her railroad bag and little suitcase full of clothes. She put on the large black hat her mother had gave her, grabbed her bags, left without closing any doors behind her, walked to the corner and caught the Melrose streetcar. She had just lost and left an old friend.

Inside her beaded pocketbook she found the folded, tattered piece of envelope with her sister's address; the address her parents had tried to hide from her.

Eloisa hopped off the trolley at Hollywood Boulevard, found a Western Union office and sent Ginny a twelve-word telegram, stating that she would be arriving on the first train from Los Angeles on Saturday.

She was determined never to see Phryne again.

8. THE SS MELVILLE DOLLAR ~ 1928-1930

Slow Boat To China

7:00 AM Wednesday, June 13, 1928

Leopold walked onto the street with just under ten dollars to his name. His duffle sack was once again serving double duty as companion and pillow, but it was nearly empty since he had pawned so much of its contents for his opium ration. He had convinced the landlord at the Ambassador to let him stay one last night and in return, the landlord could keep the advance rent Leopold had already paid for the month. He had removed the help wanted poster from the telegraph pole, and reread the details countless times. His destination was the Marine Service Bureau at Merchant Street and The Embarcadero. The poster was soliciting men of *strong back, firm spirit, and steady moral fibre* for on-board duties of varying description for the Dollar Steamship Company, and Pacific Mail, Cargo & Packet Line. It was easy enough to find the Bureau. It was a tall weatherworn brick and wood frame, four-story warehouse directly across from the massive Market Street Ferry Building that sheltered the passenger and freight terminals for the Berkley and Oakland Ferries.

It was an unusual morning; bright sun bathed San Francisco. The chatter of commerce, noisy calls of black and white gulls, steam whistles, bells, and blasting ships' horns overwhelmed his senses. Barrels and crates of goods stood loaded on hand-drawn freight wagons on the boardwalk and brick pavement. A group of a half dozen or more surly characters was gathered at the far corner of the building, using tobacco in all of its forms, sharing bawdy talk, questionable wit, tales of the high seas and war stories.

As he entered the building, someone called across the docks, "Another blackleg! Another pier jumper enters the slave market!" It was the first of many such inexplicable exchanges he would encounter in the very near future. Once inside, Leopold was summoned to a chair in front of a desk manned by a seasoned seafarer, with stiff white hair and rough bronze skin blackened by years in the sun. The sailor introduced himself as Maarten Vanderhuett, *The Dutchman*, which vindicated his heavy Germanic accent. The interview process was short and sweet. It could have been summarized as two questions: How strong are you and are you able to tie your own shoelaces? Leopold would work six four-hour shifts followed by twelve hours off and restart the clock. He would draw his monthly pay of one hundred and five dollars when he mustered in on board.

The SS Melville Dollar was to be his home for at least the next month. She would steam with the high tide at five bells (02:30) on a thirty-day schedule to the Orient, her next port of call to be Shanghai. He was hired on as a 'greaser', an oiler in the engine and boiler rooms. It was a job with questionable skills that he could thank his short oil field experience for. The position was the third rung from the bottom on the job ladder, the next lowest being 'trimmers' and 'stokers'. Those men shoveled coal into the fireboxes, moved coal by wheelbarrow, and leveled the coal within the bins to avoid the ship listing to one side. On the bottom of the totem pole were the 'firemen', the nameless few who fed the fires.

Maarten said that with his past flour mill experience and an unspoken set of skills yet to be acquired, in a year or so, he could be fortunate enough to move up the pecking order to 'donkeyman', an assistant engineer. But like anything else that gets diluted with salt water, it would depend on chance. The Dutchman mentioned that Leopold's rusty boxing skills could also be an asset, either aboard ship or in port, as circumstances may warrant. The Dutchman stressed that

Leopold's skills should only be used with discretion, and not flaunted about. He would neither be coddled, nor purposely subjected to mistreatment. Maarten mentioned that thievery, piracy, murder and mutiny were hanging offenses aboard ship. The Dutchman was the Boatswain and would, in fact, be his boss. Leopold also learned that the men who heckled him outside were union labor from the Longshoremen and Seaman's Union, chiding him as a rookie, non-union man looking for work. The union was disbanded in 1921 and had been desperately trying to reorganize.

As with any new undertaking, any new experience, an unexplainable inner tickle, a stirring of foreboding fluttered in his gut like a canary in a coal mine. It was a feeling he had experienced on more than one occasion in his lifetime, and had almost become accustomed to.

Maarten suggested that Leopold purchase two pair of dungarees, two shirts and a six or eight-inch knife with sheath. The Dutchman gave him directions to Pier 26 and shook his hand with what could best be described as a calloused piece of horsehide, nearly as wide as a dinner plate. Walking along the waterfront, Leopold wondered for the first time if he could be susceptible to sea sickness. Strangely, from somewhere deep within his childhood memories, he recalled something his father had said: *Living or dead, rock or iron, everything eventually finds its way to the sea.*

His secondary motive for going to sea was money. It seemed that the McDonough brothers demanded a fee from new police recruits. He had arranged a 'bank account' with the purser, First Mate Higsbothum, and only kept the cash he needed for toiletries, clothing and cigarettes. The first goal he had set for himself was five hundred dollars. He was determined to reach that goal and beyond.

January 2, 1929

The Pacific Ocean helped mollify his frame of mind, perhaps because it offered no means of escape, and no simplistic outlet for his frustration with life, short of casting himself upon the waves. There was no land in sight and it would appear that way for weeks on end. Quite simply, he understood that his situation was *sink or swim*. The four-hour shifts altered his sleep schedule to the point where the nightmares became few and far between. Once again, he could sleep as a child. Dawn, daylight, dusk and dark were all one. He spent his precious free time between the pages of books; reading, learning, loving, longing, and living anything he could, either passed among crew members, borrowed, bartered or bought ashore. His voyages to the Far East were not as calm as a rowboat upon on a millpond, but the stormy seas were manageable, and the squabbles amongst the crew members never became life threatening. History, tradition and respect demanded that the pewter dinnerware and crew were treated as equals: hammered, greased and salted.

Leopold had cause for celebration on New Years Day, 1929: he had been promoted one rung up the ladder to third assistant engineer. To him, it was a writ of emancipation, and not just a bump up in the ranks from the darkest dungeons aboard ship. It meant no more soot, grime or the stifling fires of the coal boilers. The heat from the furnaces languished in the engine rooms, coal bins and bunkers. The filthy blackness below decks was, more often than not, hotter than the hinges on the gates of Hell.

The SS Melville Dollar had a measured length of 493 feet, displaced 10,000 tons, and could maintain a top speed of 10½ knots. One large, black funnel spewed its soot skyward; painted with a wide, deep red band and a large white dollar sign. The freighter engaged a crew of twenty-three seamen, the majority of whom were 'red-blooded Americans'. And to make the record precise: there was the Dutch boatswain Maarten; Gaëtan, the Belgian cook; and Horace Farnsworth, the English captain. Among the lowliest positions aboard ship were five shovel and wheelbarrow men, held exclusively by exotic sailors, all of whom were either Maltese or Lithuanian, and secured from ports unknown. The very lowest were the five Chinese firemen, the unfortunates who stoked the furnaces.

SS Melville Dollar arrived in Shanghai on January 1st, three days ahead of schedule; credit given to favorable weather and winds encountered west of the Hawaiian Islands. After the cargo of lumber, silica sand and Canadian newsprint had been unloaded, the crew had a 'bank day' of shore liberty. At the mouth of the Wang Poo River, the boat people of Shanghai always swarmed around the foreign freighters, offering ferriage to the mainland, begging for handouts, hawking or bartering for trinkets, liquor, opium tar, heroin and sex.

After four dockings at Shanghai's notorious Bund waterfront, and six completed passages to and from the Orient, Leopold Throckmorton had gained some life lessons and helpful, if not completely trustworthy, friendships. Gilbert Darby, from Gig Harbor, Washington, and Harvey Jones, of points undisclosed, were his closest confidants. Harvey had been on his longest stint of sobriety since October, and while docked in Shanghai, Hong Kong, or Tientsin had acted as more of a tour guide and advisor than a seafaring sot. Gilbert was scruffy, occasionally despondent and always unkempt. He was a good-natured fellow who missed the wife he had left behind, and could be relied upon in a pinch; not in brute strength, but attitude.

The Shanghai Chinese all seemed to have been shaken and emptied from the same mold: slender, firm and physically fit people with large, slow moving brown, almond-shaped eyes and musical voices soft as fluff cotton. Nearly the entire crew of the SS Melville Dollar had disembarked in Shanghai to reconnect with civilization, often with questionable motive or disjointed desire. Captain Farnsworth also went ashore with First Mate Davey Higsbothum and Maarten, the Dutchman. All three had ducked inside one of the bars along The Bund that catered to English-speaking crews. Once back aboard ship, tongues began to wag as to the purpose of their clandestine Chinese rendezvous. Twenty-seven days later, on January 29, the reason became clear. During the early morning hours, the SS Melville Dollar had moored along the sea wall at spacious Pier 32 of San Francisco harbor, to facilitate the mechanized unloading of her cargo of Luan Philippine mahogany and bulk rice. Five units of human cargo had disembarked under the cover of murky moonlight and shifting shadows, to scurry hurriedly down the gangway. Who they were, how they were spirited aboard, where they had bunked and messed during their voyage to America remained a mystery. Nobody asked.

Leopold had thought long and hard about how he could spend his four days ashore in San Francisco, and decided to take a chance, and ride the Market Street trolley to the Delores Street Shelter of The Salvation Army at the corner of Mission Street. A brisk East wind pushed the cold winter dampness under the collar and up the sleeves of his woolen pea coat. He had a desire to plead his case to Amanda and ask her to forgive his sudden departure eight months earlier. He knew he would need to be humble as well as sincere.

He was greeted in the reception area by the familiar smiling face of Cadet Fergus Abernathy, the red-headed, spry young fellow with freckles liberally sprinkled across his fresh cheeks. The young Christian Soldier was one of the very first who Leopold had met on his road to personal restoration.

"Is Nurse Amanda working today?"

Fergus offered an instant congenial reply, "No sir. Nurse Ensign Amanda Hugg and her brothers have joined their parents, Major Aloysius and Captain Maude at the new Salvation Mission in Ciudad Juárez, Mexico. Amanda's brother Duncan has now joined our ranks as a Salvation Cadet also! I can provide you with an address if you have the desire to correspond with them."

Leopold was mildly disappointed, yet strangely relieved. He carefully fashioned his response, "Thank you, but perhaps I should visit them in person if I ever get to Mexico. It would be better ... more personal."

"Can I offer you coffee and perhaps a fresh doughnut, sir?"

He was unsure how to respond to this entire turn of events, and was caught short for a response. "No, thank you, Fergus."

Although his visit to the Shelter had turned out to be slightly disheartening, he had a sense of finality. He reached into his pant pocket, brought out a small neatly wrapped package and fumbled for his fold of bills. He pulled out a five dollar note, and passed it to the young man. "This contribution to the mission is a small token for all the help I received last year. I will always remember how graciously I was treated, so please thank your fellow soldiers and your Major for me, won't you? And please give that little package to someone you care for." He turned, didn't wait for an answer, and nibbled his lip on the way out the door. He pulled his collar up against the wind and buttoned his coat to the top.

Young Fergus called "Thank you! God Bless you, sir!".

The trolley ride back toward the waterfront was strangely quiet. The noise of the city had become muffled by his thoughts, as though cotton had been packed into his ears. He recalled his tumultuous journey and rescue from the opium, the help and guidance of Salvation Army Captain Doctor Cornwall, the dedication and tenderness of Nurse Amanda and his first eight months at sea. Although his hopes of a personal apology had been dashed, his self confidence soared at that particular moment. He was unsure of the reason. He thought to himself: *although she's gone, her memory will linger on.* He would never forget her. Perhaps San Francisco's dispassionate, damp winter wind was the breath of fresh air that he needed to drive him back to the sea and his home aboard the SS Melville Dollar. Walking up the gangway, the ship's bells welcomed him. He felt a tingle on his forearm. The Maylay tattoo artist in Singapore had advised him it could take about five weeks for her handiwork to completely heal. Inside the little packet he had left behind at the Salvation Army with Cadet Fergus was a delicately carved cross of genuine Indian ivory, hanging on a delicate, gold chain necklace.

Load Of Coal

February 18, 1930

For the past eighteen months, the freighter had carried him to varied destinations in the Far East. On average, each trip had a steaming schedule of one month each way. The west bound freight was often aluminum ingots, iron oxide and coal to Shanghai, the Philippine Islands, and Balikpapan, Borneo. Lumber from Seattle or newsprint from Vancouver were shipped to Malaysia or French Indo-China via his favored port: the British Crown Colony of Singapore. The exotic destination had such an eclectic mix of culture and citizenry that every docking was an experience packed with new discoveries. It was a mysterious place where he could find something amazing around every corner. While no two visits were ever alike, he had personal preferences. The Galway House seemed to be the only establishment in the Orient that served cold beer and white bread. Next to the Galway was a barber shop, bath house and tattoo parlor operated by two mystical bronzed-skin beauties named Safia and Uri. They were an enigma beyond his grasp.

To satisfy the need to fill empty hours aboard ship, he found a quaint little book store on the English-speaking docks of Singapore. Hidden between the haberdasheries, fruit stands, textile merchants, tobacco vendors and meat mongers, he found the small, peculiar shop of Muhammad Dulfukir. He had read countless novels, either borrowing them from various Sailors' Missions or purchasing copies from such obscure, exotic sources. It was in Singapore that he obtained a like-new copy of Jack London's *Martin Eden*; a tale that followed the journey of a self-made man from aspiring novelist, through failed relationships, personal torment, self-discovery and eventual return to the sea. He read it three times, and it had so influenced him that he decided he would leave the sea and once again try to begin a career as a police officer. He would take that chance at the next crossing that charts his ship to moor at an Embarcadero pier.

In February, the Melville Dollar was indeed steaming to its home port in San Francisco. She was seven hundred miles east of Guam, and better than eight hundred miles from Wake Island, when the main steam pipe burst in the engine room. A fire subsequently started in the portside coal bunker amidships that quickly filled below decks with a grey, choking smoke that mixed with hellish steam. Five stokers and two firemen were burned by the initial explosion and blast of steam. Four sailors remained unaccounted for.

Attempts were made to shut off the burst steam line and perhaps rescue any injured crew. Chief Engineer James Bedford tried first, but was not able to get beyond the fiddley door, and was badly scalded on his forearms and face. Captain Farnsworth, First Mate Higsbothum and Boatswain Vanderhuett jerry-rigged tarpaulins over the skylights and aft fiddley doors to act as wind catchers, attempting to push air below decks to dampen the effects of the scalding steam and to allow entry by the crew.

Third Engineer Throckmorton wrapped himself in whatever coverings he could find, sheets, burlap sacks or rags in an attempt to protect himself from the escaping steam. His first two attempts to reach the shutoff valve failed. The Dutchman then tied a rope around Leopold's waist and followed him down below. That attempt also failed, and Maarten pulled an exhausted, exasperated Leopold back above deck. The steam in the boiler room was too intense.

Nearly two hours later, the pressure had subsided enough for Leopold and Maarten to return below and close the valve to the broken line. They recovered the bodies of three Chinese firemen, and the Second Engineer, Aaron Fraser. The steam had been stopped, but relentless hot spots in the coal bins still smoldered and burned.

Leopold was the first man inside the starboard coal bunker, fighting the stubborn, smoldering embers with a shovel and hose. He was tireless, attacking the fire with unbounded energy. Captain Farnsworth had sent every able sailor below deck to fight the slow burning fires. A Somali galley swab was the only crewmember to incur injuries from the fires. The man could not swim and had constantly worn a kapok life vest. The vest proved to be a liability rather than a life saver when a burning cinder set it ablaze in a flash of flame. He was doused with water from fire hoses but suffered dangerously severe burns over his chest and head.

Twenty hours after the initial burst of the steam pipe, the coal fires had been extinguished, the steam line repaired, and the ship was under full power once again. Once the persistent fires were put out, Leopold and Maarten emerged from the holds below, covered in soot and grease, and soaked with water. They were the victors, the conquerors and were cheered by their shipmates. Leopold did not understand the accolades and cheers, but joined in on the raucous champagne and vodka celebration that followed. He had assumed that heroes were needed, and it just happened that they were he and The Dutchman. Leopold could still smell the putrid smoke and choking fumes, but he knew he was no longer in the middle of a bad dream. He was sure of it, and it felt damn good to be awake and alive.

The next afternoon, the Captain held a very brief service followed by four burials at sea. Captain Farnsworth wired Dollar Steamship headquarters in San Francisco and recommended Leopold and The Dutchman for special commendation. Two days later, the Somali sailor died from his burns.

Nearly a month had passed when the ship docked in San Francisco. On March 15, 1930, the Captain presented Leopold and Maarten with letters from company President Robert Dollar and a one hundred dollar reward, which swelled Leopold's bank roll to nine hundred dollars.

Leopold saluted and took Sea Captain Horace Farnsworth's hand, "Thank you for the good fortune while steaming with you, Captain. It has been an honor and privilege, sir, and I thank you for the opportunity to serve. This is my last port."

He had forewarned his immediate boss, Maarten, and shipmates Gilbert and Harvey that he would not be aboard for the next steaming. He gave his collection of books to the ship's cook, Arne, The Swede, but retained his now tattered copy of *Martin Eden*. Other than a tattooed forearm, the novel was his only souvenir of twenty-two months crisscrossing the Pacific Ocean aboard the SS Melville Dollar.

It was an emotional walk down the gangway onto the cobblestones of The Embarcadero and the waterfront Battery Row. It was a homecoming, a justification, and a victory march. The clock tower of the Ferry Building gleamed in the early morning sun. The fog horns of Mission Rock welcomed him.

9. HOLLYWOOD, CALIFORNIA ~ 1930

Bye, Bye Blackbird

2:00 PM, Friday, March 14

The postman announced the arrival of the afternoon mail with the click, dingle and snap of the polished brass cover over the mail slot in the door. Strewn across the floor were the morning edition of the Los Angeles Times, Abner's Director's Guild invoice for his April dues and an Air Mail envelope from Buffalo, New York, mailed Tuesday, addressed to Phryne Mandelbaum. Consuela gathered everything up and brought it out to the patio, where Phryne was reclined in a plush floral pattern art deco chaise longue, and paging through the weekly Los Angeles edition of *Variety* entertainment magazine. "Thank you, Connie. Gracias."

The LA Times' headline read: *Studios To The Rescue! New Titles Planned To Perk Up Public.* The Depression had begun, and the country was in a dire mood. Just the day before, Abner had mentioned that many new films were in the works.

Phryne wore a large-brimmed straw hat adorned with silk flowers and green ribbons, pink bedroom slippers with one-inch heels, and a rose pink satin dressing gown. On the small table next to her was a half glass of champagne cocktail, an ashtray, her cigarette holder and a pack of Marlboro.

She rolled her eyes and expressed a smirk of futility when she noticed the letter from her mother, Selene. The front of the envelope had four large red airmail postage stamps and bore several heavy cancellations received on its trip from Buffalo to the West Coast. She could only imagine what the letter was about, and immediately assumed that like so many others she had received, it would be full of trivial news, emotional tripe and unsolicited advice. She took off her new Foster Grant sunglasses, finished her drink, inserted a cigarette into the black Bakelite holder and lit it. Her lacquered nail slid under the flap and she tore open the envelope with her finger. Inside was a small newspaper clipping and a one-page, handwritten letter. Her eyes moved quickly across the letter and something struck Phryne as highly out of the ordinary. Her mother, Selene was a French immigrant in 1897 and always took pride in her penmanship. The letter was messy, bordering on scribble, with inkblots scattered across the page. After she had read the first two sentences, the reason was apparent. Bertram Truffaut had ended his life a week earlier.

Her father had been the Deposits and Asset Manager at Buffalo Savings Bank for nearly fifteen years. The bank's gleaming gold dome was a landmark of trust shining on Buffalo's lower Main Street for decades. She looked across the yard, beyond Connie's cottage, and allowed her gaze to focus on a pair of young male redwing blackbirds testing their boisterous squawks. Her thoughts wandered back to her childhood, holding her father's hand, and scurrying up the granite steps of the bank, in the hope of getting a piece of hard, shiny ribbon candy off her father's gigantic desk. She recalled the chiseled inscription on the second-most top step: *The Steps To Success.*

She reread her mother's letter, a normal reaction to bad news, if only to validate the growing grief within. She had seen all the disturbing newspaper headlines about despondent stockbrokers, bankers and investors committing suicide. The shocking Black Tuesday news about the stock market crash on October 29, 1929, was just that: unsettling and sensational. Phryne had not seen, felt or heard the Stock Market crash in Hollywood. Very few did.

The newspaper clipping her mother had included in the letter was the account of her father's suicide. Shortly before lunch on Thursday morning, March 6, Bertram Truffaut had left his job at Buffalo Savings Bank carrying his valise. Phryne remembered that her father had always packed his lunchtime sandwich in his business case.

The small, single column article continued that he had left his automobile at the bank in downtown Buffalo, and took a taxi to Goat Island State Park on the Niagara River. He was seen later in the afternoon on Luna Island throwing himself from the wooden observation bridge into the icy waters of the swiftly moving river. The last sentence in the article said that his body had not been recovered, and considering the ice cover still on Lake Erie and the ice floes in the river, recovery could be sometime later in the Spring, if at all.

She could not imagine what had driven her father to take his life. Phryne had an ache inside; not a heartache; neither was it painful suffering nor hand-wrenching anguish. Her heart had been rendered numb from all the emotional upheavals she had endured over the last twenty months. The news of her father's suicide bore credence to her belief that, with the exception of Abner, the men in her life had turned out to be nothing but disappointments. Her lost friendship with Eloisa was nothing more than an unfortunate happenstance born of a lack of worldly understanding and impatience.

Phryne filled her lungs with fresh California air, exhaled slowly and looked across the yard again to discover that the blackbirds had left. She gathered the magazine, newspaper, letters, cigarettes and empty glass. She had decided that she would fill the tub with the hottest water she could stand, pour in some bath salts, relax and wait for Abner's return from the studio. She would ask Consuela to make another cocktail. Tomorrow, in the morning, after a good night's sleep, she considered that perhaps she and her husband could leave together for Paramount Studios and she would telephone her mother in Buffalo from his office.

Phryne ultimately decided to postpone the telephone call to her mother until Monday. It certainly wasn't the type of conversation that couldn't wait, and absolutely wasn't a case of life or death; not anymore. She knew that yesterday's news had nothing to do with today or tomorrow. It just wasn't new news and no matter what, the world wasn't about to come to a drop-dead halt over a single suicide.

Abner did not go to the studio on Saturday or Sunday, but stayed home to comfort his wife as best he could. Her husband always had a way of reading her emotions and seemed to know exactly how to turn her mood around on a thin dime. He pampered Phryne, and the more she reveled in it, the better his satisfaction. Abner felt that she needed to get out of the house and get involved with something. With so much recent tragedy, free time had become her enemy and alcohol her life-blood. His wife's shine had begun to tarnish. It was time for Abner to bring out the polish, lamb's wool and chamois.

On Saturday evening, they were sitting in the parlor, each with a glass of the Saint Paul sherry. Abner was relaxed in his Morris chair, wearing his black half-slippers, his suit trousers, white shirt and black, velvet-trimmed maroon smoking jacket. Phryne sat close on the large leather ottoman with her dog Wiggins, leaning against her husband's chair with a hand on his thigh and drawing circles with her finger. She knew how to dress and did it well; nearly perfect most of the time. That evening it was a beige taffeta dress with sheer sleeves and back, a layered silk under-skirt, oxblood boots and cream stockings.

"Did you ever think about beginning a career at the studio, Sweetheart? I don't mean cosmetics or hair, I mean as a member of a troupe. A dancer, or a chorus girl if you will. You have the pins*, a great figure and the looks, Sweetheart. What do you think? You could show yourself to the world."

Phryne didn't have an immediate response. She was intrigued, and wondered exactly what her husband was talking about. He knew her wheels were turning. Her eyes sparkled and lips curled. She sat up and crossed her legs. Her stockings whooshed. "Why … what do you mean, Abe, Darling?"

"You need an outlet for your energies, Phryne. You have the form, grace and style to become an important player in the studio's future. I know you can develop your dancing. We're going to be creating an increasing number of musicals and song-and-dance films. They'll help with the national mood, and improve the studio's relations with the public. And I know they'll bring in the cash, with the lowered costs for set production, script development and story lines. Everything is getting cheaper in this economy. It would give you the opportunity to expand your horizons beyond these four walls and enjoy yourself. The money isn't at all what you should be doing this for, but it's there. I think you have the potential to shine at this, Phryne. I knew it on the day you walked into my office."

It was then that he told her that he had invited some friends for Sunday lunch and drinks outside on the patio. The climbing roses on the pergola and the urns of geraniums were in full bloom, the weather was perfect and it was just right for a casual business meeting between friends and close associates.

He explained that he had arranged the patio luncheon on Friday with Vernon Borsch, Miriam Lowenstein and Vera Ross. All three worked for Paramount; Vera was a choreographer, Vernon a dance coach and Miriam an instructor and physical trainer.

"Really, Abe? I don't know."

"Listen to me Phryne ... I know you can. You always curl a rug on the dance floor, you're a looker, smart and quick to learn. You can kick a leg as good as Lucille Day or Abigail Woods ... and those two broads ain't getting any younger. I mean, your legs go all the way up to Hanukah, Sweetheart. You got the right height and your figure can stop the traffic on Hollywood Boulevard any day of the week. You know it and I know it. You have the gams of a star. Tomorrow you'll meet Vernon, Miriam and Vera. They're good people, and I know that they'll tell you exactly what I'm telling you: that you got what it takes to be one of the best hoofers* Paramount ever cranked out. You can do it, and they'll help you. You'll be dancing on moonbeams, Phryne ... dancing on moonbeams up to the Milky Way and twinkling your toes with the stars. So what do you say? You don't have to answer right away ... think about it and take as long as you like. Really."

She pounced onto his lap from the ottoman. Wiggins, the little Yorkie, hopped to the floor, startled and bewildered. Phryne planted a kiss on Abner's lips and whispered, "We'll have the patio party tomorrow, Love. You don't have to convince me. If you and the Studio will have me, I'm in! All the way in with both feet and all of my ten toes."

St. Patrick's Day, Monday, March 17

Upon their arrival at Paramount, Phryne used the privacy of her husband's office to telephone her mother. The conversation was brief, on-point and did not reveal anything that Phryne didn't know or had not expected. Her father had not left a goodbye note or explanation, nor had the bank offered any further insight.

Her younger brother Thomas was living at home and working for the Buffalo Fire Department with Engine Company 2. She asked if her mother would like to travel to California and live with them, but as expected, the invitation was cordially declined.

When Phryne placed the trumpet ear-piece back onto the receiver, it was obvious that, other than her father's passing, there was no other news from Buffalo. For her, it reaffirmed that Hollywood was a bustling place and she had made the right choice. She thought back to her hurried departure from Buffalo a year and a half earlier. It was she who had suggested California as a destination in lieu of Leopold's plans for Cleveland or Chicago. Like so many other young women through the years, she was drawn to the dream, the possibilities and the glamour. She did not dream of being a star, but wished to be part of the excitement, the glamour and the dream itself. Every moving picture she had seen at Shea's Buffalo or stage presentation at the Hippodrome gave her the same thrill. The wonderful world of imagination captivated her. She put herself in the picture, into the glorious snow globe of fantasy, and let her dreams drift away with the make-believe snowflakes. When she was a child, the candles, candy canes and paper chains that decorated the Christmas tree meant much more to her than gifts of a fresh orange, a new pair of socks, a few pieces of rock candy or a hunk of peanut brittle. She always knew that the fancy, colorful wrapper could be the best part of the gift. As the years passed, she learned that anticipation could be better than the experience, and the attention given to unwrapping the gift was very much akin to sexual foreplay. Now, it seemed possible that maybe, just maybe, she would become an entertainer.

Despite her incidental setbacks, Phryne believed her life situation had only changed for the better since her arrival in California. She had come a long way from the beauty parlor on lower Main Street in Buffalo.

She casually wondered what sort of work Leopold might have been doing since he left. She had never wished her husband any ill will, and had not given his memory much thought other than a fleeting moment or two. Phryne knew Leopold had an endearing, secretive, sensitive side, but had fought fiercely to keep it deeply hidden, and was always very reluctant to show any hint of sympathy. Although he had been unforgiving and vengeful when he walked out of her life, she could not damn his memory. If she had been asked, she would have said that their relationship could be best described as a torrid love affair, fired with passion rather than endearment. At one time, she had high hopes for their life together, but they disappeared with the tide, and washed away like so many footprints in the sand.

The thought occurred to her that perhaps one day Leopold would see her on film, in a Paramount Picture, not as a star, but as a song and dance girl, an integral member of a chorus line in a film that would be seen all around the world and by millions of people. She felt a mysterious excitement like never before, and wondered if Leopold would recognize her. The idea intrigued her.

Immediately after lunch, she began her orientation at the Dance Studio on Lot 2. Her instructor Miriam said something that affirmed the thoughts she had earlier: "Remember Phryne, it's the footwork that makes the production presentable and memorable. It's not just the hotsy-totsy* stuff. It's all in the footwork, girl, the footwork. And to me, it looks like you know how to turn an ankle … and a head or two."

10. SAN FRANCISCO, CALIFORNIA ~ 1930

Barnacle Bill The Sailor

9 AM, Saturday, March 15

Immediately after Leopold's feet hit the cobblestones of The Embarcadero on Friday afternoon, he felt as a new man. As a caterpillar sheds its cocoon, he was ready to grow wings and start anew. Leopold got a room at the Sailor's Hospitality House at Drumm & Commercial Street, and opted for the surprisingly low daily rate of twenty five cents for a bed with bath privileges. Prices had dropped drastically over the last few months, but he had no knowledge of the effects of October's Black Tuesday. Over the past two years, the SS Melville Dollar had made ten moorings in San Francisco, and if the city had changed, it wasn't enough for him to notice.

Leopold spent Friday night showing off his checker skills in the lobby of the Hospitality House and retired early to his room, only to have difficulty falling asleep, which he blamed on his new environment and not being rocked to sleep by the waves. It seemed to make sense: if a man needs to develop 'sea legs' as he goes aboard ship, he must grow a set of 'land knees' when he returns to terra firma. He stared at the ceiling a lot that Friday night and Saturday morning, reflecting on what he had seen and done during his years upon the Pacific. He accepted the revelation that the friendships and acquaintances he had made over the past two years were much like bilge water, and once flushed they were never be seen again.

His six o'clock, Saturday morning breakfast was fried potatoes, fat back bacon, buttered biscuits and two eggs for a dollar. The Lillydale Lunch Counter called it their 'Klondike

Breakfast', but for Leopold, it was as good as a Christmas feast. The other indulgence he could not resist was a fresh deck of Chesterfield cigarettes. The return leg of any Oriental steaming often meant Chinese cigarettes, Philippine or Burmese tobacco to those sailors who did not plan ahead and purchase enough American or Canadian brands, or had lost their supply betting on checkers, poker or the number games below decks. Outside the tobacconist's shop on Market street, he lit one of his fresh American smokes, and set his feet in a westerly direction. He knew exactly which way to go. He remembered.

He was in a conquering mood, confident and in good spirits when he walked up the granite steps and into the Hall of Justice on Kearny Street. Once again, he walked to the *General Inquiries* desk like he did over two years earlier. The imposing long wooden counter and rock-hard maple bench were still there, as was the little brass sign that read *Desk Sgt. Gregory O'Rourke.*

It was early, not quite eight o'clock. Leopold stood at the counter, feeling a bit overdressed for the warm spring day with his blue-black pea coat and blue sailcloth pants. He had his tweed golf cap pushed into his coat pocket and his hands crossed at the small of his back. The policeman behind the counter was a bulky man, a soft-colored carrot top, big and heavy, but not simply fat. Regardless, he appeared that he was well capable of taking care of himself. He set his pencil down onto the page of the thick ledger spread open on the counter and looked at Leopold over the top of his wire-rimmed spectacles, which were considerably too small for his stout face. His eyes studied him, and he smiled as he spoke, "What can I do for you, sailor?"

Leopold could smell beer. "I want to become a San Francisco policeman, Sergeant O'Rourke," and looked directly into the big man's eyes. They weren't focusing. From past experience, Leopold felt some anxiety, and fought back a foreboding sense of futility. The beer could portend either a good or bad outcome to the conversation.

"Really? Why?"

Not wanting to be passed off to McDonough brothers again, "Well, I would like to help keep the peace, enforce the law and work on my observation skills, so I can tell things about people, and pick up clues, not like some two-bit gumshoe*, but a copper … like how you can tell what kind of a job a person has just by looking at him." Leopold had planted a seed of curiosity with his veiled, shallow compliment that successfully kept the desk sergeant's attention.

"What do you mean?'

"Well, for example, you knew immediately you were looking at a sailor. You could tell that I was fresh off the boat; a disenchanted, sea-sick sailor who wanted to get a job ashore. A respectable job. Like a policeman."

Slurring his first few words, O'Rourke asked, "And you think you could be good as a flatfoot*?"

Like a five-cent sideshow magician, Leopold tried to pull another trick out of his hat. He looked slyly around the empty office, and began acting out an animated euphemism that would make Elmore Leffingwell proud, "Don't tell anybody, but I know Saint Patrick's Day is Monday, tomorrow is Sunday, and you're a damn good Irish copper. I can tell."

Sergeant O'Rourke was at a loss for words. Leopold's mind and word game had worked. The big man had both hands palm-down on the counter, looking Leopold smack dab in the eye. He broke into a laugh that could very well have been heard across the bay in Oakland. "And how did you figure all that out, sailor lad?"

Leopold leaned closer, and spoke a little softer, "Well, Sergeant O'Rourke, sir, you're wearing a copper's uniform, I looked at the calendar behind you and you got red hair,

Mick." Leopold had played his cards right. In a flash, he wondered where Elmore could be.

The fellow roared once again. He laughed so loud, three heads came around the windowed partition behind he counter, wondering what could have happened. Leopold nervously feigned a quiet laugh, and watched for any sign of trouble. He was in the precarious position of being an unwitting stranger on the receiving end of an uncertain outcome; created by what could be described as a blind attempt at self-preservation in a lion's den.

The laughter subsided, the heads ducked back around the wall, and Sergeant O'Rourke eased Leopold's fear. "Take a seat there on the bench behind you there, mate. I'll tell the Chief you're here and see if he wants to see you. How's that, Barnacle Bill?" Another chuckle followed as he turned and left the counter.

It became quiet. Sitting on the bench, Leopold tried to take stock of everything that had just happened, and lock it away for analysis at some later time. Things were happening so fast, it just wasn't possible to do it now. He was cautiously optimistic about what had just happened. His spirit was refreshed, like he just flipped to the cool side of the pillow.

Sergeant O'Rourke appeared from behind the wall with a man at least his size, with four times the amount of brass and tin stuck to or pinned on his uniform. Leopold stood, his hands to his sides.

"That's the fellow, Chief. He's the sailor that wants to join our ranks."

He introduced himself, "I'm Chief Daniel Doyle. I'm the man at the top of the hill and not I'm not afraid to say that shit always rolls downhill."

Leopold felt things were starting to go his way. He stood at seaman's attention, eyes straight ahead, then rocked once on his heels and made eye contact with the Chief. "I know how gravity works, and I am willing to start at the bottom of that hill, Chief Doyle. But I won't be there long." Sergeant O'Rourke had a barely detectable smirk.

"What's your name, sailor?"

"Leopold Throckmorton, Chief Doyle."

"Do we have a Brit here among us, Sergeant O'Rourke? A Limey Brit?" The Chief looked across to his Sergeant and continued, "Throckmorton? What's that? English?"

"No, sir. It's German, and it got changed at Ellis Island when my grandparents got off the boat from Prussia. It's all Irish on my mother's side." The lie couldn't hurt; they'd never know any different.

The police chief didn't take his eyes off Leopold, "O'Rourke, what do you think? Do you think we can make a copper out of this palooka*?"

"I think he may have some detective talent, Chief." Again, there was that nearly imperceptible smirk.

The Chief spoke from deep within his barrel chest. "Throckmorton, you be back here at zero-seven-hundred on Monday. That's Saint Patrick's Day, and a better day to become a copper does not exist, let me tell you. You will be given a written examination, and a physical appraisal of your health. You will also be required to complete a fourteen week training course, and upon graduation, you can wear the uniform of a San Francisco policeman. Do you believe you are able to accomplish that?"

"Yes, Chief Doyle, I do. I know I can."

He started to speak at the moment Leopold finished. "Two more things, Throckmorton. One; there's no labor union in the San Francisco Police Department. No union, period. And two; bring a hundred dollars for the Civil Service

Examination … Do you understand these two conditions of enrollment into Police Recruit School?"

"Yes, Chief. I'll be here at seven on Monday, sir."

A handshake and a *thank you* later, Chief Doyle was back in his office.

Leopold pulled his cap out of his pocket and held onto it. "Sergeant O'Rourke, can I share a bucket of beer with you after you finish your shift? Sort of a token of thanks for your help?"

He glanced around, checking for an audience. "Sure. I know a place; The No Name, down on Battery Row. You got any idea where that is, sailor?"

"If it's the same place, I was there about two years ago but didn't see any coppers."

"It's the same place, but Chief Doyle got it cleaned up. There's no doping or whoring in there anymore. The McDonough boys keep two blocks away. I'll see you there after right after six, when my watch ends."

Fiddler's Green

Leopold walked out of the Hall of Justice with a refreshed outlook on life. He had stumbled through a long period of draught and finally it seemed that an oasis was visible on the horizon. Good fortune had come his way. He was in the right place at the right time; on-the-job drinking and Saint Patrick's Day came together in a fortuitous chain of events. He had avoided the McDonough brothers' operation completely and saved four hundred dollars in the process.

It was a flash of fate that Saint Patrick's Day fell on the very weekend that he had hung up his oil skins, pea coat and jumpers* to become a copper. And the crust of the pudding ended up to be that the mick who would give him the job believed his lie about being part Irish.

For nearly two years at sea aboard the SS Melville Dollar, he had locked himself away in self-imposed solitary confinement. He had conquered his addiction by isolation, smothered his nightmares with four hour shifts and in the process, had extinguished his burning psychological demons along with actual fires in the coal bin. Leopold understood that it was with determined persistence and just the slightest bit of good luck that it now appeared he could bring his biggest goal to fruition. He had made it his life's mission to attack the lawless forces like the ones that killed his family and separated him from his brother. He was beginning a private crusade to right wrongs.

His time at sea not only had purged him of addiction and hellish dreams, it had allowed him to reflect on where he had been and consider where he would like to be. Since he and Phryne had escaped the violence of the Black Hand in Buffalo, his biggest regret was the way he had treated her. He had come to acknowledge that he was overtly unforgiving with her. He remembered how harsh his words were and how she had begged and pleaded with him to reconsider his decision to leave. It wasn't long after they had met that he discovered what a bearcat* she was. He had savored her sexuality and was captivated by her passion for life and love, but when she disclosed her infidelity, he had been so emotionally wrought it brought him to the edge. At the time, he had felt that her transgressions were heartless and unforgivable. Admittedly, their relationship wasn't rock solid and it had seemed to be doomed from the beginning, but her sexual misdeeds and deception had rendered it, part and parcel, destroyed.

He suspected that she was still in Los Angeles, but was confident in his belief that there was no hope whatsoever for reconciliation. Phryne could not change who she was, no more than he could imagine she would have returned to Buffalo. He had never known her to be the sort of woman that would give up on a dream. She had a strong will.

There'll Be Some Changes Made

In 1922, the San Francisco Police Department had begun a first-of-its-kind training program for new police officers that was to become the pattern for police forces nationwide. Police Recruit Training School was fourteen weeks of intense physical and mental conditioning. Leopold had enrolled in a class of thirty men that had been whittled down to twenty-seven by graduation day.

On the first of ninety-seven mornings, the trainees were awakened by a uniformed man blasting a bugle within the metal walls and ceiling of the bunkhouse. He was standing in the middle of the building, allowing every decibel of *Reveille* to bounce without mercy into the eardrums of the unsuspecting recruits and echo within their craniums for the remainder of the day. He was a small man, with a pencil thin mustache, wearing thick eyeglasses and a burnt brown, woolen uniform complete with a campaign hat. Once he had their undivided attention, the bugler, Corporal Thomas Donnelly informed the recruits it was to be the only morning of such torture. From that day forward, the men were expected to be self-disciplined for morning roll call. Every morning began with calisthenics and breakfast, followed by group and individual singing performances. It was explained that the vocal work was intended to instill self-confidence when officers were exposed to public situations. It was an exhausting three and a half month course of training. A full three weeks were spent on criminal law, penal law and arrest conduct. The San Francisco Police were the best trained officers in the nation.

On July 18, 1930, an overcast Friday morning, twenty-seven men graduated from the summer class of Recruit School. Their class photograph was taken with the new officers standing on the top three steps of the Hall of Justice along with Police Chief Doyle, Mayor Rolph and Commissioner Reilly standing in the foreground. In compliance with an unwritten and unexplained uniform and personal grooming code, the top lip of each new policeman was covered with a mustache; handlebar, horseshoe, toothbrush, pencil or bush. The mayor and city commissioner were not to be upstaged, and also cultivated the wily whiskers.

Leopold Throckmorton had star #414 pinned to his coat by Chief Doyle. He accepted his rolled diploma, shook his boss' hand, and quickly ran his forefinger over each side of his mustache as a comb. He was assigned to the Mission District.

His life had changed dramatically over the past three years and this was his proudest moment. For the first time in as many years, he felt satisfied and secure with his place in the world. He had achieved his goal. The brass band started to play and the sun was breaking through the low clouds.

Amanda's memory returned for a fleeting second, and he thought about their passionate relationship of sex, coffee and doughnuts. Had she only remained in San Francisco, he might well have left the SS Melville Dollar for her and in fact, made the impetuous switch from dollar to doughnut.

11. SACRAMENTO, CALIFORNIA ~ 1930

Ain't Misbehavin'

5:30 PM, Saturday, May 12, 1928

Virginia was genuinely surprised when she received her sister's telegram. Eloisa had knocked upon the door of the house on 44th Street brokenhearted, betrayed, disgusted, disappointed and abandoned. She had seen her dreams of a new life and fresh future crushed in Los Angeles and was hoping to change things here. Inside her sister's Sacramento home there was hope. It was a two-story Victorian with a welcoming, covered porch that symbolically hugged the home from the left, across the front and all around to the right side. When her sister opened the door and welcomed her inside, Eloisa found the love and acceptance she needed.

While they were growing up in Buffalo, Virginia and Eloisa were inseparable and had shared everything from hard candy to secrets. When she arrived in Sacramento, Eloisa needed her sister more than ever. She needed their childhood bond renewed. She needed a friend and confidant: a friend she could trust and an honest confidant. The love, honesty and loyalty she'd felt with Phryne had been ripped from her.

As soon as she opened the door, Virginia immediately knew that her sister was troubled. Eloisa set her bags down, and the sisters embraced. Virginia felt Eloisa trembling, releasing her stress. They moved to the parlor and sat on a large, overstuffed sofa. Baby William was a month old, wrapped in a brushed woolen blanket and asleep in a wicker baby carrier at their feet. They shared a cup of coffee and cinnamon toast before Eloisa began her story. The revelation of her sister's arrest and subsequent incarceration had upset Virginia beyond mere surprise. It was mental anguish.

"I got arrested right there in the bakery for Pete's sake! They put the pinch on me right where I worked at the dough tables and locked me in hand irons in front of my mother and pulled me out into the shop in front of the customers. I think they were trying to make an example of me. They walked me out of the shop and into the paddy wagon. Then, to top it off, I got questioned by the BOI and charged with bootlegging and accessory to murder and got locked up in a dirty dark jail for three days and nights."

"Goodness, Ellie. I can only imagine. Father and Mother must have hit the moon."

"That's not the worst of it, Ginny. After the coppers released me, I ended up in jail at home. Really. I went back to work at the bakery and in less than two months I started to show. Father said he was putting his foot down and would not let me out of the house. I wasn't going to work anymore after that. I didn't even leave the house for Sunday church, not once. Reverend Kent came to the house. It was terrible. I spent most of my time planning my escape. I don't know where I could go, but I was planning."

Virginia was aghast. "Are you telling me that you were pregnant?" Her reaction was loud enough to wake William. He began to stir and his mother took him to her breast. Her baby latched on immediately. "You were pregnant, Ellie?" She sat wide-eyed, stunned at the revelation and waiting for details.

Eloisa's rape, pregnancy and subsequent banishment from the family were a disastrous and nearly incredible tale to hear. The Father Baker home in Lackawanna was a life saving sanctuary for young unwed mothers and their infants, but to the general public, Father Baker's carried a social stigma nearly equivalent to the plague. Like Eloisa, many young women entered the home and vanished, never to be seen again by family or friends. Virginia listened intently, hanging on each and every word of her sister's story and tried to imagine the stark atmosphere of the Protectorate. Eloisa perfectly described the hollow halls, towering ceilings, pale colors and empty echoes within the stone walls.

As evening approached the sisters moved to the kitchen to prepare dinner. Geoffrey was usually home from work sometime after six. As a rule, Saturday suppers were wieners, boiled potatoes and liberty cabbage. In pre-World War language, the meal was called frankfurters and sauerkraut. The odor permeated the entire home, and once it was ready for the table, Virginia placed everything in the oven, keeping it warm and ready for her husband.

"You know I was pregnant when I married Geoffrey, and one of the big reasons we left Buffalo was Mother and Father, not just Geoffrey's new job. He landed his promotion and transfer out here with a stroke of luck. Darn lucky. And after hearing your story, I know I had a much better time of it. I had a husband to lean on. And we left Buffalo just four weeks after our wedding."

"Your situation was quite a bit different than mine, Ginny. Still, there was no excuse for how they treated you. After you moved away, they never even mentioned you. Don't ask me to explain it, because I can't figure them out. It's Father mostly, but I can't understand why. Good golly, you were married, and to a respectable man, too. I think our parents are still living like the Puritans, for Pete's sake. And now they're living all alone and for all I try, I cannot imagine how that must be. Both put their daughters into exile, so I cannot pity either of them. When I was living there and just waiting to go into the home for women, the suppers were silent. Nobody said a word. It was like a funeral parlor. No, it wasn't … in a funeral parlor you can sometimes hear people crying. Things were actually far better at Father Baker's. The nuns, the nurses, the other mothers ... everyone ... were wonderful. There's love there. And God's love, too."

Eloisa was speaking softly, just above a whisper. She was holding William then, rocking him gently in her arms, and watching him sleep. "Our parents ... I think they only opened the first few letters you sent, Ginny. Father usually got to them first, tore them up and tossed them away. If Mother had them, she would give them to Father. But when I was in the Protectorate, she actually did smuggle one of Phryne's letters in to me. You remember her; she did Mother's and your hair for your wedding. Well, Phryne had invited me out here to visit, and that ended in total disaster, but it gave me someplace to go ... an escape route out of Buffalo."

"What do you mean by that, Ellie? It ended in disaster?"

The side door opened, and Geoffrey entered the kitchen from the driveway. He was carrying evidence of his work under his arm: a copy of the *Bee.*

"I'll explain later, Ginny."

Virginia stood, walked to her husband and gave him a peck on the lips. "Just like she said in her telegram, Ellie came for a visit today, Honey. We've been catching up and William just loves her to bits!"

Their conversation was delayed. It was dinner time. Geoffrey walked over to Eloisa, gave her a hug and welcomed her to Sacramento. Everyone moved to the dining room.

The hours after dinner passed quickly. William had his weekly bath, and nightly lap time with his father. Then it was coffee and shortbread cookies before the youngster was fed once again and readied for bed. Virginia and Eloisa set up a folding day bed in the small room off the kitchen. It was only for the night, and Virginia promised that Ellie's next nights would be spent in an upstairs bedroom. It just needed to be aired out and cleaned up.

At eight o'clock Geoffrey switched on the Philco parlor radio and all ears became glued to *Death Valley Days*, a national radio serial, followed by *The Kate Smith* musical showcase. Afterwards, the room became filled with chatter, small tidbits of personal or local news, newspaper gossip and shop talk. Geoffrey enjoyed talking about his job. He thoroughly explained the basics of the newspaper business, its inherent problems and its future prospects.

A hard working, tall, thin fellow of thirty years, he was the portrait of a single-minded newspaperman. His appearance betrayed his personality, which could be accurately summed up by the five '*W's*': who, what, when, where, and why. He was balding at the temples, and had a very thick, dark beard that constantly appeared as a two-day growth. His facial crop defied the thin, light brown hair upon his scalp. He was a good natured man with a strong commitment to his job. His work schedule was a six-day week, from five in the morning until six or later in the evening. Although the hours were grueling, he relished the work. At ten o'clock he handed baby William to Virginia, mentioned that a diaper change was needed and announced he was going to bed. "Don't stay up too late, Honey." He gave his wife a little kiss on the cheek.

The sisters still had things to talk about; Virginia was anxious to hear the rest of Ellie's story. "I'll be up in a short while, Geoff. A little while ... goodnight."

Eloisa watched as her sister washed and changed the infant. After a rinse in the toilet, baby William's diaper went into the soaking bucket to await the next day's boiling and washing. The bathroom had the unique blend of odors that betrayed the presence of a baby. Changed and clean, it was teat time for William once again. Virginia made herself comfortable on the sofa and said, "Please start again, Ellie. Tell me what the big disaster in Los Angeles was."

"Well, when I was at Father Baker's, mother brought me a letter from Phryne that invited me to stay with her in Los Angeles. I accepted, and came out on the train after I was released from Our Lady of Victory hospital. It was a five day trip, and when I arrived I was tired, but excited too. At first, everything was going just fine. There was plenty of room in the house ... it's a big house and she's got a housekeeper. She married a big movie producer after her Leopold had left, so she sure doesn't need to worry about money. She ended up losing the baby ... it died the day after birth, a little girl, born too early with immature lungs, I suppose."

"My goodness, that's terrible. Is that the disaster?"

"Goodness, no. It gets dreadfully worse. Phryne went into a depressive state, withdrew inside her shell like a turtle or a crab, and started to hit the sherry. Then one afternoon, she got a bit blotto* and told me she had cheated with Dillon, who was the man on my arm at the time."

"That's the same man who raped you?"

"I was seeing him for about a year before that happened, the rape; the time he forced himself on me. The whole thing got me so infuriated, Ginny. She betrayed me, Dillon raped me and she had something to do with it. I really think so ... she was together with him the same night he forced himself on me. And she kept it a secret from me because she knew she had done wrong, real wrong. That's the disaster. She betrayed me. She confessed and I left. Here I am."

Eloisa was talking between tears, and wiping her cheek with the back of her hand. "Phryne never told me the whole story about Leopold's departure. She never told me what drove him to leave. I cannot imagine that he would just up and leave her for no reason whatsoever. When she told me how mean Leopold was to her, I found it hard to believe. I still do.

I didn't think he was that kind of man, and I still don't. There has to be more to the story. I don't believe that he would leave Phryne just because he was feeling guilty and having bad dreams. Phryne proved that she is a woman without compassion. She clearly showed the colors of her flag when she confessed her transgressions with Dillon. She's all emotion … all emotion and no heart."

Hurdy-Gurdy Man (Monkey On A String)

Sunday, June 1, 1930

Warm spring breezes pushed the muslin curtains into the kitchen and spread the homey smell of roasting chuck roast throughout the home. Eloisa and her sister Virginia sat with steaming cups of tea at the worn, green enameled kitchen table. Each wore cotton house dresses of similar floral prints. Virginia was a bit taller and had blonde hair a shade darker than her sister's. Two day-old loaves of Eloisa's sourdough bread sat on the sideboard. For more than a year and a half she had been working the early morning to noon shift at Morella's Bakery on Bradley Street and brought home day-old or imperfect breads or rolls. Eloisa's contributions combined with Geoffrey's income from the newspaper enabled the extended family to easily weather the Depression. Other than the birth of Virginia's second child Alice, nothing had really changed at Number 13 since the day Eloisa arrived. She had refurbished the old pantry off the kitchen into her own room, finding comfort near the kitchen. There were two children underfoot in the home at all times: William, nearly two, and ten-month-old Alice.

With Sunday as his only day off, Geoffrey was nonetheless able to maintain and keep the house on 44th Street painted and in good repair. He had other duties as well. His daily twelve-hour work regimen at the Sacramento Bee harshly limited his family time to bare-boned interaction.

It was the first Sunday in June, a perfect day for an afternoon picnic at Oak Park. Geoffrey sliced off a generous portion of the pot roast and wrapped it in paper and cheesecloth. Virginia had packed a loaf of bread, two bottles of cream soda, a pint of milk and three apples into the woven basket and Eloisa had gathered the children into the Buick Master roadster. It was a day in public and everyone was displaying their Sunday best from sunglasses to laced boots and spats. Woven wide brim sun hats, cotton dresses in soft pastels, William's knickerbockers, Alice's dusty pink romper and Geoffrey's plaid golf cap defied the existence of an economic Depression. It was a fine-looking family.

Virginia's husband was truly a proud and ambitious man, a dedicated husband and father, faithful provider and the pride and joy of his socially and politically influential parents, Robert Merril Gibbons and Alberta Patrice-Rice of Pittsfield, Massachusetts. Geoffrey Lamont Gibbons was his wife's senior by eight years. An honors graduate of the Boston College class of 1916, he had earned a Bachelor's Degree in Economics. His four years at Boston exposed him to a wide spectrum of political philosophy that helped him forge his socialist views on society. During the Great War he studied at Columbia University, joined the *Peace At All Cost* movement and earned a post-graduate onionskin in journalism that had given him the opportunity for employment with *The Buffalo Daily Courier*. In Buffalo, he had displayed a knack for news, interest in socio-political issues and a diligent work ethic that quickly propelled his career. Two of the three dailies in Buffalo had merged to form the Courier Express in 1926, creating one of the top twenty papers in the country. His career was on the express trolley to success and his personal life was also moving along at a fast pace. He had met and married Virginia and transferred to Sacramento in just ten months. Her pregnancy had necessitated the marriage and placed his cross-country transfer on the fast track.

His parents graciously agreed to hold the mortgage on the house on 44th Street, which secured a firm foundation for the young family during the unforeseen hard times that were coming. But over the course of the past year, he felt his career had stagnated, and was consistently frustrated by the lack of upward mobility in the *Bee's* managerial and editorial departments. He had found it necessary to temper his ambitions and accept things as they were. The country had been suffering economically and those who were fortunate enough to be employed, understandably stayed where they were. It annoyed him that the one thing the unvarnished proletariat understood was this: the status quo.

Geoffrey Gibbons longed for the day he could cut the wire and break free from the hurdy-gurdy* men and all the organ grinders that control the unfortunate dancing monkeys of the world. He was constantly on the hunt for the next big story: an exclusive headliner that could propel him on to national, or perhaps international, recognition.

Virginia was happy with her life and was thinking about another child. She never paid much attention to her husband's world view and rarely concerned herself with what she considered to be political poppycock or empathetic economic balderdash.

On the other hand, Virginia's sister Eloisa enjoyed working with warm bread dough on the rock maple tabletops at Mamma Morella's Bakery on Bradley. It felt good to mix and shape a mass of flour, water and yeast with the new stainless steel mixers and her bare hands. Although she was comfortable with her situation, Eloisa had a disquieting sense that it could become permanent, and along with millions of her fellow Americans, she hoped better days were coming.

12. SAN FRANCISCO, CALIFORNIA ~ 1934

Between The Devil And The Deep Blue Sea

Saturday morning, June 30, 1934

Officer Throckmorton had spent his first two years on the police force as a patrolman, a beat cop in the city's Tenderloin District: an area he was somewhat familiar with. Bordered on the north by China Town, and Market Street to the south, his foot patrols up and down the blocks between Eddy Street and Union Square had worn the soles off countless pairs of shoes. He had cultivated a good deal of friendships in the neighborhood, and had gained the trust and respect of shop keepers and residents. Men and women could be on the streets in the wee morning hours walking to or from work in safety. When the soles of his shoes hit the pavement in 1930, the police stations were open to the public, and could even be considered community centers. The windows didn't have steel bars, and newer, brighter streetlights lit up the night. Most of his arrests were the occasional rowdy doxy*, drunkard or some ruffian caught in a street brawl. After a night in the calaboose*, they were freed to roam once again.

Two years on, he had traveled full circle and was stationed where his quest for a law enforcement career had started: the Hall of Justice on Kearny Street, police headquarters. He was a Bond and Bail Enforcement Officer but had been temporarily assigned to the Waterfront patrols when the strikes began earlier in the year. He was given a beat near the Embarcadero and Battery Row and was usually in the company of another officer, his shift partner Ronan O'Cain. The unionists were becoming much more active, and some could argue that their protests and picket lines were progressing toward downright belligerence. For the past month, the waterfront had become a tinderbox of unrest, starting on May 9 with a general strike, up and down the west coast that had almost completely blocked the movement of freight on the docks. The McDonough brothers played the role of friends to organized labor and were known to be giving aid and shelter to the swelling ranks of strikers. Like so many other policemen, the prickling hair at the base of his neck was a foreboding that Leopold could not ignore. The police department was braced* for trouble.

He awoke to street noise, and turned his head to discover she was still asleep, barely covered by the sheet, her form accented by sunlight poking through the cut lace curtains. Willa Tappet was a lithe, twenty-three year old hostess and weekend entertainer at *The Bear Jazz* on Pacific Street in the old Barbary Coast district. She was one of two women he had on a string, although Willa would say that it was she who held the lead. He fought the urge to rekindle the intimacy of last night and slid out of bed to make a pot of coffee. There was air in the water lines as usual, and the gurgling, surging brown liquid spitting out of the pipes woke his bed partner. "You're not going in to work this morning are you, Leo, Dear?" She pulled on her stockings, stepped into her slinky dress, slipped on her pumps and walked to the small kitchen. Her silk delicates* were still in her handbag.

He let the water run until it was a lighter shade of rust before he filled the green enameled steel percolator. "I'm afraid so, Sweetie. Afraid so. Captain wants every uniform on duty today and tomorrow. Chief Goff said now there are anarchists and communists in the city from New York just to stir up more trouble." He spooned coffee into the basket, lit a match to the gas stove and turned to face her.

She grabbed his buttocks and brought herself to him. "I wish we could be a real couple. You know what I mean. We should spend more time together." She squeezed his behind and kissed him like it was her last.

"It's the job, Sweetie … you know that. Someday we will, you'll see. Be patient." He had been using that limp apology for the better part of a year.

Willa was a beautiful woman and knew it. She took pride in her appearance and was not ashamed to say that she had been around the block a time or two. While selective with her companions and very particular about cleanliness, she nevertheless allowed more than one rooster in the henhouse. Curiously, she bragged extensively about her mastery of the ukulele, kazoo, castanets and tassels, but would never perform for anyone outside the jazz club. Leopold enjoyed her company if only for her unique sense of humor.

After a cigarette and a half cup of coffee, Willa was usually out the door. It was no different that morning.

The Van Ness Riot: Red Armbands And Night Sticks

The station alarms went off before Leopold had reached the precinct. Three short rings and two long signaled the trouble spot: The Market District. Months earlier, Police Chief Harold Goff had ordered a plan of action throughout the city that had created response squads of eight officers to be led by a ranking sergeant or minimally, a senior patrolman. Police captains made certain that all officers had at least one side arm in working order and ammunition. SFPD officers had undergone extensive training in riot control tactics over the past three months. The situation demanded it. Labor unrest had begun as soon as the weather warmed in May when the International Longshoremen's Union called a general strike from Seattle to San Francisco. It seemed that every labor organization in the United States had sent teams of agitators, demonstrators and organizers to San Francisco to make their stand with the sea at their backs.

The unions' unforeseen problem was that the police had worked up a strategy months ago, and were ready to defend the waterfront.

Leopold drove one of two Chevrolet police sedans to the corner of Redwood and Van Ness, a block from City Hall. A crowd had formed around the violence that had begun outside the offices of the *Western Worker*, a bi-monthly tabloid printed by the American Communist Party. A few fires were burning in front of the offices. Copies of the publication had been looted from inside, piled on the sidewalk and set ablaze. Flames licked upward and toward the building. The location was well known by the police and had been the scene for numerous dustups and street fights, but this particular brouhaha was on a much higher level. Sirens from additional patrol cars and the scream of Leopold's brass whistle were ignored, as were those of other officers already at the scene. Stones and bricks were being cast indiscriminately at undefined targets. The cops dodged what they could, advanced into the crowd and returned insults with whacks from their batons.

Four additional police cars loaded with officers arrived and parked alongside Leopold's and Ronan's, effectively blocking Van Ness Boulevard and Golden Gate Avenue. A half dozen mounted police atop galloping Morgans rounded the corner in front of City Hall, cutting off escape to the south. The mounted patrol, hoofs resounding on the brick pavers, gained the attention of the crowd, pushing them back up the street toward the police blockade. Long black lead-filled cudgels with leather lanyards were struck across the backs of crowbar and axe-wielding rioters. Horses whinnied and snorted from flared nostrils. Frenzied hoof beats echoed off the street or fell with a muffled thud upon the fallen few.

Tear gas grenades, the newest weapons in the police arsenal, were fired from the forward line into the mob gathered outside the newspaper office. Screams, shouts and orders were mixed into an indiscernible cauldron of noise. The first crack of a pistol was heard from someplace yards away on Leopold's right. Another followed; and another. The noise level increased with the energy of the human and equine players. The fire of human emotion fueled itself, feeding upon its own frenzied flames of violence.

Flashes of fire flared from the broken curbside windows of the Western Worker. The Fire Company could be heard coming down Ivy Street toward Redwood. The horse-drawn water pumper rolled noisily up Van Ness, and was forced to a stop one hundred yards short of its destination. The fire trucks and reserve pumper could only inch toward the burning building. The mounted police moved indiscriminately forward through the crowd, the officers swinging their batons at anyone within reach. Whistles wailed. The wounded or disabled fell to the pavement and sidewalks. The exploding crunch and crash of breaking glass bottles hitting the street below caught the attention of two officers from the Tenderloin. The coppers fired a few shots from their revolvers toward an open second story window on Redwood Street. In the alley between Ivy and Pierce, barking dogs protested in vain. A woman's scream was heard.

The noisy, unmuffled sound of the reserve pumper's coughing two-stroke gasoline engine finally signaled the readiness of the firefighters. The crowd became overcome by the drifting tear gas, and pushed toward the police cars, forcing their way between, around or over the vehicles and breaking into a full sprint away from law enforcement. Quickly, the mass of human mayhem dwindled to a few dozen walking wounded, a half dozen unmoving bodies strewn across the pavement, dazed, bloodied and beaten strikers, firemen hosing the Western Worker's storefront and exhausted, bruised, victorious policemen. The Morgans snorted and hoofed the ground. Two more Chevrolet police sedans, with screaming sirens, pulled close to the second fire pumper. A half dozen more policemen with drawn night sticks hit the street. A fresh chorus of brass whistles pierced the neighborhood. One by one, the sirens silenced. The crowd noise vanished.

Snapping embers, rising steam and hissing coals protested the firemen's wall of water. Glass windows popped and shattered from heat or water. Groans were heard coming from the fallen human forms sprawled on the street. Nearly every set of hand irons the officers brought to the violent street party had been used. Nearly two dozen individuals in steel bracelets* stood on the sidewalks, under the scrutiny of six coppers with drawn nightsticks. Policemen gathered in small clusters of two or three. The first paddy wagon arrived, driving around piles of burning newspapers, broken bricks and dazed humans. There wasn't an eye that did not feel the burn of the lingering gas. A few of the handcuffed could not help but vomit. Leopold was cursed and spat upon while he and his partner Ronan walked among the handcuffed and wounded, assessing who may or may not need to be hauled away by the medical unit. Leopold responded to the spittle and swearing with a heavy duty rap into the ribs. The blow from the business end of his night stick dropped the thug to his knees. Leopold could have ignored the transgression had the fellow not been wearing a red armband. He stood over the man, holding his night stick to the back of his neck, "You don't spit in the street, you anarchist bastard." Leopold landed another blow to the back of the prisoner's thighs with a thud.

A half hour after it began, the riot was over. A command was shouted from the running board of a patrol car by Assistant Chief Byron Burke. The cops within earshot gave him their unwavering attention. "Let's bring them in, gentlemen. Good job."

Two men who had suffered gunshot wounds and survived were later identified as Communists. One employee of the Western Worker was struck dead by a blow to the skull by an unknown assailant. A dozen or more persons were either treated at the scene or at First Presbyterian Hospital. The direst injuries were broken bones.

Nothing that occurred on the morning of June 30th had helped to ease the labor unrest in San Francisco. In the days that followed, a workers' memorial march was planned for the day of the fallen Communists' funeral.

Bloody Thursday, July 5: From The Sea To A Funeral

An uneasy truce prevailed and there were no major confrontations during the first half of the week. Mayor Angelo Rossi blamed the Van Ness rioting on Communist agitators from New York, and vowed the city would do everything possible to ensure that commerce would peacefully continue. Compared to what was coming, the Van Ness brawl was child's play, a walk in the park.

The Industrial Association and The Marine Service Bureau began housing non-union labor in temporary quarters set up in warehouses and aboard ships along the Pier. Leopold was one of about a thousand policemen assigned to the Embarcadero and waterfront while strikebreakers began to move freight from trucks, warehouses and railroad cars along the Belt Line to ships moored at the docks. Armed with gas, revolvers and riot shotguns, the police protected the non-union laborers defying the strike. Further south, the union rank and file responded by organizing picket lines to block access to freight trucks leaving from the Southern Pacific rail yards. The Riggers and Stevedores Association, International Longshoremen and the Industrial Workers of the World called for a massive parade and general city-wide strike on Thursday, July 5. A march had been planned to coordinate with the funeral of the fallen Western Worker employee. Fifteen thousand or more protestors were expected.

California Governor Frank Merriman ordered the National Guard activated in anticipation of inevitable trouble coming on July 5. Citing the backing given by the Communist Party of the United States (CPUS) to the Longshoremen and the well-publicized involvement of Socialist Party activist Sam Darcy, the governor, mayor and police chief said they would protect the interests of the public and would not kowtow to radical politics. On Wednesday afternoon 4,500 National Guard troops marched through the streets of San Francisco, south from the Presidio and Fort Mason and established a fortified military encampment along The Embarcadero near Market Street. Fortifications built from sandbags sheltered machine gun nests and mortar launchers. Tanks, armored personnel carriers, and two-ton trucks formed the forward line.

Newspapers around the country, the Chamber of Commerce, city and state government all condemned the general strike and referred to the Longshoremen, Stevedores and the IWW as radicals, anarchists and advocates of violence. The IWW earned their nickname: *the Wobblies.* President Franklin Roosevelt and National Recovery Administration (NRA) chief, General Hugh Johnson, proclaimed that the strike was "a bloody insurrection" and asked all responsible labor organizations to "run the subversive Communist influences out from their ranks like the sewer rats they are."

On Thursday, July 5, 1934, well over 15,000 people paraded four abreast in a memorial funeral march from the waterfront down Market Street to the burial graveyard on Valencia Street. Without doubt, the massive protest was organized.

The Wobblies and socialists took full credit for what they had considered an overwhelming success.

Hours later, what began as a planned funeral march and labor protest turned violent beyond expectation. Overwrought demonstrators and overzealous strikers attacked police and soldiers with bricks, railroad spikes, bottles and rocks. The mob used pry bars to loosen cobblestones directly from the street and threw them at the police line. Vastly outnumbered, law enforcement and the soldiers retreated to their fortified positions at Pier 26 and 28. With their backs to the bay, the police and military responded with teargas and gunfire. Bullets from police revolvers pinged off the brick buildings. Bursts of machinegun fire and tear gas grenades scattered the rioters into smaller mobs fleeing away from the Ferry Building, south down Market and Mission Streets. Mounted policemen charged into the violence, clubbing anyone within reach. Four National Guard tanks convinced many of the demonstrators to go home. The melee lasted for hours.

When the crowds had dissolved, and the brass whistles had quieted, over 100 people were hospitalized: a dozen police and scores of protesters had been wounded. Three men were killed by police or military gunfire. Virtually everyone at the scene suffered bumps and bruises. Nearly three hundred individuals were placed under arrest, pushing the city's jails and the Presidio's stockade to their limits. The lockups were bursting at the seams. The daunting number of arrests stretched the workload of the district attorney, judiciary calendar, and police force. Mayor Rossi promised that justice would be served, no matter the wait.

After Bloody Thursday, things calmed down. Perhaps it was a surrender, or a smack of reality. Whatever the reason, the IWW and Longshoremen's unions agreed to Federal arbitration with the Industrial Association and Marine Service Bureau. The strikes ended.

Officer Leopold Throckmorton went back to his duties in Bond and Parolee Enforcement. Because of all the recent arrests, he had expected that he could be detailed for prisoner transport and court security. His supposition was correct.

It Had To Be You

Monday, July 9: The dock dockets

Overcrowding strained the nerves and patience of the prisoners as well as the police and military personnel. Conditions were particularly harsh in the stockade at the Presidio. Military jails are austere; it's the nature of the beast. The district attorney had made some progress on the first two days of hearings, settling 57 cases of Public Disturbance, Disorderly Behavior and Hindering Law Enforcement. The court had decided it was best to focus on the Presidio population first, since that facility suffered the direst overcrowding.

The prisoner detail was one of the most straight forward of Leopold's career. He and Ronan had been tasked with picking up prisoners at the military base on the North Shore, transporting them to The Hall of Justice, and remaining with them until their cases were adjudicated as they were either remanded for lengthier prison time, bonded out or released without prejudice. There were still a few very belligerent souls who needed to be carefully restrained or physically encouraged toward better behavior, but by and large, the prisoners were subdued. Many were suffering minor scrapes and bruises, and some were dealing with more serious infections that required hospitalization or a trip to the Presidio Medical Unit and Dispensary. All of them stunk. As the days went on, it would only get worse.

The incarcerated generally professed their innocence. Many claimed to be victims of circumstance and a few raged on about the inhumane treatment of the jailors or the police. Those particular individuals, the complainers, staunch unionists or political activists, were given longer jail time for uncooperative behavior.

The jury box of Judge Felix McGrue's courtroom was occupied by fifteen despondent, handcuffed prisoners on two benches, packed like pickles in a barrel. Leopold stood at one end and his partner Ronan O'Cain at the other. The spectator gallery had perhaps two dozen people scattered across the nearly empty benches. There was one young attorney and a Wobbly lawyer at the defendants' bench and one prosecuting attorney and a legal aide sat at the District Attorney's bench. When McGrue's gavel hit the sounding block, the morning session began.

Judge McGrue was a rough-around-the-edges, no-holds-barred, shoot-from-the-hip veteran magistrate. His voice was an echoing growl. When court proceedings had begun three days earlier, he had advised the defense attorneys that, exclusive of violent offenses, he would rule from the bench to expedite the case load. The judge summarily released the vast majority of prisoners with an admonition or occasional fine. The city attorney had a list of defendants whom the police department had charged with more serious assault or coercive resist of arrest. One by one, the judge methodically reduced the number of prisoners sitting in the jury box. It seemed that everyone in the courtroom was fidgeting and awaiting recess. There were only two men remaining in the box before court would break for midday. Judge McGrue slammed his gavel down and remanded defendant number 70 to the city jail awaiting further legal action on the charge of Malicious Intent to Inflict Bodily Harm to a police officer. The bailiff escorted the hobbling prisoner out through the side entrance.

Like everyone else, Leopold stretched, cricked his neck and looked around the room. It was then that someone in the visitor's gallery had caught his attention. She looked somewhat familiar. He studied the woman wearing the pale yellow, wide-brimmed woven sun hat. He had a mysterious sense of earlier cognizance; that he had known her in some other place at some other time. She wore a turquoise, figure hugging mid-calf frock with a flared skirt and a wide, double-breasted beige collar.

She had noticed him, and cast an inquisitive look in his direction. A tender smile crossed her lips, she raised her hand and gave a short finger wave. She wore elbow-length, lace-trimmed gloves. Leopold nodded and noticed her demure smile. He looked to the judge, his partner Ronan, to the prisoners and back to the woman. Ronan had noticed the visual contact between Leopold and the woman.

Leopold recognized her and whispered under his breath, allowing his lips to form her name. "Eloisa Ashworth. Eloisa Ashworth." Their eyes found each other. He nodded. She smiled.

The moment the judge's gavel sounded the lunch recess, Leopold told his partner to go on without him and walked to the polished wood bar that separated him from the visitor's gallery. He and Eloisa stood looking at one another for a fleeting moment before he moved to the gateway and stepped into the gallery. They shared a brief but firm embrace of friendship. The courtroom emptied in a flash. Ronan watched the interaction, then turned and entered the jury room. He and Leopold had their lunch pails inside.

"What on Earth brings you to San Francisco, Eloisa Ashworth?!" She motioned for him to sit and they settled next to each other.

"Leopold Throckmorton. A cop! It's been, what? Ten years? No, six. No, seven. Seven years and you're a cop!"

"Funny how the world goes around and shakes itself up and people still end up bumping into each other. It's nice to see you, Ellie. Really nice."

"You look good, Leopold."

"Me? Hell, no. But you sure do. Real good. But tell me, what are you here for? Do you know somebody up on charges?"

She couldn't believe the happenstance, shaking her head sideways and smiling. "Leopold Throckmorton." She took both his hands. "I'm trying to calm myself. This is just unbelievable. I can't believe it."

He knew he needed to be patient. She was moving her head sideways, back and forth in feigned bewilderment, like she had just found a lost kitten.

He studied her. He was captivated. His thoughts flashed. He was examining her, profiling her and finding the category she would best fit into. She was no longer the Eloisa he had known in Buffalo. A woman was sitting next to him, not a girl trying to push beyond her teenage years and yearning for adventure. Her lips glistened. She had changed. She was downright, stunningly good-looking and much more than attractive. Her eyes sparkled. She was alluring … that was the word he was looking for: alluring ... with the body of a hand-carved ship's figurehead. An alluring woman, steaming forward, unafraid of anything that lie ahead, be it on stormy or calm seas.

His thoughts were as quick as lightning. He could see that she was built. Head to toe … ship-shape. Her voice interrupted his examination.

"I'm here for somebody, Leopold." She sounded anxious.

"Who? Are you waiting for someone?"

"My brother-in-law. You see, I'm living in Sacramento with my sister, her husband and their two children. He's at the

Presidio, under arrest. My sister stayed behind with the children and I took the train down here yesterday. Now I'm waiting for his court appearance so I can stand in evidence for him or maybe bail him out."

He detected nervous anticipation in her words.

"What's his name?"

"You can help? No one could tell me when he was due in court or when his hearing was coming up."

"What's his name, Eloisa?"

"Geoffrey, it's Geoffrey ... Geoffrey Gibbons. He's a reporter for the Sacramento Bee newspaper and he was arrested during the riot and shouldn't be locked up. It was a mistake, it had to be. He was here reporting for the newspaper. The paper telephoned the police but got the hinky* run-around, the brush-off treatment and couldn't get anywhere. They gave me a letter that says he was only doing his job and reporting the news."

Leopold took out his notebook, writing as he spoke: "Geoffrey Gibbons."

"That's right. Geoffrey Gibbons, a reporter for the Sacramento Bee. That would be wonderful if you could hurry his case along, Leopold. Really. Me and my sister and his children would appreciate it."

"I'll see if I can spring him for the afternoon docket. Would that be all right? This afternoon?"

"Wonderful. That would be wonderful ... do you think you can do that? Get his case moved forward, I mean?"

"I'll try."

"Thank you so much! Thank you!" They stood. She kissed him on the cheek. They had each other's hands.

He glanced to the clock over the jury room door: ten past twelve. "Me and Ronan will be back with the next bunch about one o'clock. I'll see if I can brace* your Geoffrey. No promises, but I'll try." He smiled at her, nodded and squeezed her hands before he turned and walked to the jury room, his partner and his lunch.

Eloisa watched him walk away and could only marvel at the circumstance that caused their paths to cross after so many years. She wanted to turn the page, and read the rest of the story. But first, she needed to get the book.

Flat Foot Floogie With The Floy Floy

After six quick bites out of his liverwurst and onion sandwich, Leopold and his partner were out the back door of The Hall of Justice and ready to pick up the next load. Leopold's thoughts were rolling every which way, like waves in a typhoon. He didn't know what to make of it all. "You drive, Ronan. I need to think."

Ronan had to ask, "So, who was the good looking dame back there in court, buddy?" He jerked the Ford paddy wagon into gear.

"Somebody from a long time ago … seems like a lifetime … seven years ago back in Buffalo. She's living out here with her sister up in Sacramento and she's looking to get her newspaper reporter brother-in-law out of the Presidio lock-up. I told her I'd try to round him up."

"A reporter?"

"So she says."

There was no further conversation the rest of the way to the North Shore military base.

A two-stripe corporal was seated behind the stockade dispatch desk. Leopold decided to dig up a line of hokum,

"Hey, Corporal. Judge McGrue wants me to round up somebody by the name of Geoffrey Gibbons. Judge says he needs him to testify in court about a wounded Army trooper, Smith, Schmitz, or Smiths, or something like that. You know anybody wounded in your ranks who answers to the name Smith?" Ronan was stone faced.

The corporal looked annoyed. "Can't say that I do. But I guess I better try to help a wounded soldier, one of our own, or maybe he's a Marine. Yeah, that's it. Must be a Marine. That's why I don't know him."

Leopold agreed, "Good thinking, Corporal. Must be. Do you think you could grab this Gibbons for the judge?"

The young soldier pushed his chair back from the desk, "Don't worry, I'll get him. Your regular load is waiting back at the fence and ready for you; another fifteen. The extra bum will make it sixteen." He pushed a clipboard across his desk, "Sign the check-out sheet here, for the fifteen. I'll bring this Gibbons goon around in a little bit, and add him on."

In five minutes, Leopold and Ronan had the prisoner van loaded with its handcuffed human cargo and ready to leave for the courthouse. They stood smoking cigarettes, waiting at the gate.

The corporal came around the back of the barb-wired compound and through the gravel yard. He was walking behind Geoffrey Gibbons and pushing a night stick into his ribs. "It took me a minute to find him; he didn't want to answer, then I had to add him to the manifest and get the lieutenant's signature. Sorry for the delay, coppers." He rudely shoved Gibbons toward the police hack.

Leopold thanked him. "Thanks, Corporal. I know the judge appreciates it, and so do we." He gave the soldier a make-shift salute.

Ronan opened the back door, encouraged the additional prisoner inside, and set the padlock.

Seated, and back inside the truck, Ronan laughed, "You got more shit than a racehorse. You know that, don't you Leopold?"

"Yeah, I know." He turned and looked through the observation window. Gibbons looked like a broken man, exactly like the other fifteen in the van.

At the Hall of Justice, inside Courtroom A, nearly three hours had passed. Judge Felix McGrue worked down the list and brought his gavel to the desk fifteen times, passing judgment on fifteen lives.

Eloisa came to the edge of the bench. She and only one other remained in the gallery. There were no further cases scheduled after her brother-in-law's, so the other spectator was either a nosey body or member of a union. She nodded once again to Leopold. It was apparent that she was very grateful. Geoffrey Gibbons had spotted her almost as soon as he was seated in the jury box. It was evident he was happy to see her.

The bailiff walked him to the defendant bench and the two attorneys waiting there. In mere moments, the judge began. Gibbons' suit was torn and soiled beyond any point of salvation. The left sleeve was torn away, and like all the other inmates, he had no belt, tie or shoelaces. He had scrapes and bruises on his visible skin.

Judge McGrue spoke in a drawn-out, low, toneless drone. His voice sounded like a bow drawn across a bass fiddle. "District Attorney, do you have any specific charges to bear for this prisoner?"

"Participating in Public Disturbance, Your Honor."

"Mister Gibbons, were you wearing that suit on July 5th?"

"Yes, I was."

"Where do you live, Mister Gibbons?"

"Sacramento, Your Honor."

"Are you an organizer or officer in a labor union, Mister Gibbons?"

"No, I'm a reporter, Your Honor. A reporter for the Sacramento Bee. I came down here just for the day, to report on the funeral and protest march."

The judge looked annoyed. "Then what happened? Didn't you show your press identification?"

"I did. It was taken from me and thrown to the ground by a policeman. I reached to pick it and my armband up and I was beat across my back by his Billy club."

The defense attorneys whispered to each other, nodded, and whispered again. Leopold and Ronan exchanged glances. Eloisa looked quickly to Leopold and back to Geoffrey.

"What armband, Mister Gibbons? Do newspapermen wear armbands now?"

"No, Your Honor. It was a red and black armband I got from a union officer. I was wearing it in solidarity and mourning for the Western Worker newspaperman who was killed."

Leopold and Ronan shook their heads in disbelief. Eloisa looked worried.

Judge McGrue folded his arms on the bench, leaned forward and looked over the top of his spectacles. "You, Mister Gibbons, may be a damn fine newspaper reporter for the Sacramento Bee. The press is a bastion of freedom in this country. Reporters for the press have the right to move freely to lawfully report the news. I believe that you, Mister Gibbons were exercising that right. However, you also freely acted the idiot."

Mumbles and whispers floated in the courtroom. Geoffrey Gibbons was surprised. Eloisa was flabbergasted. Leopold,

Ronan and the District Attorney were amused. The judge was annoyed.

"You were ill-advised to wear a Communist armband and march in a demonstration that was advocating anarchy and supporting the lawless labor stoppage called by the Wobblies, Communists and other un-American union mobs, Mister Gibbons."

"You're guilty of being an idiot. The case is dismissed. Go home, Mister Gibbons. Do your job. Don't be an idiot." His gavel hit the sounder with a smack. "Court is adjourned until nine o'clock tomorrow morning."

Everyone stood. The judge exited through the door behind the bench. Chairs were pushed back, papers gathered, brief cases buckled shut, and shoes shuffled on the wooden floor.

"Good night, Ronan. I'd love to have a beer, but not tonight. See you tomorrow morning, bud."

"Yeah sure. See you in the morning. We'll do it all over again."

Leopold watched the reunion between Eloisa and her brother-in-law. He was amused by the look on her face as Geoffrey came close to her. He, like all the inmates, had an obnoxious odor. They stayed at arms' length. Eloisa motioned Leopold over.

"Geoffrey, this is a friend of mine from Buffalo, believe it or not. He was the one that helped move your case forward."

It was apparent that Geoffrey had no interest in starting a conversation. He acknowledged Leopold with a nod, an abbreviated smile and simply, "Thank you for your assistance." Leopold detected arrogance.

"When are you going back to Sacramento, Mister Gibbons?" Leopold was hoping he could spend some more time with Eloisa, and was poking for an excuse to do so. He used charity as a tool to achieve his goal. "You're about my size, and I could let you borrow a pair of pants and a shirt … maybe even a jacket. Yeah, I think I could do that … a jacket, too." Geoffrey was four inches shorter than Leopold's six-feet-two.

Geoffrey was resentful, "I do not need help from a flat foot."

Eloisa interrupted, "Come on now, that sounds good, doesn't it Geoffrey? You can shower or take a hot bath at the hotel and change into some clean clothes before dinner." She knew just how irritating her brother-in-law could be at times.

"I will take you up on your offer to get cleaned up, Ellie, thanks. But I am not staying in this town a minute longer than I have to, and I certainly do not need dinner. I can grab a hotdog or hamburger at the station. I am going back to Sacramento on the next train, because surely, I am not going to sit on this story. They are not going to sweep their murdering violence and corrupt power under the rug. I will not let them. And I am sure that Virginia, William and Alice are waiting for me to come home."

When Leopold heard that statement about corruption and violence, he knew the judge was right. This fellow was an idiot; the worse kind: an indignant idiot. He decided to talk around him, and not to him.

"Where are you staying Ellie?"

"The Whitcomb. The Hotel Whitcomb on Market Street."

"All right, I know where that is … I'll tell you what … I'll scoot to my place and grab a few things that Geoffrey can wear for his trip back and then I can run over to the hotel and drop them off. How's that?"

Geoffrey protested. "I do not need that, Eloisa. I do not need to borrow clothing."

"Don't be silly, Geoff. You can't ride the train to Sacramento looking like a bum. That's an argument you will not win." She picked up her handbag. "Leopold, I'm in room 202. Just come on up and knock. We'll both be there waiting for you. Thank you." She turned, ready to leave, and gave Leopold a little wave. "Come on, Geoffrey. Let's hop a streetcar, telephone Ginny and get you cleaned up." Eloisa wasn't in the mood for nonsense. Geoffrey's protests were beaten back by Eloisa's persistence and his lack of sleep in the stockade.

Leopold didn't want this surprising new connection to be bogged down with petty, pointless arguments or a conflict of personalities. He was happy to see that Eloisa seemed to have a handle on her brother-in-law. He couldn't explain it: he was happy to see Eloisa.

When My Dreamboat Comes Home

Monday, July 9, 6 PM

Leopold had a two-room, one bath apartment on Ross Avenue, a short, five minute trolley ride from The Hall of Justice. It was small, and bright, with two double sash windows in the living room, and one in the kitchen. He never had much company, and couldn't see the point in concealing the obvious, so he kept the Murphy bed pulled down from the wall.

He took a fast shower, so fast the water never warmed, shaved, trimmed his mustache with nail scissors and put on his Saturday night suit and grey fedora. Deep in his closet, he found a high-collared white cotton shirt, a pair of dungarees and a worn summer jacket for Geoffrey. He thought twice about it, and decided to go ahead and donate a pair of Y-front undershorts and cotton socks to the cause. Everything went into two paper sacks.

He felt that he was walking a thin line, and didn't want to offend a complete stranger, neither on the short nor the high end of charity; especially a stranger who had already expressed his disdain for cops; more than once. He also didn't want to let Eloisa believe he was too callous to help.

When he knocked the door of room 202, Leopold had decided to ignore any veiled insults thrown by the reporter from Sacramento, and be as gracious as possible.

"Leopold! Come in! I just knew you'd be here to help. Come on in and sit down. Let me take those." She took the bags, walked to the bathroom door, knocked, looked away and set them inside. "Here's your clothes, Geoff! Leopold just arrived."

He could hear the shower running. He thought: *My God, she's absolutely radiant.*

"Sit down, sit down."

He sat on the nearest of two upholstered arm chairs, and Eloisa took the other.

"Well, Geoffrey telephoned my sister … his wife Ginny, right after we got back here, and good gracious how happy everyone is now! He's leaving tonight on the seven-thirty *Capital Express.* To tell the truth, I don't think he can wait a minute longer to get back to work at the Bee."

"So … you're leaving too?"

"Well, maybe I'm being too bold, but how about you and I have dinner and share stories? I mean, it's been seven years. The hotel room is paid for and Geoffrey is leaving right away and I can catch the morning train, at eight-thirty. I have already asked Ginny what she thinks and she said it would be perfectly all right if two old friends did that; have dinner and talk, I mean. What do you think?"

"I think it's 1934 and who cares? It's all part of Roosevelt's New Deal: Geoffrey leaves for Sacramento and you and I have dinner."

She nodded in agreement, smiled, crossed her legs and blushed. "Good!"

'Blue Skies' on the patio

All three took the Market and Third Street trolley to the Southern Pacific Depot, where Geoffrey was to catch the Capital Express. He had decided not to wear Leopold's old jacket and simply settled for the shirt and dungarees. He had cleaned up quite well, and the shower evidently brightened his mood. He actually found the graciousness to thank Leopold for his help and mentioned that he appreciated the socks and underwear. Eloisa had sacrificed a pair of her shoelaces and mooched a safety pin from the hotel to help secure his pants. His grouchy outlook having been washed down the drain, he was actually cheerful and quite happy to be on his way home.

He gave his sister-in-law a brief hug. "Then you should be coming back sometime tomorrow, Eloisa?"

"Absolutely ... I'll be on the eight-thirty train." She had every intention to catch that train. "Give Ginny and the children my love."

He surprised Leopold when he reached out and shook his hand. "I apologize for barking like at bulldog at you before. I was on the edge but, let me say thanks for helping Ellie get me out of the can. And thanks again for the clean things."

"You're welcome. Perhaps we'll see each other again someday. But not in a court room."

Geoffrey nodded and turned toward the movement on the platform. The bell was sounding, and passengers were on the move. It was time for the Express to leave the station. He took two steps, turned, waved and started away. The conductor called his last warning, "Come ….. aboard!" Feet shuffled, luggage bobbed and people scurried into the rail cars.

With a rush of stream and a screech of iron on steel, the locomotive slowly began to huff its way out of the station.

Leopold looked at his pocket watch; exactly half-past seven. "Time for dinner, Ellie."

She took his arm, "Let's walk, Leopold. It's a beautiful evening."

It was an atypical night in San Francisco. A warm breeze from the South kept the fog and dampness out in the bay. A few wispy clouds were scattered across a peaceful, heavenly blue sky. About an hour of daylight remained.

Leopold was mesmerized by her soft voice. Her scent left him mystified and the rhythm of her footsteps and whisper of her dress created a melody that locked in his mind.

She moved her hand down to his and felt his grasp drink up every fear she ever had. She was allowing him to lead her by the hand and it felt good. She sensed she had found a guardian.

They had walked eight blocks to Market Street and managed to talk about nothing. The riots, the courtroom and Geoffrey's ordeal were the topics. It was uncanny, as if they knew there was simply too much personal news and private information to simply dump it all on the street in plain sight and public view.

When Leopold suggested that they dine at the hotel, Eloisa only mildly protested the cost, but agreed without persuasion. "In truth, Ellie, this is the first time I have set foot inside a ritzy place in many, many years. So, I feel that I'm way overdue for a night out."

"That's my story, Leopold. Exactly the same. White napkins and tablecloths are things I haven't seen in quite a while. Quite a while."

The dining room at the Whitcomb was opulent. Tall windows dressed with soft plum drapes, richly patterned silvery grey carpeting, subtle mustard pressed tin walls and two fireplaces with massive black andirons.

They didn't fuss over their selection from the menu and quickly decided on the *Grand Mere Chicken Casserole* and a bottle of Rhine. Leopold was amused at the pre-prohibition wine label, 'Gundlach Sonoma Rhine Farm, San Francisco, California, 1917.'

Their conversation didn't uncover any deep secrets over dinner, and only served to fill in the empty spots with chatter about her sister's home, children and life in Sacramento. Leopold skimmed over his two years at sea, told a few mild police department war stories and anecdotes from his time at the Police Recruit School. They shared a small plate of pistachio ice cream and lady fingers for desert.

A dance band started at nine o'clock on the outdoor patio, which drew most of the dining customers outside. For Leopold, it was an unexpected pleasant diversion and an opportunity to extend the evening. He suggested they follow the crowd and Eloisa enthusiastically agreed.

"More wine?"

She smiled, nodded and feigned a shiver.

"Here, take my jacket."

"No, no, I can run upstairs and get my wrap." She reached for her pocketbook.

"I can get it, Ellie. Where is it?"

"I left it on the bed, of course."

"Give me the key, I'll get it and be right back. Don't argue."

She watched him walk away. His baggy slacks didn't hide all of his muscles or his swagger. She had forgotten how handsome he was.

Inside her room, he found her beige shawl right on the bed, next to her woven railroad suitcase. He brought it to his face, brushed it against his cheek and smelled her before he caught himself. *I will not act the fool*, he thought.

As soon as he was back at the table, he covered her shoulders, and extended his hand for a dance. The band had just begun '*Blue Skies*'. He held her. They danced on air; her head in the clouds and his thoughts on the wind. She believed they had danced through two tunes. It was actually five.

They did manage to return to their table and taste another glass of the Rhine. Eventually, it was Eloisa who took the first step onto the ice. "So much time has passed that we are bound to make a little mess of things, Leopold. I think it's time to get the rug beaters out and kick up some dust." She took another sip of wine, getting ready to take the second step. "I came out here in early 1928 and met up with Phryne. So when I first saw you in the courthouse, I knew you were no longer married. She found a lawyer and divorced you soon after you had left."

"Did you spend much time in Los Angeles?"

"Not at all. A month at the most, I think. When I got there, Phryne had a job and enjoyed a life of her own. I knew I couldn't fit in, so I left to stay with my sister in Sacramento and I've stayed there ever since and haven't heard a single word from her. From Phryne, I mean." The wine played tricks with her words. She was actually trying to be much more explanatory.

"Los Angeles is custom-made for custom-made people. Not everyone can be custom-made. I didn't fit that mold either, Ellie."

"Tell me about you. What have you been doing for these last seven years?"

"Quite a lot. I've worked an oil field, drank, smoked, dreamed, sniffed, boxed, got lost, got found, went to sea and read books. I sailed the Pacific, managed not to drown myself and came back on dry land to be a cop. Here I am."

"And here you are. And me too." Her eyes twinkled. "Do you have anyone special in your life now?"

"No. Nobody's in my life. I've had acquaintances, but I haven't let anyone in the front door. How about you?"

"You haven't let anyone in the front door, eh? Well, I can do you one better than that. I haven't even seen anybody on the sidewalk. Not even the milkman."

The soft humor was welcome. Wine has its way at times.

"To be perfectly honest, Leopold, I've been too afraid to let anyone get close. Some people, friends and even my family, have deeply hurt me. And Dillon Cafferty destroyed me more than you could ever know, and certainly more than I could have imagined. Oh, I've been to the pictures once or twice, and held hands, but I have lost faith in men. And up until today, I could never trust a man, much less a cop. You helped me change that today."

"Would you like to talk about it?"

"Not tonight, Leopold. Let's not knead that dough just yet. How about we just have our wine and be thankful that our paths have crossed when they did. I hope someday I might see some movement on my sidewalk."

In between dances, he talked about exotic ports of call, strange characters in far-away places, secret cargo, typhoons, and life and death at sea. He discovered that she was still working in a bakery and becoming bored with living as a bump on a log in her sister's home. He also learned that her opinion of Geoffrey was very close to that of Judge McGrue, but not quite as harsh. Rather than an idiot, she classified her brother-in-law as an idealistic, socialistic dreamer. His great redeeming quality was that he was a loving and unselfish provider for his family. Leopold had to agree that was indeed a very good quality for a husband.

The band quit playing at eleven o'clock. The patio and lounge were closing at midnight. Eloisa and Leopold knew the night would not last forever. His duty watch began at seven and her train left at half-past eight.

He squeezed the last drops out of their second bottle of wine. They held hands on the table.

"Thank you, Eloisa. I've had the best time tonight. It was wonderful to spend time with you."

"I think I need a copper to walk me to my room."

"That I can do."

He helped her up, held her close to his side, slipped his arm around her waist and his hand on her warm belly. She covered it with hers and picked up her pocketbook with the other. They walked across the lobby as one, moving in perfect unison. She kissed him in the elevator. The door opened and closed at the second floor. She wouldn't let him go. He moved his hands to her hips and pulled her to him. The elevator opened again at the lobby. Leopold asked the new passenger, "Press number two for me, the second floor, buddy. Thanks."

Her quiet little giggle brought him an inexplicable sense of joy; a joy of innocence, a joy of expectation. When the lift stopped once again at the second floor they got off, walked down the hall and stopped outside room 202. Her blue eyes filled his heart.

"I think we should say *good night*, Leopold."

"You're right, Ellie. I agree. Let's do this right."

"Maybe I could come down on the train and visit soon, maybe next weekend? I could spend all day, it's only a little over two hours on the train. And we could get to know each other all over again."

"That sounds good, next weekend. I should be scheduled off watch next Saturday and Sunday with all the overtime and double tours that Ronan and I have been pulling; provided there's no more trouble in the streets. And it would be only fair if I paid for your room since you're riding the train."

"Well, come on in, and I can write down Ginny's telephone number." She unlocked the door. Inside, she walked to the bedside table, took a sheet of writing paper out of the drawer, and wrote the number. "This is the number to reach my sister's house, and it's a six-party line, so if you don't get through at once, try again and let it ring and ring. They're supposed to hang up if they hear you ring more than five times. I'm usually home by two, and if not, Ginny should be there. So, telephone me, please, and tell me if it's all right. If you have the day off, I mean. We could go to a picture or something." They were making plans like first lovers.

He tore the bottom half off the paper, picked up the pencil and wrote an address and a telephone number. "This is my address, 13 Ross Avenue, number 3, on the first floor. And this is the number for the landlord's blower, and I think it could be a party line, too. So if you need me, telephone me at that number and he should get a message to me."

They kissed again. It was a connection that neither apprehensive Leopold nor disenchanted Eloisa saw coming.

In the lobby, he asked the desk clerk to ring her bell at seven o'clock. She had a train to catch.

Back at Ross Avenue, Leopold found it very difficult to fall asleep that night. But he didn't mind. He felt invigorated. It had been a long time. For the first time in years, his thoughts were in the future rather than the past.

In room 202 at the Whitcomb, Eloisa also had trouble sleeping. She too, was thinking about the weekend to come.

Tain't No Sin

Saturday morning, July 14

It had been ages since Leopold donned a new suit and fedora. It was a double-breasted, dark blue, fitted wool tweed jacket with wide shoulders paired with high-waist, fitted slacks. He was only slightly nervous about scuffing his uncomfortably tight, new ivory wing-tip oxfords. Had it not been for an outgoing J.C. Penney saleslady and her helpful suggestions, he could still be lost in the store.

He stood on the platform waiting for Eloisa. Squealing, hissing air brakes and straining steel announced the arrival of a Berkshire 2-8-4 locomotive into Southern Pacific's Townsend Station. The monstrous black iron hulk released a gush of steam in surrendering exasperation as the Capital Express came to a halt.

Eloisa exited the rail car, carefully descending three narrow, precarious iron steps. The large brim on her soft rose hat bounced with every step, the heels of her pumps clicked and the center pleats of her floral print, mid-calf dress captured her form as she stepped, almost skipping, toward him. Standing in front of him, in the flesh, the sight of her was so much better than the image he had locked in his memory from Monday night. He took her railroad bag and gave her a firm hug across her shoulders. The suitcase felt like it was packed full and he wondered if she had considered staying both nights of the weekend. He could only guess.

Her lips touched his cheek. "I'm glad we could meet up again Leopold, I really am. I'm glad you have the weekend.

As I told you on the telephone, I have been looking forward to seeing you again." She noticed she had left her mark on his cheek, "Oopsy daisy." She reached for her handkerchief and Leopold pulled away. "I mussed your cheek with lipstick."

"Well, you're not going to wipe it off are you?"

"Why not? It's embarrassing for a man to walk around like that."

"With a woman as beautiful as you on my arm, it's not just a lipstick smudge. It's a badge of honor." He stood facing her, and set her bag down. "Stand still, Ellie. I'm going to show you how to aim your kisses." His lips touched hers.

"You're good, Leopold. Right on target." She twittered*.

On the trolley to the Whitcomb, Leopold suggested that after lunch they could go to the matinee film showing at the Globe. "I haven't been to a picture show in years … many years. I think the last one I saw was some old silent flipper with Buster Keaton. Like I said, it seems like a hundred years ago and I think I paid sixty-five cents. Now it costs just two bits."

"What's showing? A new one?"

"I have no idea."

She giggled. Her little laugh had enamored him on Monday, and she had unknowingly just made it her own adorable trademark.

Over lunch, Leopold asked about Geoffrey's newspaper article covering the riots on Bloody Thursday. "How did that end up? Did he get his name in big print on the front page? I was thinking about him, but I don't read newspapers. There's too much bad news. As a matter of fact, that's all they print: bad news."

"His San Francisco adventure was a big waste of time and money. The paper actually reimbursed him for the hotel room; well, actually, they paid Geoffrey even though he was in jail and he paid me back. But they didn't even print the story he wrote, and that really upset him. They printed a tiny three inch, single column story hidden on page two about his arrest and time in the Army stockade. He didn't even get a 'by-line'. Sometimes the poor man feels he's just pounding his head against the wall."

"Nobody wants old news, I suppose."

"But I have some news you might like, Leopold. Evidently he had been thinking about you, too. He remembered our ordeal from years ago, and he wired someone he knows back in Buffalo at the Courier and asked if there was anything more about that night you lost your family." Leopold sat expressionless. "I'm sorry, I didn't intend to…"

"It's all right, Ellie. Go ahead. Really, it's all right." He had bitten the inside of his cheek, and shamed himself under his breath, '*Damn it*'.

She hesitated a few seconds, watching for a reaction and waiting to be certain she could continue. "Well, Geoffrey found out that the Detroit police had found your brother, Nicholas in 1928 by a stroke of dumb luck. Somebody had seen the FBI wanted list and found the name *Throckmorton* on a Detroit marriage license. It seems your brother had married in Detroit and was working at a machine shop. The FBI had thought it was you at first, but then discovered that their mistake was really good for their investigation. They questioned Nicholas about that night, they knew he was at work, but they wanted to find out what he knew about the whole dustup. So it's good to know your brother safely left Buffalo."

Not knowing what to expect, she was nervously watching his expression. She saw a good one; he showed relief. "And they closed their investigation completely about six months later, after they questioned him, or in police talk: interviewed him. And they dropped the charges against you and Phryne, just like they did in my case."

"Charges? You and me and Phryne were up on charges? I never knew anything about charges." This was news to him; the kind you do not read in newspapers. He twisted in his chair, and pushed away his bowl of barley soup. "What kind of charges did they bring against us, Eloisa? Damn it! I'm a cop."

"I was charged with accessory to murder for the Customs agent and rum running. They arrested me and put me in jail for three days. That's probably why I felt sympathy for Geoffrey when he was in jail … I have an idea what it's like. I have experience."

She started by repeating the charges, explaining that they had been dropped and reassured him that the case had been closed. "First of all, Leopold, remember that all this was seven years ago and it's long forgotten as far as I know."

He listened to her story and felt compassion with every harsh detail. She told of her arrest, interrogation, incarceration and eventual, unceremonious release. She told how embarrassed her parents had been and how they had isolated her at home.

She stopped short of her pregnancy, thinking it was too much at once, knowing fully well she would be obligated to disclose it sooner rather than later.

"It's no wonder you came out here to Los Angeles to see Phryne. She was all you had left, wasn't she?"

Eloisa had to think about that; Leopold was right. The hurt from years ago came back. She tortured herself by not telling him everything. "I suppose you're right. At the time, she was the only friend I had left."

It was Saturday, and the dining room crowd was not businessmen and bankers, but predominately shoppers and a few bluenose* East Coast tourists. He put a match to a cigarette and offered her one. She declined, and he sat back into his chair, slowly drew in the smoke and exhaled more slowly. His coffee had cooled beyond drinkability. "Well, Ellie, I'll tell you what ... I think that your story had more news than your brother-in-law's dribble. But they probably would not print your story either, would they?"

"Probably not."

"Not because it isn't a good story ... but because it wouldn't sell newspapers. Nobody wants to read the truth. Bullshit sells better. I have learned a couple things in the last eight years: newspapers print bad news, fires can burn twice, and you can't take back words or bullets."

He pulled the chain on his pocket watch, gazed at the dial and crushed out his cigarette. He looked across the table and offered her his hand. "It's about that time. Let's go to the pictures, Ellie."

Cocktails For Two

After a ten-minute newsreel featuring the men and machines behind the ongoing construction of Boulder Dam, the feature film began. *Murder at the Vanities* was a new musical murder mystery set in a Broadway playhouse, staring Jack Oakie and Kitty Carlisle.

Leopold and Eloisa had expected nothing more than an hour and a half of innocuous entertainment. Ten minutes into the marquee presentation, they were at the edge of their seats. What they witnessed was a scene featuring conversation between female characters standing and seated in a dressing room when a familiar face flashed across the screen. Another ten minutes passed, and that face was on screen once again; this time in the front row of a top-hat dancing troupe. After a third appearance, Leopold and Eloisa were convinced that it was indeed Phryne. When the initial surprise had waned, they shared a smile and could only agree that Phryne was living her dream. She was a dancer in no less than six scenes, and during the final song and dance number, she could be seen repeatedly front and center. There wasn't much to be said about the film, but they both agreed that, good or bad, Phryne had never failed to amaze.

After the film, they rode the streetcar to the Garrison Tavern and Restaurant at the foot of Beale Street. A gracious example of an antebellum Southern mansion, it was an unusual treasure a block away from the cobblestones of The Embarcadero. It stood facing the East, fronted by verandas on each of the two floors, with large white Doric columns. Standing at the top step, Leopold pointed out Pier 26 and mentioned he had often steamed from there on the Melville Dollar. He had made six o'clock dinner reservations at the Garrison for the second floor dining room.

Inside, Eloisa's eyes touched everything. The polished wood staircase in the foyer was twelve feet wide and led directly to the stained-glass doors of the upstairs lounge. Inside, the maître d' found a quiet corner table away from the doorway and bar. Eloisa was dazzled with the opulence. After the waiter took their drink order she asked, "I don't think I was ever in a place quite like this. Are you trying to impress me or sweep me off my feet?"

"Both. And to top it off, we're having cocktails for two."

"Like the picture we just watched, right?" There was that giggle of hers again.

"The film was good, and Phryne proved she can dance, but that last number, '*Cocktails for Two*', was simply horrendous, despite Duke Ellington and his band. The music and dancing were fantastic, but that song ... what a vocal mess. Like I said, the melody was grand, Duke did it up, but those lyrics in the song were so discombobulated, it felt like a cheap, painful hangover."

A door had opened. The film had given Eloisa the opportunity to talk to Leopold about Phryne. "When I left Los Angeles, I should have known she would end up in show business. She had a cosmetics job at Paramount already, and I worked at the canteen for a short time."

"Really? You both worked at the same movie studio? Together?"

That was the opening that Eloisa was waiting for. She knew eventually she would need to tell Leopold everything, but was genuinely concerned about wounding him. She remembered Phryne's account of his dreams. They had more than an hour before dinner, and it was about to be consumed by hidden history.

One by one, she began dragging all the skeletons out of the closet. She started with Phryne's divorce, subsequent marriage to Abner, their Hollywood lifestyle and her devastating admission of infidelity with Dillon. From time to time, she would take a sip of her Bee's Knees* cocktail. She kept her eyes on Leopold. She wanted her sincerity to smooth the disturbing revelations. When she disclosed the premature birth and death of Millicent Mae, Leopold needed time to recover from his shock, sorrow and sympathy for Phryne. Eloisa moved her chair and sat next to him.

Leopold expressed his regret, "Phryne didn't deserve the way I treated her. I was a beast, the worst kind: unforgiving and heartless."

Eloisa would not allow him to take all the blame for walking out on his wife. "Phryne's adulterous dalliance with Dillon not only hurt you, but it also destroyed my friendship with her. She completely shattered the trust we shared."

"You're being far too generous in the forgiveness of my character. I was wrong. I weakened, and allowed myself to be led along a path to self-destruction and damnation."

"While you may think all that is true, you must take credit when credit is due. You recognized your shortcomings. You found the strength to pull yourself out of the cesspool, Leopold, and you did. And who's to judge? Phryne's in pictures now because you called it off."

It wasn't a pleasant conversation, but pulling the covers off stark secrets seldom is. She finished with full disclosure of her rape, pregnancy, banishment to the Protectorate and giving up her newborn for adoption.

The conversation was a mixed smorgasbord of life events spanning a period of six years. Leopold saw Eloisa in a new light. He not only felt compassion for her, but admiration of her character and appreciation of her bravery.

Leopold nursed a bottle of Presidio Pilsner listening to her epic. When it was his turn at bat, he stood and put his jacket over the back of his chair. He lit a Chesterfield and began with his destructive guilt, desertion of his wife and his dive into the ocean of opium that was Chinatown.

The afternoon was a dizzying recollection of past experiences that gave credence to their individual resilience.

He finished his story by recalling his recovery at the Salvation Army Shelter, nearly two years at sea, his fascination with a fictional character named Martin Eden, and ending with his graduation from the police Recruit School.

"Here I am, and there you are. It's like we've taken our lives down a road that went full circle, isn't it Ellie?"

"Not quite. Maybe we will end up being the biggest bumps on that road." Her giggle heartened him.

He raised his glass of beer, and she her cocktail.

"I have one thing to say about those bumps, Ellie."

"Well, let's hear it."

"Hang on, honey."

For the first time that afternoon, they laughed together. A quiet settled when it ended. Their eyes met and a link was formed. They felt it. Seconds flashed by. Something had passed between them. He gave the waiter a beckoning wave, and ordered another Bee's Knees and a beer.

Something caught her eye. "What's that on your arm? I can almost see it through your shirt."

"Oh, that's some needle work I had done in the Orient. A reminder of my seadog days." He unbuttoned the sleeve, folded up the cuff and set his forearm on the table.

She recognized the tattoo for what it was. "A life preserver with your ship's name … the SS Melville Dollar, right? Silly me … at first I thought it was a doughnut."

Her words gave him pause.

"I never thought of it that way, Ellie. But I imagine it could be. It could be a doughnut." He took her hand. "We should do this again. And again. And perhaps more. It feels good to feel good again."

Her sweet little twitter precluded her statement. "I think you may have more than a tattoo up your sleeve, sailor."

(fade to black)

Continued with:

The Flying Phaeton

The End Notes

Chapter One:

The Bureau of Investigation (BOI) was created in 1908, prompted by the 1901 assassination of President William McKinley in Buffalo, New York, and the need for an autonomous investigative service. President Theodore Roosevelt ordered its creation by Attorney General Charles Bonaparte. In 1924, a young J. Edgar Hoover was named as director, and tasked to put the Bureau's house in order. The BOI of 1927 was a meager national force of about 200 Special Agents. At best, it was inefficient, ill-equipped, undertrained, plagued by political corruption, outwitted and outgunned by organized crime. In 1935 its name was changed to the Federal Bureau of Investigation, the FBI of today.

Wire transmission of photographs or drawings was not available until the later 1930s. Until then, police agencies relied on the Post Office Department to deliver likenesses of suspects and wanted posters across the nation.

Bootleggers were an inventive bunch of criminals. One criminal entrepreneur had invented a system to fill all four of his 1925 Auburn Roadster's tire inner tubes with bootleg whiskey. The system that Dillon Cafferty used (bladders inside the seat cushions and the addition of heavy-duty leaf springs on the Pierce Arrow) was perhaps one of the most ingenious, deviously efficient, deviant method any of the Canadian or American authorities had encountered.

Chapter Two:

Famous Players was created in 1915, became Famous Players Paramount in 1927 and eventually morphed into

Paramount Pictures. Its big stars were Mary Pickford, Rudolf Valentino, Clara Bow, Gloria Swanson and Douglas Fairbanks Sr.

Maybelline mascara was invented in 1915 by nineteen-year-old Tom Williams after he saw his sister applying a mixture of petroleum jelly and coal dust to her eye lashes. The young man perfected this recipe with his chemistry set and named the product after his sister, Mabel. For years, women had often darkened their lashes and eyebrows, using chimney soot, boot polish or pitch. Williams called his new product *Maybelline Cake Mascara: "the first modern eye cosmetic for everyday use"* It was marketed with the first brush for application.

Lipstick & Nail Polish were only available in deep red until the mid-1930s.

Bay Rum aftershave was 58% grain alcohol and was often consumed as drink during Prohibition.

Labor Day became an official holiday in the United States and Canada (Labour Day) in 1894, by decrees from President Grover Cleveland and Prime Minister John Macdonald.

Chapter Three:

Long Beach Oil Fields were discovered in 1921. The Los Angeles basin oil field was enormously productive in the 1920s, with hundreds of oil derricks covering Signal Hill. In 1923 the field produced over 68 million barrels of oil, making it one of the world's richest and most productive.

Hobos tramps, and bums had a communication system that exists to some extent today. Called 'signs', it was a type of hieroglyphics that provided a means to warn of police presence, the best hideouts, dangerous locations or animals, and where to find the best handouts or rides. Chalk on a fence or rock, charcoal or even scratches on the earth were their mediums of choice. Hobos considered themselves as migrant workers; tramps only worked when forced to; bums did not work at all.

Chapter Four:

Pre-Code Hollywood was wild, raucous and without censorship. The movies made up until 1934 were a reflection of life in the hills north of Los Angeles. The *Motion Picture Production Code* was passed as an industry standard in 1930 but was not enforced until four years later. Most film aficionados still long for the 'good old days'.

Organized Crime flourished unabated in 1920s Los Angeles. Joseph *Iron Man* Ardizzone and Jack Dragna controlled the city during Prohibition. Liquor, gambling and prostitution flourished under the blind eye of bought-and-paid-for police.

Chapter Five:

Father Nelson Baker was ordained in 1876. He was a civil war veteran of the battle of Gettysburg, successful businessman, and member of the St. Vincent DePaul Society. Buffalo was a growing metropolis at the turn of the century, and during the expansion of the Erie Canal and waterfront construction, thousands of infant bones were discovered. In 1906, horrified by these grim discoveries, Father Baker opened Our Lady of Victory Infant Home to house and care for abandoned babies and their socially stigmatized, unwed mothers. A true architectural wonder, the Basilica of Our Lady of Victory is a national shrine. Father Baker was named Venerable by Pope Benedict XVI in 2011.

Childbirth in 1928: Dr. Joseph DeLee believed that childbirth was a 'damaging' and 'morbid' pathologic process. He suggested procedures to save women from the 'evils' that were 'natural to labor'. When labor begins, obstetricians should sedate the mother, allow the cervix to dilate, administer ether, cut an episiotomy, use forceps to deliver the baby, remove the placenta, administer medications to contract the uterus, and stitch the episiotomy. His article was published in the *American Journal of Obstetrics and Gynecology*. All of DeLee's interventions became routine for decades in the United States. Hospital stays were generally five to seven days.

Horsehair was very widely used in the 19th and early 20th centuries in upholstery, hats and gloves. It was commonly used in women's undergarments blended with either cotton or silk wefts in the fabric weave.

Chapter Six:

San Francisco had a population of 600,000 in 1930 compared to Los Angeles' total 1,200,000 and Buffalo at 574,000.

Los Angeles carried out several mass deportations of Mexican nationals during the 20s and 30s. In 1930 and '31 alone, Los Angeles County deported approximately 23,000 Mexicans. Thousands were actually American citizens.

The Yellow Peril was a term of convenience used to justify quotas or even bans on Asian immigration. The 1921 Emergency Quota Act and the Immigration Act of 1924 restricted immigration with regard to national origin.

The McDonough brothers controlled San Francisco from 1910 until the onset of the Second World War in 1941. Pete and Tom earned the moniker *Kings of the Tenderloin*, a reference to their boyhood home in the *Cow Hollow* district of the city. Their control over San Francisco was so effective, Al Capone once said, "The more lucrative forms of crime were so highly organized and well protected that outsiders couldn't break into San Francisco." (quite the endorsement).

The police, politicians and labor unions all respected the McDonough's influence.

Vinyl records were first commercially produced by Victor Recording Company in 1930. Previously, records were wax or shellac.

Chinatown The Hall of Justice, Portsmouth Square, City Hall, The Corner, Battery Row and The No Name were all within a half-mile radius of one another.

The League of Nations ordained the first international treaty on the prohibition of opium by including it in the 1919 Treaty of Versailles that the dictated terms ending World War I.

The Salvation Army of the United States ministered to home-sick troops in Europe during the American deployment of World War I. The young women officers, who came to be known as *Doughnut Girls*, caught the attention of the troops and the American public. Ironically, US Infantrymen during WWI were referred to as *Doughboys* with uncertain origin. Could that moniker be a reference to the copious amount of doughnuts the American soldier managed to consume?

Chapter Seven:

Lunchtime in the 1920s: The sandwich was an art form!

Sardine Sandwich: Mix to taste: chopped olives, hard-boiled egg yolks, drained sardines cleaned of tails, season with lemon juice, salt and paprika. Very tasty on white bread.

Pine Tree Sandwich: Slice white bread and cut into pine tree shapes. Prepare a mixture of soft butter and finely chopped parsley. Spread mix on pine needle area of bread and pour melted sweet chocolate over the trunk part.

Emergency Sandwich: Chop six sweet pickles and five hard boiled eggs. Blend together two tablespoons of peanut butter, one tablespoon of prepared mustard and mix into the pickles and eggs. Add vinegar to make a spreadable mixture. Very good on whole wheat or rye bread.

It's all in the name: *Tea table* became *coffee table* before it was *cocktail table* in the 50s and 60s and back again to *coffee table*. Cheers!

Morris chairs were a popular addition to any home at the turn of the century. This new invention was a reclining chair. Hello you lazy boy!

Dominion Day was a fixed holiday on July 1st throughout Canada. It was renamed as *Canada Day* in 1982.

Fergie's Foam was the 4.2% beer that could be legally served on draught in Ontario, Canada during Prohibition. Today's 'light beer' is 3.2% alcohol.

Trojan brand condoms were first introduced in 1916. In 1930, natural rubber was replaced with Latex. Earlier, condoms were made from linen or sheep intestines. "Lambskins" were thinner, and more expensive.

RMS Lusitania was a passenger vessel torpedoed by a German U-boat in 1915 causing the deaths of 1,198 passengers and crew. The sinking helped change American sentiment prompting US entry into WWI in 1917.

Chapter Eight:

The Dollar Steamship Company was the largest and most successful United States shipping firm at its zenith in the 1920s, and its signature white dollar sign mounted on red-banded stacks was recognized world-wide. The company slogan was *The Orient and around the world.* Founded by Robert Dollar, a Scotch immigrant in 1910, his company was headquartered in San Francisco. Many of the freighters carried the names of family members. The company pioneered round-the-world passenger travel with the introduction of *American Presidents Line* in the mid-1920s. Those ships carried the names of U.S. Presidents.

Doughnuts originated in America sometime in the mid-19th century (1850+), most likely as an import from European immigrants. The Dutch call them: *oliekoek* (oil cake), Norwegians: *smultring* (lard ring). A delight for any connoisseur, the little round cakes with the hole in the middle are deep-fired in oil or lard. *Donut* is the 'Americanized' form of *doughnut*. The phrase "bet you a dollar to a doughnut" refers to a sure thing, a sure bet, and was first mentioned in the later part of the 19th century.

Knot is a nautical speed. One knot equals 1.14 miles per hour. The SS Melville Dollar and sister ship SS Esther Dollar could race along at 10½ knots; 12 miles an hour.

Kapok was a highly flammable, fluffy plant fiber used in life jackets. Repeat: highly flammable. The material replaced earlier, bulky life jackets made of cork.

Chapter Nine:

Chaise longue is not a chaise lounge, but is often used as one. The chaise longue is an upholstered piece of furniture, and very cosmopolitan.

Champagne Cocktail is 8 oz. champagne, 1½ oz. cognac, 1 sugar cube and a dash of bitters. Garnish with an orange slice and red or green maraschino cherry.

Foster Grant sunglasses were introduced in 1929 by Sam Foster.

Hollywood studios ground out an average of 800 films a year during the 20's and 30's. Today, it's about 300.

Chapter Ten:

Chief Daniel O'Brien started the San Francisco Police Recruit Academy in 1922; the first such training school to be established in the United States. It consisted of fourteen weeks of indoctrination that included boxing, swimming, wrestling, firearms use, jumping, running and even talking and singing. The course not only taught police skills, but self-confidence.

Oil skins are an integral part of a sailor's water resistant clothing. In the 1920s they were duck cloth soaked in linseed oil.

Pea coat is a double breasted, large collar, heavy woolen jacket usually worn by sailors.

Chapter Eleven:

Courier Express: The *Buffalo Daily Courier* and the *Buffalo Morning Express* merged in 1926. Samuel Langhorne Clemens was an editor and part-owner of the paper from 1869 to 1871. He is better known by his pseudonym, Mark Twain and the characters he created such as Huckleberry Finn, Becky Thatcher and Injun Joe.

Chapter Twelve:

Summertime 1934 was a violent period in San Francisco history. The events detailed in this chapter are paralleled by actual events. A certain degree of editorial license was used to protect the actual individuals involved regardless of culpable guilt or presumed innocence.

The Wobblies and Longshoremen rank-and-file membership discovered after their lengthy strike, that what is agreed to on paper can be a disaster in practice. The monetary gains won by a strike seldom replace what was lost, and rarely come close. The longshoremen won (?) some demands: a wage increase to 95¢ cents an hour and a six-hour work day at 30 hours per week ($28.50). Prior to the strike, they had worked 40 hours per week at 85¢ per hour ($34.00). The arbitration also granted the employers the right to automate and mechanize the work. The union lost their demand for union-controlled hiring that would have banned non-union workers. William Dudley (Big Bill) Haywood, was a principal founder and leader of the Industrial Workers of the World *(The Wobblies - IWW)*. He was also a principal member of the Executive Committee of the Socialist Party of America.

Flat Foot Floogie With the Floy Floy was a song written by the scat duo of Slim & Slam: Bulee 'Slim' Gaillard and Leroy 'Slam' Stewart. Scat singing is a version of jazz that allows the vocalist to change or invent words. 'Floogie' was originally intended to be 'floozie' (term for a prostitute) and was changed to 'floogie' so as not to have the recording banned. She would have flat feet from walking the pavement. Slim & Slam never revealed what 'floy floy' was, but most certainly it was a quality that a professional floogie would have.

Murphy beds were an inspired patented improvement over pull-down beds. William Lawrence Murphy developed his cantilever design in San Francisco in 1900. His innovation enabled the bed to be pulled down, unfolded and closed easier.

The New Deal was President Franklin Delano Roosevelt's plan to involve government in the economic recovery out of the Great Depression. Federal work-for-wages programs began and Social Security was established.

Murder at the Vanities was a 1933 'pre-code' Paramount musical released into national distribution June 1, 1934. Duke Ellington and his orchestra appear in a highlighted performance. Thinly veiled topless showgirls, strong drug reference (a featured performance of the song 'Sweet Marijuana'), strong sexual innuendos and cursing reveals the movie industry prior to Hays Code censorship. Lucille Ball, Ann Sheridan (dancing girls) and Alan Ladd (song-and-dance man) are among the unlisted stars. They weren't quite yet famous in 1933.

The Odd Stuff

To sum up the *Dollar To Doughnut* era, here's a quote by Lois Long, a reporter and columnist for *The New Yorker* magazine, best known for her coverage of the flapper lifestyle during The Roaring Twenties and Jazzy Thirties: *"Tomorrow we may die, so let's get drunk and make love."* On December 23, 1940, *The New York Times* proclaimed that during the 1920s *"gin was the national drink and sex the national obsession"*. Have times changed?

The BOI (FBI in 1935) despite popular belief to the contrary, fought organized crime with its hands tied in the 1920s. Organized crime was just that: organized. Charges of murder, extortion and arson disappeared with the witnesses.

Al Capone was hounded by police all over the country. For example, he never carried cash and was charged with vagrancy in Miami in 1930 and once again in Chicago. Contempt of Court charges for feigning illness and perjury were nothing more than harassment. His eventual incarceration in 1932 was effected not by the BOI but the Internal Revenue Service. He served seven years for tax evasion, and eventually died of heart failure, brought on by the complications of syphilis, gonorrhea, and cocaine addiction in 1947.

Baby Face Nelson (Lester Gillis) died in a shootout with BOI agents in 1934. **John Dillinger** died of BOI gunshot wounds: ambushed while exiting a movie theatre in 1934. **Pretty Boy Floyd** (Charles Floyd) was similarly gunned down in an Ohio corn field in 1934. **Bonnie and Clyde** (Bonnie Parker and Clyde Barrow) drove into a Texas Highway Patrol ambush in 1934, and died without firing a shot. Their 1934 Ford was riddled with over 100 bullet holes, and together they died from 43 wounds. All members of the police posse suffered temporary deafness from the gunfire. **Dutch Schultz** (Arthur

Flegenheimer) escaped prosecution and the BOI. He was shot by a fellow gangster in Newark, New Jersey, and was caught 'with his pants down' in 1935; killed while standing at a urinal.

Lucky Luciano (Charles Salvatore Lucania) was probably the most powerful mob boss of all time, and could only be prosecuted on what many considered trumped-up charges of pandering. Imprisoned in 1936 at Ossining, New York (Sing-Sing) he struck a deal with US Navy Intelligence during WW II and assisted the government in the fight against Axis spies on the New York and New Jersey waterfronts. After the war, his sentence was commuted and he was deported to Italy, where he died of a heart attack in 1962.

Two Bits could be explained here (or not): Robert Louis Stevenson (authored *Treasure Island* and created *Jekyll & Hyde*) explained his experience with 'bits' in *Across the Plains*: "In the Pacific States they have made a bolder push for complexity, and settle their affairs by a coin that no longer exists– the BIT, or old Mexican *real*. The supposed value of the bit is twelve and a half cents, eight to the dollar. When it comes to two bits, the quarter-dollar stands for the required amount. But how about an odd bit? The nearest coin to it is a dime, which is, short by a fifth. That, then, is called a SHORT bit. If you have one, you lay it triumphantly down, and save two and a half cents. But if you have not, and lay down a quarter, the bar-keeper or shopman [sic] calmly tenders you a dime by way of change; and thus you have paid what is called a LONG BIT, and lost two and a half cents, or even, by comparison with a short bit, five cents." Try to put that on your debit card.

Da Hong = Big Red = 达宏

Sing Lee = Victorious Profit = 利李

Wong Wai was a Chinese national living in San Francisco who dealt in opium and aphrodisiacs during the 1920s and

1930s. In 1935, he was convicted of smuggling young girls from Asia to the West coast for prostitution. *Wong Wai*; really, you cannot make this stuff up.

Hillcrest Country Club (opened 1920) was exclusively Jewish well into the 1950s until Danny Thomas (a Lebanese Christian) became a member.

SS Canadiana *(The Crystal Beach Boat)* was a passenger ferry built by Buffalo Dry Dock Corp. It carried visitors between Crystal Beach, Ontario and Buffalo, NY from 1910 until 1956. Capacity in 1910 was 3500 persons (many standing) was later reduced to 1800 seated.

Telephone service could be best described as 'disconnected' until after World War II. Competing companies and manual switching meant that only very limited dial service was available. In 1926, Los Angeles had 123,000 telephones for 1,200,000 people. Waiting lists were as long as a telephone pole was tall. Businesses got priority.

Bee's Knees cocktail was a potent blend of 2 parts gin, 1 part honey, and 4 parts mineral water.

"... you may have more than a tattoo up your sleeve ..."
~ Eloisa Ashworth 1934

Art by Amy.©

The Glossary

Slang, Jazz & Hip Lingo

Every era has its own favorite words. Here are some from the late 1920s and early 1930s. Hipsters are cool, aren't they? Remember that when you 'twitter'.

Alley ape	Criminals lurking in dark alleys
Bit	12½ cents; *2 bits = 25¢*
Babe, dame, doll	Female
Bearcat	Fiery, promiscuous female
Bee's Knees	Great, sweet (named after drink)
Bell bottom	Sailor
Bindle	A hobo's sack of belongings
Blotto	Tipsy, drunk
Blower	Telephone
Bluenose	A prude
Booze hound	Drunkard, alcoholic
Brace	Grab, get hold of
Bracelets	Handcuffs
Breezer	Car without windows or roof
Brodie	Mess, trouble, failure
Bumping gums	Talking nonsense, lies
Butter and egg man	The money man; a sugar-daddy
Calaboose	Jail
Chicago overcoat	Coffin
Chin wag	Talk, discuss
Chippy	Woman with low moral behavior
Cinder dick, bull	Railroad detective, railroad cop
Clip joint	Where customers get cheated

Coolie	Chinese (derogatory)
Copper	Policeman, cop
Crumb	A fink, a loser
Cupid's bow	Lipstick look, a inverted bow
Dangle	Leave in a hurry
Delicates	Panties
Deck	Pack of cigarettes
Dizzy	In love
Doughboy	US soldier (WWI)
Doxy, doxies	Dockside prostitute
Dumb Dora	Female patsy (derogatory)
Fin	Five dollar bill
Flatfoot	Beat policeman, patrols on foot
Flimflam	Swindle, cheat
Flophouse	Cheap rooming house
G-man	Federal agent
Gams	Legs
(Get your) ashes hauled	Jazz term: to have coitus
Gold Digger	Woman looking for a rich man
Goon, gorilla, (guappo)	Gunmen, Mafia-type (derogatory)
Grifter	Con man or woman
Gum it up	To cause trouble
Gumshoe	Private detective
Haywire	Out of control, confused
Heebie jeebies	The shakes; nervous fits
Hinky	Phony, fake
Hit the pipe	Smoke opium
Hokum	Nonsense, lies
Hotsquat	The electric chair
Hooch	Bootleg whiskey

Hood	Hoodlum
Hoofer	Dancer
Hoosegow	Jail, prison
Hotsy-totsy	Pleasing, arousing
Hurdy-gurdy man	Street entertainer, organ grinder
Joint	Bar; (slang) jail
Juice	Flashy, with attitude
Jumper	Thick cable stitch pull over
Lam (on the)	On the run from police
Lambskins	Condoms; from sheep intestines
Lock-up	Jail
Make tracks	Leave in a hurry
Mick	Irish (derogatory)
Mouthpiece	Attorney
Moxie	Pep, vigor (after the drink Moxie)
Muffin	Female (derogatory)
Okie	Oklahoma native (derogatory)
Patsy	Innocent man taking the blame
Pachucos	Flashy young Mexican men
Palooka	Inexperienced fellow
Pins	Legs
Positootly	Of course!
Pro skirt	Prostitute
Pug	Boxer (pugilist)
QT	Quiet, secretly
Rattler	Freight train
Ring-a-ding	A good time
Rube	An unsophisticated person
Sawbuck	$10 bill
Screw	Police, prison guard

Shell shock	War nerves, PTSD
Shylock	Cheater, loan shark
Sideways (person)	Oriental (derogatory)
Skittles	*Nine pins:* a bowling game
Snake charmer	A woman used as a decoy
Stable	Group of women, party girls
Sweet mama, tomato	Attractive woman
Tapster	Bartender
Toodles	Bye-bye (French: *à tout à l'heure* = see you later; right away)
Trip for biscuits	A trip or task for nothing
Trouble boy	Gangster
Twitter	Giggle
Viper	Drug user or dealer
Wheat, wheatie	Country boy not used to city life
Whoopee	Sex, coitus
Willikers	Golly, gee whiz
Yellow	Oriental (derogatory)
Yellow Peril	Chinese immigration influx
Zotzed	Killed, dead, unconscious

"Toodles."

~ Phryne Mandelbaum 1928

The Music 1920-1934

Who's Sorry Now	Karen Elson
Jailhouse Blues	Ottilie Patterson
The Prisoner's Song	Loudon Wainwright III
Makin' Whoopee	Lucy Ann Polk & Les Brown Band
Single Girl, Married Girl	Harvey Reid & Joyce Anderson
Don't Put a Tax on the Beautiful Girls	Nicole Reynolds
No One Man is Ever Going To Worry Me	Sophie Tucker
Nice Work if You Can Get It	The Andrews Sisters
Hallelujah! I'm a Bum	Harry McClintock
Waiting For a Train	Jimmie Dale Gilmore
I Double Dare You	Annette Hanshaw
(I Want A) Butter and Egg Man*	Turk Murphy & His Chicago Jazz Band
Strutt Miss Lizzie	David Johansen
All Alone	Chaim Tannenbaum
I'm Gonna Sit Right Down And Write Myself A Letter	Oh! Sister!
Love Me or Leave Me	Billie Holiday
Take a Whiff On Me	Hattie Hart & Memphis Jug Band
Chinatown, My Chinatown	The Jugalug String Band
I'll See You in My Dreams	Matt Berringer

Get Happy!	Dorothy Collins
My Melancholy Baby	Mildred Bailey
Everybody Loves My Baby	Vince Giordano
Slow Boat to China	Kay Starr
Load of Coal	Jelly Roll Morton
Bye Bye Blackbird	Diana Krall
Barnacle Bill the Sailor	Louis Prima & Keely Smith
Fiddlers' Green	Seán Cannon
There'll be Some Changes Made	Kathy Brier
Ain't Misbehavin'	Eva Taylor
Hurdy Gurdy Man	Tommy Dorsey, Louis Armstrong
Between the Devil and the Deep Blue Sea	Helen Forest & The Benny Goodman Orchestra
It Had to be You	Bing Crosby
Flat Foot Floogie With the Floy Floy	Benny Goodman & His Orchestra
When My Dreamboat Comes Home	Jaye P. Morgan
Tain't no Sin	Otillie Patterson & Chris Barber's Jazz Wizzards
Cocktails for Two	Duke Ellington

Post script

The title spring:

(from Chapter 10): Amanda's memory returned for a fleeting second, and he thought about their passionate relationship of sex, coffee and doughnuts. Had she only remained in San Francisco, he might well have left the SS Melville Dollar for her and in fact, made the impetuous switch from <u>dollar</u> <u>to</u> <u>doughnut</u>.

This novel contains 100% recycled post-consumer thought.

"It could be a doughnut."

Thank you!

Edward R Hackemer

Made in the USA
Coppell, TX
16 July 2021

59026119R00144